INVISIBLE STRINGS

NALEDI MASHISHI

Legend Press Ltd, 51 Gower Street, London, WC1E 6HJ
info@legendpress.co.uk | www.legendpress.co.uk

 British Library Cataloguing in Publication Data available.

First published by Blackbird Books in 2021 | 593 Zone 4, SeshegoPolokwane 0742, South Africa | www.blackbirdbooks.africa

Print ISBN 9781915643582
Ebook ISBN 9781915643599
Set in Times. Printed in the UK by Severn Print
Cover design by Gudrun Jobst | www.yotedesign.com

Naledi Mashishi is an author, and masters student based in London, UK. She holds journalism degrees from Rhodes University and the University of the Witwatersrand. She has previously worked as a fact-checking researcher for Africa Check. In 2019 she was the recipient of the Casa Lorde Writer's Residency hosted by Blackbird Books and Eunice Ngogodo Own Voices Initiative.

Invisible Strings is her debut novel.

Follow Naledi on Twitter
@naledimashishi

and Instagram
naledimashishi

This book is dedicated to my grandfather,
Madala Mphahlele

My love for storytelling began when you sat down next to me and let me tell long winded stories about spiders. For that I am forever grateful. I wish you were still here to read this one.

PART ONE

GHOSTS

ONE

For the past two years, Kgethi had been drowning in a vast, darkening sea. Above her she saw the light of her pre-pregnancy world rapidly dimming. The colours of her varsity life characterised by late night McDonald's, cheap fast fashion, and rooftop parties receded from her. She watched as her daydreams of being a rich and famous Top Billing presenter staying in world-class hotels, rubbing shoulders with local and international celebrities, and following in the footsteps of fashion icon Bonang Matheba floated away. Her pregnancy had formed a ball and chain around her ankles, dragging her towards a life of diaper changes, nighttime feedings, domestic tedium. She found her dreams now locked away in safes with no keys. She entered motherhood with a chest full of water, never quite able to accept that this was it. This was her new life.

The only thing that still connected her to her old life was a delicate gold bracelet with links shaped like palm leaves. It was a cheap costume piece bought from the type of accessory store that sold earrings which turned ears green. But when Kgethi looked at the bracelet she remembered the day she had walked into a store in Braamfontein, wearing a crop top that showed off her impossibly flat stomach, and spotted it. She remembered how it used to clink against the plastic cups she held as she moved through a crowded dance floor. How she used to play with it when she sat bored in a lecture hall and when she flirted with the cute boys on campus. The bracelet was a lifeline, a final reminder that nearly three years ago she had once been a girl with an enviable, slim body and a real life. She looked at the bracelet and reminded herself of who she used to be.

Naturally, she was furious when the bracelet went missing. She rummaged through her drawers and failed to find it. Her confusion quickly transitioned to annoyance as she realised what must have happened. Valuables in Johannesburg had a tendency to grow legs. They walked out of pockets, bags, and through windows silently. If you were particularly unlucky they were forcibly surrendered by the persuasive power of a loaded gun. Her gold leaf bracelet had vanished. She searched through her wardrobe then looked under her bed.

'What's going on?' Her mother's voice said.

Kgethi looked up at her doorway. 'I can't find my bracelet. The gold leaf one. Have you seen it anywhere?'

'No,' she said with an unsympathetic look. 'Where did you last see it?'

'I don't know! I just wore it two days ago!' She said, cursing loudly again.

'Well I'm sure it'll turn up.'

She wasn't so sure. The missing bracelet soured her mood, which worsened when she was forced to go grocery shopping with her two-year-old daughter. There was nothing that represented the tedium Kgethi's life had been reduced to more than the strip malls of northern Johannesburg. They were uniform in appearance with the same supermarkets, the same try-hard trendy coffee shops, and the same kitschy home stores where suburban white women bought Live Laugh Love wall decor. She hated them.

She supposed she should have been grateful Thato didn't make the whole ordeal harder. Kgethi would watch as other two-year-olds threw tantrums over chocolates but her child never did. Thato had always been peaceful. As a baby she hardly cried. She slept through the night from birth, didn't suffer from colic or diarrhea or any of the other ailments common to babies. She was often so quiet for such long periods of time that it was easy for the residents of the house to forget that she was there.

Kgethi used to watch over that quiet, squishy, powder-scented blob of a human and will herself to feel something. She willed herself to wash the baby, change diapers, breastfeed, and carry out all the other duties that came with motherhood, but she only performed them out of obligation. There was a part of her that almost wished Thato would cry more. Or vomit. Or do something that demonstrated that there was a real person with real thoughts and feelings wrapped under the layers of blanket and baby fat. Instead she felt nothing.

'You're lucky, you know,' her mother once told her. 'She's a very easy baby.'

Kgethi said nothing. Thato wasn't just easy. She was barely human. She was a bundle of flesh that took quietly and gave nothing back. It was as though Thato had sensed that she was unplanned and had resolved to move through life causing as little fuss as possible. She walked quietly next to Kgethi, holding her hand while they approached Woolworths. Kgethi turned around to take out a trolley. When she looked back Thato was gone. She blinked. 'Thato?' Panic set in. She looked around and saw the Thato running into a store they had visited the previous week. Oh for fuck's sake, she thought before setting off after her. 'Thato! Thato come back here,' she yelled. She ran into the store after her and grabbed her by the arm. 'Thato! Why would you run off like that?' She hissed.

'Excuse me, Miss,' the cashier said. As Kgethi looked up at her a glint of gold caught her eye. She looked closer and there in her hand was the gold leaf bracelet. 'I think this belongs to you?' She said. 'You might have dropped it the last time you were here?'

Kgethi was stunned. She looked from the bracelet to Thato. But... how? She took the bracelet, grabbed Thato's hand and left. She couldn't stop thinking about the incident and what it meant. How could Thato have known? Kgethi hadn't been with her the last time she had visited that shop.

* * *

She stared through the kitchen window as Thato played in the garden. She was chasing after the white butterflies which had descended on the city like a cloud as they migrated north. Behind her was the mulberry tree where Kgethi had once spat out the black-red fruits her mother had collected in a bowl. Next to that was the pedestrian gate that a fifteen-year-old Kgethi had snuck out of in the black of night to go clubbing. Maybe, she thought, I'm just overthinking this. Maybe she was going crazy and God knows, she thought, it wouldn't be the first time. She was the same person who had deluded herself about Luvuyo. Thinking the party boy with more cocaine than sense, with whom she had spent drunken nights of fun would step up once she told him she was pregnant with his child. Instead the asshole had blocked her on all his social media accounts.

Her own father had been even worse. He had shaken from anger when she had first told him. 'How could you be so irresponsible?' He had thundered, banging his fist against the table. The day she told him it had been the three of them in house, which was unusual. He had been under strict instruction to come alone. The last thing both Kgethi and her mother had wanted was to see him trailing in with that woman. They sat at the kitchen table forming a triangle.

'Do you know what a condom is Mamokgethi?' He had shouted at her. 'All you needed to do was use a condom! Just one!'

She could feel herself shrinking smaller under his gaze. 'Dad, I did!'

'Obviously you didn't otherwise you wouldn't be here! Who is the father?'

The room was so silent the three of them could hear the distant wall clock ticking in the living room.

'She doesn't know,' Mom said. 'The baby doesn't have a father.'

He looked from Kgethi to her mother incredulously. Then he laughed. 'That's fantastic! No, really. Not only is my daughter pregnant, she's a common whore too!'

'Don't you speak to her like that!' Mom snapped. 'I'm not going to tolerate you disrespecting her in my house! Whether you like it or not she is still your daughter and maybe if you'd actually played your part in raising her instead of chasing after anything in a skirt you could have had more of an influence on the person she is today!'

'Oh, don't start with that rubbish, Mahlatse! I tried to make it work but she insisted on acting like a spoilt brat and disrespecting my wife, probably because of your influence—'

'Okay, no!' Kgethi burst, her voice ricocheting off the walls. They both turned to look at her. She could feel her heart thumping against her chest. It felt like she was 15 again. 'You see this, what you guys are doing right now, we're not going to do this. Dad, I didn't ask you to come here so that you and Mom can re-enact your divorce. That sucked enough the first time, thanks.'

'Kgethi, I think you're the last person to talk now,' her father said in a dangerously low voice.

'Why? I'm the reason we're all here right? Look Dad, I'm sorry I got pregnant. It's not like I wanted to, trust me I didn't but we're here now and the baby is coming. And I just thought you should hear about it from me.'

He gave her mother a scalding look. 'You don't seem upset to hear this,' he said. 'Almost as though you think this is okay.'

'Don't you dare, Itumeleng. Obviously I'm livid. I didn't want this for her. I don't want this for her. I couldn't even look at her when she told me but we're here now. This baby is coming whether we like it or not so it's better we all just... get on with the program.'

'Well, I'm not getting on with any program. I'm not contributing a cent towards this child. I don't want to see this child and I definitely don't want it in my house.'

Kgethi almost laughed. God he was so predictable. I shouldn't have bothered, she thought.

'Come on now, Itumeleng,' Mahlatse said, irritation seeping into her voice.

'No! That's my decision,' he turned back to Kgethi. 'You decided you were grown enough to make a baby, now you must be grown enough to raise it. I raised you and I'm raising two boys that I chose to make so I don't want to raise any more!'

Kgethi snorted. 'Oh please, Dad. Your idea of raising a baby is playing with it every two weeks and then handing it to its mom to do the actual parenting. No one's asking you to do anything! We just thought you should know.'

This final disrespect was too much for him. He stood up and announced that now that Kgethi was of age he had no further legal obligations towards her and certainly not towards her child. He had a wife now and children he needed to focus his energies on 'instead of this train wreck' he said with an accusing finger. Then he walked out in a huff.

Well he can fuck right off, Kgethi thought to herself. But if she was being honest, her father's rejection stung.

She would have let Thato's newfound ability go until her mother walked in one day wide-eyed with astonishment that Thato had found a missing set of keys. As the weeks went on, she found everything lost: old receipts that were needed to return an item or validate a warranty, jewelry that hadn't been seen in years, stationery, and even old remote controls. All anyone had to do was ask Thato where something was and she would toddle off and return with it a few minutes later. Once they tested her powers after her mother's car was hijacked in the parking lot of a shopping complex. Thato simply shrugged her shoulders and said, 'Gone'.

News of her ability began to spread through the family. Aunts Kgethi's mother never spoke to outside of obligatory family functions rang her up wanting Thato to find something or other. Even Uncle Molefi who usually kept himself scarce around children made the unprecedented move of picking up the toddler one day and babysitting her while she found his missing vinyl records.

Her mom came to her one day with a strange request. She had been approached by an old friend of hers who wanted Thato to find her missing wedding ring. The next day the woman came to the house for tea, kneeled down before Thato and asked her, 'Baby girl, where's my wedding ring?' Thato had taken a moment before looking up at her and responding, 'Outside house'. The woman had a semi-detached cottage where her domestic worker lived. She reported a few days later that after she questioned the domestic worker the woman had broken down in tears and confessed that she had taken it under pressure from her boyfriend. She was fired on the spot.

Kgethi didn't think too much about Thato's powers. They sank into the background noise of her life until one day, Kgethi got a message on Facebook that brought them back into sharp focus. The message was written, 'Cc, my name is Philani Simelane. I heard ur little girl finds missing things. Pls can u help me find something important I lost?' She stared at the message for a few seconds. The profile picture was of a stranger. She went onto his profile and saw they had no friends in common. She was stunned. Her chest tightened. Who was this man? Where did he come from and how did he know about Thato? She ignored the message. Three days later another one came, this time from a strange woman she had never seen before.

She walked in public with Thato feeling as though every eye was watching them. When she made eye contact with a stranger she wondered, 'Did they know too?'. Strange sounds turned into voices whispering her and Thato's names. She hadn't felt this aware of herself since she was pregnant. When the third message came she knew she had to tell her mother. It seemed unavoidable now that people would find out. Kgethi had an idea.

'Maybe we should start charging people?' Kgethi proposed. 'We could make some real money.'

But Mom wouldn't hear of it. 'We're not going to start selling your daughter. Please man, Kgethi.'

'Why not?'

'Because it's exploitative!' She snapped. 'And anyway I don't think it's safe. Can you imagine what could happen if people found out she has this ability? Someone could take her or, or...' she went silent.

Kgethi stared at her mother. What the hell were they going to do? The strangeness of it all turned them into unlikely allies in a relationship which had turned cold the moment Kgethi had come home pregnant. Her mother had treated every moment of her pregnancy as a punishment. Every time Kgethi complained of her body aches and exhaustion, or the persistent stares she got in public, or the cost of antenatal care, maternity clothes, and baby supplies, her mother would say in a dismissive tone, 'Well if you'd just used a condom you wouldn't be in this situation now would you?'

Every time Kgethi looked at her she saw disappointment in her face. She had seen it before, of course. Like the time Kgethi snuck alcohol into high school and nearly got expelled. Or the time her mother got a call from another teacher complaining of Kgethi's behaviour. Or the numerous times her parents had been called into the principal's office because of something Kgethi had done. But there was something about this disappointment that stuck. Kgethi had really fucked up this time, and her mother reminded her of it daily.

And then came Thato. Kgethi watched the anger melt away from her mother's face as she held Thato, fed her expressed milk using a bottle, played peekaboo with her, and sang her to sleep. She snapped at Kgethi when she bottle fed at the wrong angle, nagged her about breastfeeding instead because 'It's better for the baby', and lifted Thato away from her when she held her without properly supporting her neck. Well, looks like she finally got the daughter she wanted, Kgethi thought cynically. Now she felt Thato's powers hanging between them like a heavy rope binding their waists together. She saw the uncertainty she felt mirrored in her mother's face.

'What should we do?' She asked.

Her mother shrugged. 'I don't know. I think we must stop telling people about Thato's powers. Let's just keep it between us. No more letting Thato help people who aren't our immediate family.'

Ntatemogolo insisted on them bringing her to his home in Soweto to find his pipe, which had gone missing a few days prior. Kgethi hated going to his house. He always looked over her tight, revealing clothes with a disapproving stare before asking why she didn't cover up more. He scoffed at her attempts at Setswana often muttering something she pretended not to understand. When he found out she was pregnant he became unbearable. 'If you just disciplined her like I told you to this wouldn't have happened, Mahlatse,' Kgethi once overheard him telling her mother. 'She doesn't even know who the father is! What decent man is going to want to marry her now?'

Unfortunately for Kgethi, he was also unavoidable.

When they arrived, Ntatemogolo had hardly greeted them before stretching out his arms. 'Bring her to me,' he had said. 'I want to see her.' Kgethi handed Thato to him. Instead of clinging to her as most babies do when a stranger tries to take them from their mother, Thato went willingly. At two-years-old, Thato had a keener sense than most adults of where she was wanted and where she was not. She stared at him with big, curious eyes as he took her. He looked at her and chuckled.

'Such a big forehead! You can tell this one is going to be very intelligent!' He looked at her a moment longer. 'You know something Mahlatse?'

'Yes, Papa?' Kgethi's mother responded.

'She looks exactly like Dineo!'

Her mother stiffened, in the way she always did whenever Aunt Dineo was mentioned. Kgethi wouldn't know. She had never met her aunt who had gone missing or died (depending on who told the story) before she was born. All she knew about her aunt was the pictures she had seen, the name she had taken as her middle name, and the half-memories her mother always started telling before her grief prevented her from continuing. Kgethi looked at Thato and supposed she could see the link. She vaguely remembered round curious eyes and a slanting forehead in the faded photographs she had seen.

'I think she looks a bit more like Kgethi,' her mother said.

'Hhayi, no,' Ntatemogolo interjected. 'It is as if I'm holding Neo again. If Sylvia was here she would say the same thing. She used to say that Neo was the oldest looking baby she had ever seen,' he said with a smile. 'And she was right! Neo was wise beyond her years even at three months old!'

There was a moment of silence. Kgethi detached the way she usually did whenever discussion of her aunt and grandmother came up, but not before noticing the look on her mother's face. She looked heavy. As though she were sinking into the floor.

TWO

Kgethi had given birth to her aunt. There was no sense in Mahlatse denying it any longer. She had frozen in shock when she saw the same features in her granddaughter's face that she had last seen over 20 years ago in her sister. It was as if Dineo had returned to their lives through Kgethi's womb.

On the cold June morning of Thato's birth, the wound of Dineo's disappearance grew a little bigger. Looking at Thato was painful at first. Every time she had to help Kgethi with washing Thato or feeding her the split second of recognition cut into her like a knife. As time went on the pain Mahlatse initially felt went away. She had long accepted that the burden of raising Thato fell squarely on her shoulders. But what she hadn't anticipated was the level of indifference Kgethi displayed. She approached everything from feedings to diaper changes to bathing in a half-hearted manner. She would complain about the cost of formula only to come home with a head full of fresh waist length micro braids that cost God knows how much. 'I'm allowed to do my hair, Mom. Don't judge me just because I don't want a chiskop like yours!' She said defensively when Mahlatse brought it up. Kgethi seemed completely disinterested in raising her own child and it irritated Mahlatse beyond measure.

She remembered how difficult Kgethi had been. She had cried all night every night for the whole of her first year. She was in hospital every other week for some ailment or another.

She was a fussy baby, quick to start shrieking and slow to calm down. Mahlatse had been so tired and stressed she could barely remember her own name. To make matters worse, she was largely alone. Her own husband had refused to do his fair share of parenting, saying that the baby he had insisted on creating was 'too much'. She had never missed her own mother more than she did in those first few months.

Thato on the other hand had been a joy to look after, and Mahlatse couldn't help thinking how much easier things might have been if Kgethi had been more like this. The rage she'd initially felt towards Kgethi for getting pregnant had slowly slipped away, with love towards her granddaughter taking its place. But there was something about Thato's powers that unsettled her. The rest of the family however, was indifferent. They did not bother to find an explanation for why Thato had the abilities she had and decided it was nothing worth worrying about. They were simply thankful that they now had what few people did: a reliable way to find their missing items. Perhaps if it had stayed this way, if her abilities ended there, Mahlatse might have been able to stop herself from pondering them too much. However, as Thato grew, so did her powers.

One evening shortly after Thato's fifth birthday, Mahlatse and Kgethi were sitting in the living room together watching Grey's Anatomy as they did every week. Mahlatse was half-watching, half-knitting a small beanie for her granddaughter. Thato had been put to bed. As the two of them sat they started to hear the pitter patter of tiny steps making their way towards the living room.

'Oh God, she's awake,' Kgethi said, managing to pause the show just as Thato walked in. There were wet tracks of tears running from her eyes to her chin.

'Thato, why aren't you in bed?' Kgethi asked, barely masking the irritation in her voice.

'Kgethi don't snap at her like that,' Mahlatse said. She put down her knitting needles, picked Thato up and placed her on her lap. 'Baby girl, did you have a bad dream?'

She wiped away her tears. 'Yes, Koko,' she said.

'What happened?'

Thato looked up at her and said, 'I saw you driving. You stopped at a robot and a man in a big white car bashed you.'

'Oh sweetie, it was just a bad dream! No one is going to crash into Koko, don't worry. Now let's go back to bed, okay?'

A few days later Mahlatse was running late for a meeting. She desperately needed to sell a house to make up for the dip in her sales over the past few months. It was hardly her fault, the housing market was on the decline, but still, she was rushing to make a good impression. The couple she was meeting were absurdly wealthy and their idea of a good family home involved no less than a swimming pool, a tennis court, a big yard for the dogs, and four bedrooms to fill with future children. She had a house in mind that would generate enough in commission to pay her growing pile of bills. If she could sell it.

She was thinking of the house at a traffic light when suddenly she was knocked from behind. Her body lurched forward and snapped back from the force of the seatbelt, banging her head against the headrest. She was only just registering the pain in her neck when a woman knocked on her window.

'Are you alright ma'am?' The woman yelled.

She turned and saw the reddened face of a man who had planted the nose of his white bakkie into the back of her car. When she looked into the face of the man she saw Thato's worried eyes staring back at her. She was so spooked by the incident that she decided not to tell anyone the full story. 'I got hit by some housewife driving an SUV,' she told Kgethi when she asked. She told Ntatemogolo and Molefi there had been an accident but mentioned nothing of the dream. It was a coincidence. It was deja vu. It meant nothing, she reassured herself.

A few months later, Kgethi walked into the house looking pale as though she had seen a ghost. 'Mom, the freakiest thing just happened!'

Mahlatse felt the apprehension churning inside her but tried to remain calm. 'What happened?'

Kgethi sat down at the kitchen table. 'You know Precious, right? The Zimbabwean girl I work with?'

'Uh… yes?'

'Well, she told me today that last night she got held up by some guys on her way to the taxi rank. They took her wallet and phone and gave her shit for being Zimbabwean.

'Here's where it gets really weird. Two days ago Thato told me that she had a dream about a lady getting robbed on her way to get a taxi. And she described the lady in the dream as being really thin and short with dark skin and long braids.

'Mom, that's exactly what Precious looks like! And Thato has never seen her before! Like, I've never even described her. That's so weird right?'

Mahlatse paused. 'This isn't the first time she's done something like this.'

'What do you mean?'

Mahlatse turned to her daughter. 'My car accident. It wasn't a woman in a Range that hit me. It was a man in a white bakkie. A big one.'

Kgethi looked at her in disbelief. 'But then why did you lie about it?'

'Because I… I didn't want to admit…' she struggled to find the words. 'I'm starting to get worried. If she's getting visions then… well it might be a sign she has the calling.'

Kgethi rolled her eyes. Mahlatse knew that telling her daughter about callings was like telling her the tooth fairy existed. Kgethi had come back from one semester of psychology at Wits insisting that what people termed callings were actually mental illnesses like schizophrenia or bipolar disorder.

'You'd have to be at least a little crazy to think a bunch of dead people are telling you to be a sangoma,' she used to say. Mahlatse found her dismissiveness extremely irritating and narrow-minded.

'I think you're overreacting, Mom,' she finally said.

'Maybe, but maybe don't tell people just to be safe,' Mahlatse said. 'Especially Ntatemogolo.'

THREE

It took Thato a few years to see she was different. At first, she thought everyone else was just like her. She thought everyone saw the world as she did connected through shining gold threads. In her mind, everyone else's dreams like hers had a tendency to come true.

She would gaze through the window of her Mummy's car and see shining gold threads spooling off the homeless people who begged at intersections. They weaved between the cars at peak hour traffic dragging their threads of missing things behind them. Everyone had strings. They waved in the wind like jellyfish tentacles. They were all gold in colour. Some looked thick like the ropes she swung from on the school playground. Some were thin and delicate like spiderwebs. She saw some shine bright in the sun while others looked faded like old pictures. Everywhere she looked she saw living puppets tethered to their losses as they walked down the streets.

The strings made up her world along with the high walls guarding the homes of her neighbourhood, the jacaranda trees which shed purple flowers onto the roads, the sounds of the giant hadedas cawing in the morning, and the taxis swaying up and down the streets like drunk men. She saw the threads reflected through the tall mirrored skyscrapers in Sandton. If she stood very close to a person's string she could see exactly where the missing thing was.

Thato was like a helper. Like one of Santa's little elves. It gave her a warm feeling to know she could help her family so much, even though she was so small. She liked how happy she made the grown-ups around her when she helped them find a missing thing. The strings were one thing. When she was six the dreams started. Those scared her. Seeing the man bash into Koko upset her so much she started crying. Seeing a woman get mugged by a big group of bad men shouting ugly things at her gave her nightmares. She told Koko and Mummy, because they always told her that if anything bad happened she must go to them. At first, Koko told her that her dreams were just that, bad dreams. Then they started looking at her different. She felt a nervous lump in her tummy. Was there something wrong with her?

One day, she had a bad dream scarier than all the others put together. She was standing on a road in the middle of nowhere at nighttime. There were rows of yellow sunflowers taller than her on both sides of the road. The big sunflower heads were bowed like they knew something awful was about to happen and they didn't want to see. Suddenly, she heard shouting. The footsteps of someone running towards her. Dogs barking and running too. She turned around and saw a boy. He ran out of the sunflower field behind her holding a few sunflower heads. He ran past Thato towards the field on the other side of the road.

Bang!

She jumped from the sound and covered her ears. It echoed all around her, making shockwaves she felt running through her body, making a ringing sound in her ear. She looked up and saw the boy fall. He hit the ground. The sunflowers scattered around him. She saw a dark wet patch grow on the boy's back. She screamed when she heard someone come up behind her. It was a tall man holding a gun. He walked towards the boy and bent over him. He kicked him once with his heavy boot, turned around, and walked back into the field. Thato heard what sounded like a car starting far behind her. She tried to move her legs but couldn't. She felt like she'd turned into ice. There was no one on the road besides her and the boy. She heard soft footsteps and turned to see a white dog with gray spots and the outline of a ribcage showing through its skin running past her.

She woke up in a cold sweat. Her heart was thumping so hard it felt like it would jump out of her chest. In the corner of her room was a shadow, and the shadow was shaped like a person. She turned on her bedside lamp. The shadow was the boy. She could see the wall through him, like he was made out of glass. Blood trickled from a dark, wet spot on his chest. He was crying and with each sob blood poured out his mouth. She wrapped her arms around herself, too scared to scream or cry. She pinched herself. No, she wasn't dreaming. This was real. The boy was real. His crying rang in her ear. The air around her smelled like coins. She hid herself under the sheets. 'Please go away, please go away, please go away, please...' she whispered. She felt like she was under there forever. She had never been more scared in her life. She lay shivering under her blanket until the crying stopped. The coin smell went away. She looked up and he was gone. She didn't go back to sleep that night. She didn't sleep for the whole week.

She didn't want to tell anyone what happened. She wanted to pretend it hadn't. But after it did she started seeing see-through people everywhere. Some of them looked at her. Some walked past her, leaving cold air behind. No one else ever saw them. She saw Mummy and Koko walk straight through two. Some weren't so bad. There were grey old people who smiled at her as they walked past. There were children, some with ugly sores from being hit by cars or thin bodies with no hair at all who would pull funny faces at her before running away laughing. There were women Mummy's age, Koko's age, some with dark wet holes in them, some thin and sick-looking, who would hug her tight before turning into air.

Then there were the bad ones. They were usually the men. She was once chased away from the swimming pool area by a big man with blood on his face who was laughing at her like one of the bad guys in cartoons. There was a drunk man who wobbled from side to side on the street swearing at everyone from his Mom to the drivers, to Thato. There was even a man who gave her a look that made her want to crawl away and said, 'Come on, give me some pussy one last time. I bet you're nice and tight,' before walking away laughing. Thato didn't know what that meant but it scared her. At first, she thought other kids saw the see-through people too. She told a boy in her class about one of the bald kids with bruised eyes who'd wanted to play with her.

'Oh, you mean like an imaginary friend? I have one too,' he said. 'Mine is named Charlie and he looks like a big purple horse with moth wings!'

So that's what they were called! Imaginary friends! So many kids in school had one that it made Thato feel better about hers. Even her teacher smiled at her and asked her more about her imaginary friends when she mentioned them. The smile turned into a frown when Thato told her how many had dark stains from blood, open holes, and were falling over like in the old cartoons when they drank too much. Thato thought she was in trouble for sure when the teacher called Mummy in. 'What did you do?' Mummy hissed at her the night before the meeting. She didn't say anything. She looked at the floor and tried not to cry.

She felt heavy the whole day at school before the meeting. As though her legs had been filled up with rocks. And when Mummy arrived in the afternoon, they went to the teacher's office. Thato stayed at the back of the room playing with toys while Mummy sat at the teacher's desk. She could still hear everything. The teacher sat behind her desk and asked in a serious voice, 'Is everything okay at home? Is there a member of the family who drinks a bit too much in front of Thato? Were you aware Ms Pule, that Thato has been having such disturbing thoughts? Because really, if this continues, I'm bound by law to call child protective services.'

Mummy smiled at her and told her that everything was just fine at home. That apart from the odd glass of wine no one drank in front of Thato. That she was aware Thato had an active imagination, but she would speak to her at home just to make sure she was alright. Once they were out of the teacher's eyesight, Mummy pulled her behind the car, looked around to make sure no one was listening, and crouched low until they were eye to eye.

'Thato!' She said in a panicked whisper. 'What did you tell them?'

Thato looked down at her shoes. She could feel the hot tears starting in her eyes. She'd been naughty and now she was in trouble. She could tell.

'Come on, Thato. Don't cry. Then they really will think I'm abusing you. Just tell me what you said to Teacher,' she said.

'I... I told her about my imaginary friends.'

'What imaginary friends? Since when do you have imaginary friends?'

Thato didn't respond.

'Okay, can you at least tell me what you said about them?'

Thato shifted her feet. She kept looking at the ground. 'I... I told her some of them have blood and holes and stuff.'

Silence. 'I'm sorry, what?'

'Mhmmm,' tears slowly started running down Thato's cheeks.

'Okay, okay, calm down. Calm down! Just tell me everything about these imaginary friends.'

So Thato told her, starting with the boy in the corner of her room, to the bald children, to the drunk men shouting weird, scary things at her. At first she was so nervous she had a hard time getting the words out. When she saw that Mummy's eyes weren't rolling like normal but were stuck on her face, sucking up her words like sponges, it became easier to tell the truth. Mummy looked away for a moment and took a sharp breath. Then she turned back to Thato and put her hands on her shoulders.

'Listen to me, Thato. You can't go around telling people that, okay? Especially not white people. They freak out when they hear these kinds of things because they don't understand like we do, get it? So from now on whenever something weird happens to you I want you to come and tell me or Koko okay?'

She nodded her head. The next week when the teacher asked her about her imaginary friends she told her about a big purple horse with moth wings.

FOUR

Molefi didn't like children. There were two things in life he knew for a fact he never wanted: marriage and children. Which is why he wasn't as excited as his friends were when same-sex marriage was legalised back in 2006. Sure, he could see why objectively it was a good thing. Equal rights and all that. He attended every same-sex marriage he was invited to and ensured he bought one of the nicer gifts on the wedding registry. But personally, he was unmoved by being presented with an option he had never had any interest in taking. And as for kids, well, it was harder to argue why someone would want them than why they wouldn't. Little screaming terrorists the lot of them. They did nothing but break things, make everything dirty, and suck up all peace, spontaneity, and their parents' money.

Molefi liked knowing he could fly off to Europe at a moment's notice (which he did, twice) without having to worry about a babysitter or term dates. He liked knowing he could buy beautiful Carrol Boyes glassware without worrying about some brat flinging a soccer ball around the room and breaking it. He always found good excuses to get out of toddlers' birthday parties and christenings. He attended the baby showers of only his closest family and friends. He had perfected the art of holding a baby for approximately five seconds before returning it to its mother. There was only one baby he feared when it came he would be completely unable to avoid. The worst baby. His sister's.

He had always felt that Kgethi was an excessively spoilt, excessively difficult child. She had cried too much as a baby, shrieking for hours until Molefi had to leave to protect his sanity. He would arrive at his sister's house only to be greeted by a woman so exhausted she could barely stand, wearing sweatpants and dark circles under her eyes, while a persistent wailing went on in the background. She threw thunderous tantrums in public. As she grew older the tantrums turned to pouting. The screaming turned to snide comments, unreasonable demands, and cruel jokes. Molefi would look from Kgethi to Mahlatse, at the small almond eyes, wide nose, and rounded face they shared, and wondered how it was possible for a child to look like her mother's clone but in every way that mattered act exactly like her asshole of a father. When Kgethi became pregnant he expected the child to be exactly the same. Instead she gave birth to her polar opposite. Molefi had never thought before he met Thato that it was possible for a child to be so peaceful. It wasn't just that she never cried or threw tantrums. She had a weightlessness to her that he had only heard of children having but had never seen. It was as though baby Kgethi had absorbed all of her parents' unhappiness in the womb and carried it throughout her life whereas Thato had been born free. There was, of course, the awkward question of her gifts. By her eighth birthday it was an open family secret that she was able to see the dead. Mahlatse was not pleased.

'It's getting worse, Molefi,' she said to him. 'I'm really starting to think this child is being called.'

'She's eight years old,' he said dismissively in between drags of his cigarette. 'Badimo aren't the nicest bunch but I don't think they're that cruel.'

They were sitting at what had become their favourite restaurant on Vilakazi Street. Molefi never failed to marvel at how much the street had changed. What had once been a quiet residential road the three of them walked as children had transformed into a tourist magnet and one of the hottest pieces of real estate in Soweto. Both Nelson Mandela and Archbishop Desmond Tutu had once owned houses on the street, making it the only street in the world where two Nobel Peace Prize laureates had once lived. Tourists flocked to gawk at the beloved former president's house in particular where, if you looked closely, you could still see the holes blasted open by Apartheid police bullets decades ago.

Now the street was bustling with tourist-priced restaurants and merchants hawking off authentic African souvenirs. On the same street where Molefi had once only heard languages like isiZulu, seSotho, and xiTsonga he now heard French, German, and Chinese. Red-faced tourists marched up and down the street carrying DSLR cameras and locally produced hand-beaded bags in tow. The emerging black middle class, desperate to escape the claustrophobic whiteness of the suburbs, arrived in droves every weekend to drink beer, eat their food and speak the languages that had raised them.

Molefi came every time he needed a good dose of nostalgia. No matter what had happened, the good and the ugly, Soweto was his home and there was still no place where he felt more at ease than here. This street was filled with the memories of his childhood and most importantly, of his sister. He would glance at a house still standing on the road and remember how he and Dineo used to walk past it together. These memories weighed heavy as a burden on him yet he chased them away. He looked across at his sister and still thought of how strange it was that it was Mahlatse he was sitting across from and not Dineo. Growing up they had never been terribly close. They had never understood each other. She had instinctually known from a young age he wasn't quite like other boys and he had always known her as a dizzy, daydreaming child with strange habits who was irritatingly absent-minded. But over time they had forged a strong bond through their mutual grief. Now Molefi couldn't imagine a life without their relationship.

'I just worry about her, Molefi,' Mahlatse continued. 'I worry about what these powers could mean.'

'They might not mean anything. Sometimes people just have abilities and they never get called,' he said, taking a drag. 'Like you remember Aus' Rosalia? Who lived two streets away?'

Mahlatse's face was blank.

'Hhayi man, Mahlatse, Aus' Rosalia! The one with the dreams'

'Ohh her!' Mahlatse finally said. 'I remember her! Mama once didn't let me go out because Aus' Rosalia told her she had a bad dream about me!'

'Yes! The dream lady! Remember she used to go around telling women they were pregnant because she dreamt of ripe fruit? And all the women she spoke to were in fact pregnant. She was never wrong. But she also never had a calling. For all you know, Thato could be like that.'

Molefi had still never told Mahlatse about the day he had overheard Aus' Rosalia tell Dineo that she'd dreamt of her.

'And what if she isn't?'

He rolled his eyes. 'Really, Hlatse! You need to relax before you worry yourself into an early grave. We should all be grateful we have a child with such useful gifts who wants to help out. Unlike that other one.'

Mahlatse made a face. He ignored it. 'And besides,' he continued. 'As long as we don't go around whispering her powers into everyone's ears I don't see what the problem could possibly be. What's the worst that could happen?'

Mahlatse opened her mouth as if to respond and paused instead. As he finished his cigarette they overheard a blonde American woman at the next table say earnestly, 'Excuse me, could I have a glass of oom-kom-bow-tee?'

They made eye contact with each other and started giggling. 'Oh poor things,' Molefi said. 'They can't help it, can they?'

'They really can't,' Mahlatse said. 'and that's why Papa can't stand the well-meaning whites.'

'That one can't stand most things,' Molefi interjected. 'He can't even stand fun. Mama always said there were only two times she ever saw him dance. On their wedding day—'

'—and the day Verwoerd died,' they said in unison before laughing again. Their laughter was replaced by an awkward pause as the memory of what else their father couldn't stand seeped in.

Their father was a traditional man through and through who rejected most white, Western things. In his household English was treated like a weed. Their father believed that if a few seedlings of English were allowed to grow in his children's throats they would begin to root, wrapping themselves around tongues and choking any Setswana words they encountered until they withered away. As a result English had been banned. The tsotsitaal that was spoken in the neighbourhood was banned as well. 'It's a nonsense language,' their father would say. Only pure Setswana was spoken in his house.

In retrospect perhaps he had been right about that one thing. Mahlatse had been different, treating English as a coat to be mended at home so that it could be whipped out and worn in professional settings. Molefi had watched as his sister encouraged his niece to speak English in her home, never bothering to correct her when Kgethi responded to Setswana with English. As a result, he'd winced whenever he heard Kgethi speak Setswana with a strange accent, poor grammar, and limited vocabulary. How ironic, he'd think, for him to agree with his father's traditionalism when decades prior it had torn him apart.

After a long moment Mahlatse looked at him sympathetically. 'He'll come around, you know,' she offered.

Molefi scoffed. He wasn't sure who she was trying to convince, him or herself. 'It's been over twenty years, Hlatse,' he said. 'I highly doubt that.'

* * *

Johannesburg was a city permeated by colonial influence in every corner and reflected most brightly in its architecture. In the older, central suburbs you saw hints of 19th century Holland while in the newer northern suburbs Tuscany reigned. Molefi hated the north. The buildings, the traffic, the people, it was all unbearably trendy and unjustifiably overpriced. He instead fell in love with the character of Old Johannesburg. The twisting jacaranda-tree lined roads, green ivy clinging to walls, decades-old homes with high tin pressed ceilings and wooden floors, and the strips of shops boasting antique furniture and second-hand books all appealed to him.

Once he had made his money as a corporate lawyer in New Johannesburg, he bought the house of his dreams in the Old. It was late 2018 and the president's resignation earlier that year had done little to save an economy in tatters. Molefi was one of the few that benefitted from this change in events. The economic downturn had a knock-on effect on real estate, turning the property market into one that favoured buyers. Molefi was almost giddy when he bought his dream house for a steal from desperate owners who were anxious to emigrate. It had a large yard, cottage in the back, swimming pool, wide open rooms, and great French windows. He fell in love with it the moment he saw it, but he knew a move from his Sandton townhouse would not be possible without Thato's help. Molefi rejected the term hoarder. He simply loved to have a house full of beautiful things which he collected during his travels. From books, to photographs, to ornaments, to vinyl records, he loved having a home that was tastefully full. Naturally, this made moving a nightmare. At least it would be if he didn't have a niece with a natural gift for finding missing things.

He asked Kgethi if he could borrow Thato for the day. He figured he could handle a seven-year-old child on his own. They were at that cute age where they no longer threw tantrums and did not yet have the irritatingly sarcastic tongue that came naturally to teenagers. Since Kgethi never said no to someone who wanted to take Thato away, she accepted. Molefi watched as the little girl ran from him to the house fetching various objects and reminding him where he left others. When they arrived at the new house he allowed her to carry light objects while the movers he hired carried the heavier furniture. He allowed her to take a break and watched as she ran into the garden, chasing after the butterflies. He smiled as he looked at her. If he could have a child and be guaranteed that it would turn out like Thato, maybe he could try it. Just one.

She paused and bent over with a furrow in her little face. She picked up a small feathery thing. Molefi was confused before realising what it was. With horror, he stepped down from his patio and moved towards her.

'Thato! Put that down! That's dirty,' he yelled at her.

'But Uncle Molefi, it's hurt. Look,' she said holding up the pathetic bird. It was flapping weakly but its wing was lame and its legs were crooked at a grotesque angle. It didn't look like it would live.

'Come now, Thato. Put that down!' He wanted to smack it out of her hands but didn't want to touch it. Who knew what kind of bacteria that disgusting creature was hosting? He reached out for her but she ran away from him.

'I want to help it!' She turned her back from him.

Once again he was reminded why he didn't want children. 'I'm not playing with you. You need to put that thing down now. It'll make you sick!'

She turned around, faced him, and opened her hands. Molefi froze in shock. The little bird chirped and stood in her hand perfectly whole. She thrust it into the air and it flew, beyond the trees and into the sky, far beyond sight.

PART TWO

THE REBIRTH OF SOLOMON KHUMALO

FIVE

On the front cover of the May 2019 issue of Time magazine was an aerial shot that at first glance appeared to be a split frame photo. In fact it was a single image. On the left side was lush green grass and trees, tennis courts, and rooftops covering sizable homes. On the right were small, sprawling grey rectangles bunched up together, one on top of another, separated by narrow walkways. The left and the right are separated only by a road. There is one headline. It reads: The World's Most Unequal Country. On the left was Sandton, the richest square mile in Africa, where prosperity, glass and metal skyscrapers, five-star restaurants and outrageous amounts of wealth were tightly concentrated.

Solomon Khumalo was raised on the right. Alexandra was where he was born and raised but his life there felt like the consequence of an unlucky draw. He always felt like he didn't truly belong in Alex. Over the years, the burgeoning economic capital of the country had attracted a mad rush of economic migrants into Gauteng, from villages and small towns. Many of them settled in Alex because of its close proximity to Sandton. Solomon noticed the influx. Many of his neighbours, including his own mother, were building homes in their small backyards and renting them out, bringing more people to his street. He found himself feeling more cramped. Or perhaps more restless.

He would gaze at the Sandton skyline and know in his gut

that he belonged there. When he went into Sandton with his mother he felt a yearning for the clean streets there, not like the ones at home where people threw rubbish out until it grew into large piles the municipality refused to collect. He would walk the streets from home to school and back, passing by the children who played in the streets, the old ladies clutching their Bibles and handbags as they walked to their prayer circles, the women in bathrobes and doeks sitting on crates swapping stories, the men who gathered around televisions in taverns clasping bottles of beer and cheering on their soccer teams, and knew that he couldn't stay here forever. If I lived in Sandton, I'd be dropped off at school in a Lamborghini every day, he'd think to himself. He would sometimes watch Top Billing with his mother and see the gigantic mansions people lived in with swimming pools, tennis courts, and kitchens the size of his whole home. One day, he told himself, I'll live in a house just like that. He would imagine himself driving a Bentley, laughing with a beautiful woman whose neck was choked with diamonds and perfume. He could see himself standing in his rooftop penthouse apartment in the Michaelangelo overlooking it all, overlooking Alex, and thinking about how he would write long speeches telling an adoring audience that he had made it, and so could they.

The last thing he wanted was to be like Bhut' Nelson, who had lived his entire 75-year-old life in one house just up the road. The only thing he had ever achieved was the old Toyota Cressida he bought just after Apartheid ended that was rusting away in front of his house. The car that had once been the ultimate success symbol driven by businessmen and gangsters alike was now a noisy collection of spare parts that spewed thick fumes as it rattled slowly down streets. Solomon would look Bhut' Nelson in the face and feel a shiver run up his spine. I'm going to be better, he'd think. I'm going to do more.

'There's only one way you'll leave this place,' his mother would tell him. 'You must study hard in school and put your trust in God.'

His parents had different approaches to his dreams. His father had scoffed at them, saying, 'The problem with all these black elites is they take their money and go spend it on white businesses, buying houses in white neighbourhoods, instead of staying here and improving things for the next generation of black children. Then they turn around and come to us with big smiles and bigger promises during elections. They only remember us when it's time to get votes.'

His father, Mthobisi, was allegedly a Mkhonto we Sizwe veteran. Allegedly, because no one, not even Solomon, could be sure that any of his stories of exile were true. He dutifully collected his veteran's grant every month, but when you asked him about life in exile he would sometimes say he was in Botswana, other times in Angola, and other times as far away as the Soviet Union. Solomon once tried to look up the Soviet Union on the map at school. No matter how much he searched, he couldn't see it anywhere. This for him was solid evidence of his father's lies.

One of the earliest memories he had of his father was when at five years old, he clasped his mother's hand as his parents stood in the longest line he had ever known to vote for the first time. He knew his parents were going to vote for Nelson Mandela. It was all they had talked about for months. They could hardly contain their excitement. His father was giving long, impassioned speeches to anyone who cared to listen about how hard they had fought and how much they had sacrificed to reach that moment. After they voted, they went outside and showed their ink-marked thumbs to the cheers from the people outside waiting for their turns.

Solomon's father was a big talker. He was always the first to speak at community meetings. He would hold long lectures at taverns, on street corners, and in any other place he could find a captive audience. And he always did. People were taken by how clearly he articulated their struggles. They laughed at his jokes, hung on in suspense when he told them about his near-miss escapes from the SADF, and nodded in agreement every time he spoke about the greed, corruption, and incompetence of the government. They marveled at his recollection of historical facts, how he quoted the likes of Steve Biko, Robert Sobukwe, and Thomas Sankara from memory, and how he detailed the pitfalls of capitalism and the evils of white supremacy.

He had often been elected as a community representative whenever a politician (always close to elections) had offered to speak to the residents of Alex and hear their concerns. He had been interviewed by journalists looking for a good soundbite more times than anyone could count. He had been encouraged every municipal election to run for ward councillor, to which he always replied, 'Thank you comrades, but I have no desire to be part of the system.' As he grew into a teenager the excuse began to sound like a cop-out to Solomon. He looked at his father with the same wide-eyed admiration everyone else did when he spoke. When he joked Solomon laughed. When he broke down in detail how the government had wasted the money allocated for the Alexandra Renewal Project, Solomon's chest swelled with pride. When he spoke to other kids at school he found himself trying to copy the same mannerisms and cadences his father adopted while speaking.

But when Mthobisi stepped off his podium he revealed himself for what he was. A fraud. He hadn't held a job in years, instead relying on the veteran's grant which he drank away at the tavern every month. Solomon would hear him stumble home at night drunk, singing old struggle songs and banging about in the kitchen. Whenever Solomon asked his father for anything, even something as small as coming to church to watch him play Joseph in the nativity play, he'd make a big show saying, 'Hey, my boy is going to be the next John Kani! You'll see!' And then he would never show up. As far as Solomon was concerned, he was all talk and no action. Solomon often thought to himself that his father didn't refuse to occupy a political position because he didn't want to be part of the system. He refused to because he knew he would fail. Solomon would look at his father stumbling home wearing clothes stained with his own vomit and think to himself, this isn't a man. He refused to be anything like him.

SIX

While his father was the dreamer who lived in the clouds, Solomon's mother, Patricia, kept her family's feet firmly planted on the ground. She was a government employee at a nearby Home Affairs office. The job gave the family enough money and benefits to live in a four-room brick house with a wall surrounding it and a long drop in the yard. Like most of their neighbours, she had built a one-room home in their little yard which she rented out. The tenants would range from young, new matriculants fresh out of their rural villages to entire families who had trekked across the national borders. 'We need the extra money,' she had explained to Solomon and his siblings. He hated it still.

Some of the tenants were loud with annoying, disruptive habits and he hated having to share the long drop. When too many people used it, it stank fiercely, especially in the summer months, attracting many flies that buzzed about his legs and ears. There was only one tenant Solomon had liked who had moved in when he was 13. She had been a pretty, soft-spoken young woman who had moved from Lesotho to work as a domestic worker in one of the Sandton suburbs. The bedroom Solomon shared with his siblings faced hers and he soon realised that she did not always close her curtains completely. He snuck out a few times when his mother wasn't home to watch the tenant getting dressed through the curtain crack hoping to catch a glimpse of her breasts without being caught by his mother.

His mother was a praying woman. She would pray in the mornings, pray before every meal, and pray loudly every evening before retiring to bed. She would force her three children to take turns reading aloud from the battered, dog-eared Bible she kept in the home. She gave each of her children biblical names. Solomon for her eldest, Isaac for her second, and Mary for her only daughter. Mthobisi hated the names. He thought they were too white, too colonised, but he had been so drunk during the birth of each of his children that by the time he sobered up his wife had already written their names on the birth certificate.

Every Sunday morning while Mthobisi snored off the previous night's drink, she dressed herself and her children up and made them take two taxis with her to St Mary's Cathedral. The cathedral was located in the middle of Johannesburg CBD. The CBD had once been the economic heartbeat of the city, but was now a rubbish filled, urine scented, crime-ridden, dilapidated shell of its former glory. Men urinated openly against the cathedral walls. The brown stone walls of the church were turning grey from grime. Even entering the church required manoeuvring through the hooting, densely packed cars on the road driving as and how they pleased.

Inside the cathedral was an entirely different story. The air was thick from the smell of incense. The church was modeled after Renaissance architecture, with white walls curving into a ceiling so high it was impossible to touch, rows and rows of dark wood pews culminating in a golden altar, stained glass windows and an enormous brass organ at the back. Above the altar stood an enormous statue of Jesus dying on the cross with a grief-stricken Mary next to him. The statue of Jesus with his bright red bleeding wounds, ribs sticking through his skin, and agonised expression frightened Solomon and his siblings. So did the part of the ceremony where congregants were called up to eat the flesh of Christ and drink his blood. When he was still small, Solomon had wondered if the real Jesus was tied up in a basement and every week the kindly-looking deacon would go downstairs with a knife to cut off some of his flesh and drain some of his blood. The idea terrified him.

Solomon and his siblings were relieved when their mother sent them two stories up to the room that housed the Sunday school. Instead of staring at tortured Jesus, they got to play with other children, listen to Bible stories, and sing songs. The songs were his favorite part. They would stand in a circle during worship while the Sunday school teacher stood in the middle leading them all in song. The sound of a dozen little voices would ring out:

> Father Abraham had many sons,
> Many sons had Father Abraham.
> I am one of them, and so are you,
> So let's just praise the Lord
> One arm!

Then all the children would lift one arm and sing the verse again, swinging their arms wildly until they added another arm, and then a leg, and then another, until they were marching in place like giggling soldiers, bobbing their heads, turning around, and finally collapsing on the ground in fits of laughter. Solomon liked Sunday school. He didn't like having to go down for communion, where he'd watch all the adults drink Jesus's blood and eat his flesh. He didn't like having to sit still as an old man in a long cream robe clutched his forehead and prayed. Most of all he hated fidgeting through the unbearably boring final minutes of the church service.

'Mama, why do we keep going there?' He asked one morning. 'Why don't we go to a church that's closer?'

His mother looked at him briefly before telling him to stop asking questions and just get dressed. It wasn't until a few days later that she explained. The cathedral was nearly a hundred years old, making it one of the oldest in the country.

It had been one of the few cathedrals to allow congregants of all races to attend services during Apartheid. Archbishop Desmond Tutu had preached there as the first black deacon of the cathedral and the country. The funerals of anti-Apartheid activists like Oliver Tambo had been held there.

'There is history living in that church, Solomon. It has always welcomed people like us, even when other churches didn't. Do you understand?'

He didn't quite understand why she favoured that church over the numerous churches nearby that had always welcomed and even been run by black people. But he didn't say anything. He didn't want to upset her and he didn't want to sound like his father. He and his siblings eventually outgrew Sunday school and were pronounced old enough to sit in the pews with their mother. It was here that they watched the purple, red, and white robed procession march down the aisle at the beginning of every service, heard the choir warbling a song written in old school English, and held back the urge to cough as someone swung back and forth a golden thurible with thick plumes of incense emanating from its holes.

It was here that he learned religion was a routine. The service followed a formula that took no less than three books to complete. There was a navy blue book detailing the service that told them what to chant in unison and when. There was a maroon book that told them what to sing, and a black Bible for them to follow the readings. Every service followed the same pattern. Here is where we stand and sing. Here is where we shake hands with strangers sitting around us and tell them 'peace be with you' with fake smiles plastered on our faces. Here is where we stand in a line to receive the body and blood. He resented it. Not just because it bored him to tears but because it felt pointless. The songs they sang were ancient and written in an English he barely understood, like:

> Be Thou my vision, O Lord of my heart
> Naught be all else to me, save that Thou art!

Thou my best thought, by day or by night
Waking or sleeping, Thy presence my light!

When he kneeled on the old faux-leather cushions and chanted, 'We believe in one God, the Father, the Almighty, maker of heaven and earth, of all that is seen and unseen...' along with the others, it didn't feel like he was speaking to any higher power. It felt like he was ticking a box, and after this box would come another. His mother liked the box ticking. She was a woman who found security in routines, both on the weekend and during the week. She woke up at the same time, ate at the same time, and prayed at the same time. On Saturday mornings at exactly 7 am Solomon would be woken up by the sound of Joyous Celebration being blasted on the old CD player and knew it was time for him and his siblings to wake up, eat breakfast, and help his mother clean the house. She was a woman who believed in the power of prayer and expected her children to believe in it too.

'You need to pray every day, Solly. Whether you're having a good day or a bad day, whether you want to ask Him for help or thank Him for something He's done, pray to him and you'll see all the blessings He'll send to you,' she would say.

One Saturday afternoon he was standing outside with her helping her hang the laundry out to dry. He was 12 at the time. The wind was blowing quite fiercely and as he looked at her weather-beaten face and her calloused hands fight against the wind, a thought came to him.

'Mama, how sure are you that God listens to our prayers?' He asked her.

'What a strange question,' she said as she picked up another shirt from the pile of washed clothing in his arms.

'I'm very sure. I feel His presence in the room whenever I pray. For months I prayed that Auntie Cynthia give birth to a healthy baby. She had a very difficult pregnancy. Last week she gave birth to a healthy baby boy.

'I prayed that God would help me find the money to buy

Mary's school uniform and he did. I even prayed for you to do well at school and now look how well you're doing. And it's all because of God. I asked Him and He answered.'

'And he listens to every prayer?'

'Yes. Every one.'

He knew that what he was about to ask danced the thin line between curiosity and rudeness before it left his mouth. But he still asked, 'Did you ever pray for Apartheid to end?'

His mother looked at him sideways before answering, 'Yes we did. We prayed every day that it would end. And He ended it. And now you get to grow up without any Apartheid laws or police or any of that.'

'But Apartheid went on forever! Why did He take so long? What was He doing the whole time?'

She stopped. She turned to face him fully. When he saw a cloud passing over her face he knew he had gone too far.

'That's enough from you now. How dare you question the Lord? He does everything in his own time. For His own reasons. Everything happened as it should have and now look, are we still living under Apartheid?'

She gave him a look so fierce he knew there was only one acceptable answer. 'I… no.'

'Exactly!' She snatched another shirt from the pile and turned to peg it with a huff. 'You shouldn't let those kinds of thoughts into your head, Solomon. You'll find that they come straight from the Devil.'

They continued in silence after that. Solomon learned that day that there are certain questions one could ask and certain questions one couldn't.

SEVEN

Solomon's mother constantly reminded him, 'I want you to be grateful for how blessed you are. You have food on your plate, a roof over your head, clothes to wear, and a mattress to sleep on.' She always told him he was in a better position than a lot of other kids. He could have been part of the Congolese family of four that moved into their backroom when he was 14. The two kids were frail with big bellies from lack of food and barely literate from lack of schooling. They couldn't be admitted into any school until their family received their refugee papers. They had been waiting three years. He could have been one of the kids living in a shack rather than a brick house who lived in fear of their house burning down when the winter chill set in and people started using fires to keep themselves warm. Or one of the kids living on the banks of the Jukskei River who would be washed away when the river swelled from the rains.

It was hard for him to feel grateful when he looked at the shiny German cars that drove past Alex. When he knew they still had to go without. When they ate dinner together he would see that his mother's portion was much smaller than everyone else's. While everyone else had a piece of meat, his own mother's plate only had pap and cabbage. 'I don't like eating meat that much,' she'd say when he questioned her. Yet whenever they went to a wedding or funeral, he would watch as she piled chicken, beef stew, and mogodu onto her plate.

Their school uniforms were second-hand from a flea market and threadbare. On rainy days he could feel his socks get wet as the water seeped into the holes in his shoes. There were months, particularly close to month end, where he and his siblings would have to rely on the feeding scheme at school for another meal. He would sometimes overhear his mother worrying with friends about how she would pay a certain bill. One afternoon he came home early and overheard his mother crying in her bedroom. I'm going to take her out of here, he thought to himself. When he was rich enough one day he'd move her into a nice home in the suburbs, hire a woman to clean her home every day, and make it so she'd never have to worry about bills again.

When a community member delivered some university application forms to his high school he took a few. His academics had never been perfect, and he'd had to repeat Grades 5 and 9, but other than that he'd generally scraped through. He took forms for the University of Johannesburg, Wits University, and the University of KwaZulu-Natal. He had no idea how he would pay tuition if he got in.

'Don't worry mfethu, you can just get onto NSFAS,' a neighbour who was attending UJ told him. 'That's what I did. They cover everything, fees, res, they even give you a book allowance and some spending money. You just have to pay them back when you get a job.'

'How do you get it?' He'd asked.

'You have to get in somewhere first. Then you can apply. Come to me once you get in and I'll help you out.'

From then, Solomon kept dreaming about the day he would walk up to his neighbour, acceptance letter in hand, and say, 'Look mfethu, I got in. Please help me apply for NSFAS.' Getting into university was a feat few achieved. Whenever someone got in it was a big deal. Their mother would brag everywhere from church, to the taxi rank, to the hair salon. 'Did I tell you Vuyo got into Wits? Yes, Vuyo! My Vuyo. I always knew he'd get in! He's going to be the first graduate in the family!' The mothers would boast to everyone who had ears. Solomon pictured his mother swaggering about the streets of Alex, telling everyone, 'My Solly got into Wits! My boy is going to be a big, big businessman one day! You'll see!' He closed his eyes and pictured her gathering her church friends to form a prayer circle for him the night before he had to go register. He could already hear her voice leading the prayer, crooning, 'Lord, may you watch over Solomon. May you grant him the knowledge he needs to pass – with distinction.'

There was only one problem. He didn't get into Wits. He didn't get in anywhere. He passed well enough to earn his matric certificate and absolutely nothing else. He felt like his whole world come crashing around him when he saw Higher Certificate next to his pass in the papers. Not even Diploma. Higher certificate. What would he do with a higher certificate?

'Cheer up, Solo,' his best friend Bongani had said to him. 'At least you passed!'

They had gone to read the paper together. All around them were classmates who were crying tears of joy or sadness at the news of their own performance.

Solomon didn't even want to look at him. Bongani had at least gotten a diploma pass. Bongani! Solomon still remembered when he could barely read back in Grade 5. He had arrived at their school fresh from KwaZulu-Natal as a slow-witted boy who towered over all the other kids and was so wide he almost filled up a two-seater desk by himself. His size and dark skin tone had made him the object of ridicule among his classmates. They laughed at him during break time, told him he looked like a burnt up Oros man, and replaced his name with a cruel new moniker: Sdudla. Solomon who had been the smallest boy in class was forced by the teacher to sit next to him. After weeks of helping Bongani make sense of the work the teacher scribbled on the board, the two became close friends. How had that same boy who had once been so dependent on Solomon passed better than him?

'What am I going to do now? At least you can apply for a diploma!'

'But where am I going to get money to do a diploma?' Bongani replied. 'Don't worry, we'll find something.'

That was the thing about Bongani. He always tried to be positive even when positivity was pointless. Solomon wasn't so sure. How was he going to tell his mother? He entered his home with his head bowed, the paper folded under his arm, trying to make as little noise as he possibly could. Unfortunately his mother had ears so sharp they could pick up a mouse scurrying across the floor. Within seconds she was upon him, 'So did you pass? How many distinctions did you get?' She said quickly, snatching the paper away from him.

Within seconds her smile turned into shocked silence. She looked at him with disappointed eyes. 'You didn't even get one? Not even one?' She said to him in disbelief. She was distraught. 'Your brother and sister were looking up to you. How could you let them down like this?'

His father's reaction to the news was quite different. 'Don't worry, my boy,' he'd said. 'At least you got your matric. That's something. And that university would have just taught you how to serve some white man. They don't teach independent, revolutionary thinkers there. Just how to be another cog in the capitalist machine.' He'd wanted to snatch the beer bottle out his father's hand and throw it in his face.

He did the only thing he could do. He went out searching for a job. Everywhere he turned the potential employers either wanted a degree or experience or both. He even needed experience to be a petrol attendant at the nearby station. 'Do you know how many applications I get every day from kids just like you?' Asked the garage owner when Solomon begged him for a job. 'I get at least ten. No, 20. All of you are the same. All you have to your name is matric. Well, matric doesn't mean anything anymore, my boy. You should have gotten yourself a diploma, or better yet, a degree!' The man laughed at him before telling him to get out. Solomon looked back at the garage as he walked away, vowing that when he was rich, he'd never ever buy his petrol there.

'You could always come work with me,' Bongani had said to him. 'I don't make a lot but it's something and I think they're looking for new guys now anyway. If you give me your CV I can ask.'

Bongani found work pushing trolleys at Benmore Gardens, one of the fancy malls in Sandton. He had grown into an astonishingly tall, strong man and was often called on to help people carry heavy bags and boxes to their cars for loose change. Solomon had considered it. He closed his eyes and pictured himself pushing around trolleys all day, begging rich white ladies with big glasses and irritated expressions to let him help them pack their groceries into the boots of their SUVs. He imagined them turning up their noses at him as they dropped a R2 coin into his open palms for his efforts, making sure not to touch him, and reaching for their hand sanitiser if they did. He didn't think he could bear the humiliation.

He got a brief stint as a security guard during the World Cup. It had been difficult for him to stand outside the stadium in the cold while listening to the audience cheer on his soccer heroes like Ronaldo, Messi, and Robinho as they played only metres away. But during those moments he reminded himself, 'I'm doing this to help Mama. I'm doing this so I'm not like my father.' When the World Cup ended, he tried to make himself useful. He would offer to do odd jobs like wash people's cars, but so few people owned cars and so many people wanted to wash them for extra money that even that proved unsustainable. He settled on walking his siblings to school and back to feel a sense of purpose. There had been so many stories of young girls being kidnapped, raped, and murdered that he would escort his sister everywhere. She soon grew tired of him. 'Why can't you get a real job so you can leave me alone?' She would moan. The complaint would twist his stomach into knots. He felt like a failure.

One day, he was on his way to a recruitment agency in

Randburg he heard could help those with only matric when he stumbled across a job advert outside a second-hand car dealership: Hiring a general worker. Must have matric. Driver's license and experience in car sales desirable. Must be available to start **immediately**.

He stared at the advert for some time. Yes, he had no driver's license and what did he know about car sales? Then again, the advert never said he needed those things, only that they were desirable. The only thing he needed was a matric certificate, which he held a certified copy of in his hand right that moment along with his CV. He knew that if he gave it up he would have to scrape together money for another photocopy. But if there was ever a time God was giving him a sign it was right then. He walked inside.

The dealership was a near-empty stark white room with white tiles and sagging brown sofas in one corner, and a counter at the very end. There was a framed picture of a large, dark skinned man with a grey beard on the wall. He recognised him as TD Jakes, an American pastor. Solomon's mother often watched his sermons when they played on SABC 2. He stood awkwardly in the store. He wasn't entirely sure what to do. Should he ring the bell on the counter? Should he yell to see if anyone was in?

'I'll be with you in a moment!' Yelled a heavily accented voice.

A few moments later a man emerged behind the counter. He was a tall, broad man. Solomon had always been among the smallest boys in his class but he was still shocked at how much this man towered over him. He was dark-skinned with a wide torso and full bushy beard. He looked as though he were nearing 40, although he could have been younger.

'Hello,' he said. 'Do you want to buy a car?'

Solomon realised that the man had a heavy Nigerian accent, as though he had stepped off a plane from Lagos the day before. He had met Nigerians before in passing. There were some who owned businesses just outside the Pan African

Mall. He had always heard his parents complain bitterly saying they brought drugs in and trafficked women out. But he'd never really interacted with them.

'I... uh... no. I wanted to apply for a job,' he replied. He briefly worried he would mess up his English, but then thought that perhaps a Nigerian man would have sympathy for a person who spoke it as a second language. 'I saw the ad outside?'

'You sound like you are not sure whether or not you saw an ad outside.'

'Uh...' he wasn't sure how to proceed. 'No, sir I'm sure. I saw it. It's there.'

'Hmm. Very well then. Do you have your CV?'

'I do, sir. And I have my matric certificate. A certified copy, sir,' he said, holding it up proudly as though it were an access pass.

'You are quite eager, aren't you? Leave them on the counter. If I like you, I'll call you in for an interview.'

He left his CV and certificate on the counter. He didn't move. When the man realised he wasn't leaving he gave him a confused look.

'What's the matter with you?'

'Please sir, I need this job.'

The man cocked his head. 'What did you say?'

'Please sir, I have been unemployed a whole year. I need this job. I'm a good worker. I work hard. I'm good with my hands. I'll do whatever you need me to do. Please give me chance. I swear I won't let you down.'

The man scowled. He snapped at him, 'I gave you a simple instruction! I told you if I like you I'll call you. Don't come here and beg in my store. Get out!' Solomon left with his tail between his legs. I blew it, he thought. A few days later he received a phone call. It was from the store owner calling him in for an interview.

EIGHT

Solomon would always joke that he received two different educations. The first was at school. The second was working for Mr Ife. Every morning when he arrived at Mr Ife's car dealership he would put on blue overalls and prepare for a day of hard work. As a general worker he washed the cars, matched the license discs to cars, helped strip parts off and moved in deliveries of new parts for the mechanic. There was a cleaning lady who came in twice a week but on the other days the task of keeping the offices, kitchen, toilet, and workshop neat fell on him.

The mechanic was another Nigerian, about ten years younger than Mr Ife, named Abiola. When together the two of them spoke a language Solomon had never heard in his life. They claimed it was pidgin English, but it was sounded so different from any English Solomon had ever heard that he was convinced it was an entirely different language. Mr Ife was a man with a large voice and an even larger personality. While Solomon studied cars under the skillful hand of Abiola he could hear Mr Ife on the phone in the office either laughing or swearing with his great booming voice. They would hear his voice carry all the way to the back of the workshop every time he greeted a new client.

Mr Ife was never confronted by a sale he could not close. If the client complained that the car was too expensive, he would list off all the new parts of the car. 'In fact, you will even save money by buying this car because it is practically a new car at half the price. That is how well we have fixed it,' he would say. At the end of the exchange the dealership coffers would be a few thousand rands fuller. When he made a particularly good sale he brought a big crate of beer to the dealership. Solomon found him and Abiola sitting in the yard cracking open bottles of Black Label among the old car parts that needed to be sent to the scrap yard. Mr Ife called out to him, 'Hey, Solly, come out and have a beer with us. It's on me!'

Solomon walked forward and felt himself numbing over when he looked at the beers. 'Thanks boss, but can I have a Coke instead?'

Mr Ife gave him a baffled look. 'You don't drink beer?'

'No, sir.'

'Why not? What kind of man doesn't drink beer?' He turned to Abiola. 'Abiola, have you ever heard of a man that doesn't drink beer?'

Abiola shook his head.

'I don't like to drink alcohol sir,' Solomon explained. 'Can I have a Coke instead?'

Mr Ife gave him another look before saying, 'I guess that means more for me then. Go look in the fridge to see if there's Coke in there.'

Solomon went and returned with a Coke. He sat and spoke with them but watching them drink beer made him feel uneasy. He would look at a beer bottle and imagine he saw his own father's hands clasped around it.

One day during Solomon's lunch break Mr Ife announced that he needed to take the rest of the afternoon off to go to a doctor's appointment. 'Solly my boy, I think it's time that you start helping with the car sales.'

Solomon was shocked. 'Car sales? But I don't know how to sell a car!'

'Sure you do. You have seen me do it haven't you?' When Solomon looked at him blankly he sighed. 'Look, you must just ask the customer what kind of qualities they are looking for in a car and what is their price range. Then you must find a car that best matches what they are asking for.

'And you must really make the car sound good. Tell them its mileage, what parts of the car we have replaced, the car's reliability, safety features, maintenance costs, all those things.'

Solomon still looked unsure.

'You will be fine, my boy,' Mr Ife said, placing a hand on his shoulder. 'You've seen me do it a million times before. I have faith in you.'

Less than two hours after he left, Solomon's first customer came walking through the door. He was an impatient looking man with a reddish complexion, a sizable pot belly, and small, sharp blue eyes. The man didn't speak, he barked, 'You the owner here?' Solomon was taken aback by the sharpness of his voice. The man intimidated him.

'No. Mr Ife has gone to the doctor. But I can help.'

He looked around with his nose scrunched up. 'Is there anyone here who can speak proper English?'

Solomon cringed. Proper English. He became only that much more aware of his accent. He wanted to get away from the man but instead forced an awkward chuckle and said, 'I can speak proper English, sir.'

The man looked at him stoney faced. 'Fine then, I guess you'll do. I'm looking for a car.' He wanted a bakkie no older than five years and had less than 50,000 kilometres on the clock. It was a tough criteria for Solomon to meet, as most of the cars in Mr Ife's shop were older, and he only made it tougher. He didn't want a Toyota. 'They're too easy to steal. It'll be here today, gone tomorrow,' he said. He didn't like the look of the other two bakkies Solomon showed him. He complained about another Nissan stating that the safety features on that particular model weren't good. Solomon was exhausted by the time he showed him a final car. Surprisingly, this was one he actually liked.

'What did you say the mileage on this one was again, boy?'

Solomon faltered. The mileage on the car was 77,000, a good 20,000 kms higher than the man was interested in. If he told him that, he would walk out of the shop and never return. Solomon had to close the sale. Mr Ife would be upset with him if he didn't.

'It's about 45,000,' he said quickly.

The man paused. His already red face deepened into mauve. 'Boy,' he said in a voice that could cut stone. 'Look here. Look here and tell me what that says.' He pointed a pudgy finger at the dashboard. There in clear digital figures was the number 77,000.

'Well? What does it say boy?'

'I... uh.' Solomon felt his face becoming hot. He wanted to crawl into a hole and stay there forever.

'Since you obviously don't know how to read, it says 77,000. And how much did you just say was on the clock?'

He couldn't answer. His throat turned to sand. The man launched into a tirade littered with 'you people' this and 'you people' that. Abiola had to come out to try calm him down. The man left in a huff, vowing never to return and to tell everyone he knew not to bother with their dealership. When Mr Ife found out the next day he was not impressed.

'How could you do such a stupid thing?' He bellowed. 'How could you lie about something as obvious as the mileage? The mileage? That's the easiest thing to check!'

'I'm s-s-sorry, sir,' he stuttered. He was sure he had done it now. He was sure Mr Ife was going to fire him.

Mr Ife sighed. They were sitting in his air-conditioned office. Mr Ife was on one side of his dark wood desk and Solomon was shrinking in his seat on the other.

'Solomon, I want you to listen to me,' he said in a stern voice, his eyes steely fixed on Solomon's face. 'You never, never tell outright lies to customers. A lie can always be found out. We don't lie here. We soften.

'We say, 'Yes sir, the mileage is a little high but this model has only had one owner who took very good care of it. Kept it in mint condition. Besides a scratch here and there it's had no serious accidents. It was owned by an honest, hard-working man just like yourself, sir.' Do you understand where I'm going with this?'

'Yes, Mr Ife.'

Mr Ife sat back and looked at Solomon closely. There was a long, pregnant pause.

'Do you know why I hired you?' He said after some time. Solomon shook his head.

'It's because I could see this one, he's very determined. You might not have gone to university but neither did I. I came here 12 years ago with nothing in my back pocket except a few bucks and my passport. And I worked. Yes I worked! I was a bouncer for one of these white nightclubs. I worked my way up until I opened up my own corner shop. It wasn't much, just a general store, but I saved up every penny and started it cash.'

'Do you still have it?' He had never heard of it until then.

He shook his head sadly. 'No. A bunch of hooligans burnt it down years ago in these xenophobic attacks. But you know,' he said, getting worked up. 'The one thing I don't like about this country is South Africans think they're better than everyone else. Yes Solomon, I'm talking about your countrymen. They keep saying, 'Oh the foreigners are taking our jobs, they're taking our women', but I never took any South African's job.

'I made a good, honest living and worked for everything I have. Every Nigerian, every foreigner here I know did the same. The problem is there are too many who don't want to do the work. I hired another South African guy who just stopped showing up. Stopped, just like that,' he said clicking his fingers for emphasis.

'Which is why I hired you. Because I could see, okay this one, he is serious. He actually wants to work. And you've been working very hard, haven't you? Which is why I don't want to have to cut you off over a thing like this. You made a mistake.

But I will not tolerate another. If I ever catch you telling lies to a customer again, I cut you off. You understand?'

Solomon felt the relief set in as he realised he wasn't getting fired. 'Yes, Mr Ife,' he said with more energy than before.

'Good. Now go help Abiola in the shop.'

Several months passed before Mr Ife felt confident enough to have Solomon attempt to sell cars again. In that time Solomon listened carefully to Mr. Ife, taking notes during every sale.\When he had the chance to sell cars again, he didn't lie. He softened. He emphasised the good over the bad. He smoothed over the bumps that each car had. And it worked. He closed his first sale. And then another. And another. After two months he was promoted to a salesman. And he was just as good, maybe a little better, than Mr Ife.

NINE

Under the watchful eyes of his mother he and his siblings continued to attend St Mary's Cathedral every Sunday morning. About two-thirds of the cathedral pews sat empty each service, but what the congregation lacked in size it made up in commitment. Patricia was one of those loyal to the church who formed part of a tight knit community, often staying behind long after the service had ended to speak with her friends there. She hoped that her children would form part of the same community. They had other plans. Once Solomon began matric, he would use his studies as an excuse not to go to church. This excuse became more successful the closer and closer he came to his final exams only to blow up in his face once he failed to get into university.

'You see, this is what happens when you don't want to go to church,' his mother had said to him. 'You should have asked God to give you a space at a university. Did you even pray like I told you to?'

He was embarrassed to admit he hadn't. During his months of unemployment he frequently turned to the Bible for answers and had never been more dutiful in his prayers than in the weeks that followed submitting his CV. Once he started working for Mr Ife, his job became his new excuse. It wasn't quite as effective. Mr Ife was as committed to the Christian faith as Solomon's mother, and so the dealership was closed on Sundays. But that didn't stop Solomon from lying anyway.

That isn't to say he wasn't a Christian. He had been baptised in the Anglican church and confirmed in that same church shortly after he turned sixteen. He wasn't reluctant to go to church because he wasn't a good Christian. He was tired of the mind-numbing boredom that came with church. He had visited a few others close by. He didn't know how it was possible but somehow the Catholic church had been even worse than what he was used to. While the Methodist ones were less-paint-by the numbers, none of the sermons spoke to his soul. He found he much preferred reading the Bible and praying on his own.

Once he started doing well at work, he truly believed that a significant factor in his success was his months of prayer. Maybe Mama was right, he'd think. Perhaps by praying every day in those months and waiting patiently for God to deliver, his blessings were finally multiplying, pouring down all over him like soft summer rain. His mother certainly thought so. She invited her prayer circle to the house the week before he started at work to pray over him. They had circled him, each pressing one hand against his body while his mother said, 'Lord, please watch over Solomon. Give his hands the strength to work and guide him, so he sees nothing but success in his future.' When he was promoted she jumped up and down clapping her hands. 'You see, my child! You see! I told you that if you worked hard God would watch over you and look now!'

His siblings congratulated him. His father stayed with his back turned, watching the fuzzy TV. Solomon had bought a new TV a few months ago but it sat in his parents' bedroom gathering dust. His father refused to watch it. His father had always been warm towards him. He'd flinched whenever Solomon had returned his greeting with a hard, icy look. But now there was something cold growing between them. His father looked at him like he was an intruder. Something alien that was posing as his son. The tension only grew after Solomon was promoted. His father's drinking became worse.

He would stumble drunk into the house in the early hours of the afternoon making unreasonable demands, slurring and shouting at Solomon, 'So you think you're the man of the house now?'

So he packed up his bags and he left. He found an apartment closer to work in Randburg to share with a childhood friend of his named Mmusi who was attending an advertising school not too far away. The apartment wasn't terribly big. It was situated close enough to a bar for them to hear the thud-thud-thud of loud music being played well into the early hours of the morning. His roommate's bathroom habits left a lot to be desired. But it was the first space Solomon had ever been in which was truly his. He would often stare out of his bedroom window onto the street and the apartment buildings across the road and take in the fact that at the age of 21, he had made it. He was out of Alex.

A few months after moving in he was returning home from work when he saw a woman struggling with balancing several shopping bags as she searched for her keys. She was young, in her 20s, slim and light-skinned. He could see her small breasts poking through her thin vest. She was wearing a red patterned doek tied in such a way that her afro poked through the front. He had noticed that more women were starting to wear their hair naturally. He much preferred it to the stiff shiny weaves he had seen.

'Excuse me, Miss,' he said. 'Do you need help?'

She turned to him. She had doe eyes and high cheekbones. He could feel his face warming up and butterflies fluttering in his stomach as he looked at her. His legs turned to jelly and his throat turned to sand.

'Uh, no thanks. I've got it,' she said, fishing her keys out her handbag and sticking them in the door.

'Are you sure? It looks like you're struggling a bit there.'

She looked at him as though meaning to reject him again. But something in her hesitated. She looked weary of him, conflicted by whether or not she could trust him.

'Don't worry, I'm not like a creep or anything,' he quickly said. 'I live right upstairs. Number 34.'

'You mean with Mmusi?'

Oh no, he thought. What if she's dating him? As far as he knew Mmusi didn't have a girlfriend but he could never be entirely sure. 'Uh, yeah. How do you know him?'

'We have a couple of classes together,' she looked him up and down one last time before facing towards him, as if finally determining he was reasonably safe. 'I'm Nobuhle by the way.'

'I'm Solomon,' he said, awkwardly extending his hand. Instead of offering hers she gave him a plastic bag in return. 'You said you'd help me with these, right? You can take this one.'

He didn't know what it was about her. It may have been the easy manner in which they were able to speak — quick-witted, meaningful, and above all interesting. It may have been the wealth of knowledge she had at her fingertips on literature and music or the foreign films she introduced him to, but before long he felt himself falling. He felt weightless when he was near her. There was no image that had imprinted itself more firmly in his mind than her smile. She was the first girlfriend he had ever had. The first woman he had ever bought dinner, and movie tickets, and even the odd gift. She burned holes in his pocket but for once he didn't mind because what he gave her he gave freely.

One night when they were sharing a pizza she said to him, 'I want you to come to my church with me.'

He looked up at her. 'Your church? Why?'

'Because you mentioned that you don't really go to church anymore and I think maybe you just haven't found the right one. Mine is like, completely different. It's a lot more... engaging. You really feel the spirit moving through you.'

He chuckled. 'What? Are you worried I'm going straight to hell?'

'Well, maybe. It's important to go to church you know. Plus there's such a great community there.'

'You sound like my mother.'

'Solo, I'm being serious.' All hint of humour had left her face. He sat up and wiped the smile of his. 'Just try it out? Just come with me once. And if you don't like it, you don't have to go back? Okay?'

He sighed. He felt himself give in under the weight of her hopeful stare. 'Okay, fine. I'll try it once. But if it's like my mom's church I'm not going back.'

It was nothing like his mother's church. First, it looked nothing like the grand Renaissance-inspired cathedral he was used to. There were no organs or golden altars or stained glass windows. No tortured Jesus watching over him. It was a plain auditorium inside an ugly, brown, angular building. It had rows of plastic chairs instead of pews, and an elevated platform with a podium. The only detail that gave it away as a church was the simple, dark wooden cross mounted on the wall. Second, it was loud. He heard the muffled but distinct sound of a multitude of voices singing. Once an usher opened the heavy doors the singing was deafening. People of all ages and genders were standing up, bashing the faux-leather pillows in tune. He heard high pitched female voices singing: Ukholo lwami ndonyuka nalo

And all the other voices joining in unison:

Ukholo lwami ndonyuka nalo
Ndilubambe ngesandla
Ndiyongena nalo ekhaya ezulwini

He looked around in wonder. The song was one he had heard a hundred times at church services and funerals and weddings, but he had never heard it being sung before with so much volume and life. He had never seen so many people crowded into a church before. There was a body for every seat in the auditorium, up in the gallery, and spilled over into the walkways. Nobuhle grabbed onto him as the two of them snaked through the congregation, careful to avoid wayward elbows and pillows and small children staring up at them through between their parents' legs, until they had squished into a small corner. The only hint of familiarity were the two Bible readings and the reading of the gospel. There were no blue prayer books, no reading aloud in unison of words written in bold, no checklist routine for Solomon to mentally tick. Instead there was the same rapturous singing and seamless transition from one song into the next.

Then, a slender man with a shiny bald head and thick tortoiseshell reading glasses stood in front of the congregation. By that point the room was so packed the air had turned stuffy. Solomon turned and saw old ladies fanning themselves with the pew leaflets. The man didn't wear robes. Instead he wore a dark grey suit and was armed only with the Bible.

'Sanibonani!' He said in a voice that boomed into every corner of the room.

'Sawubona,' the congregation responded.

'Kumnandi ukuba lapha!'

'Ukuba lapha kumnandi!'

The pastor spoke as though he had tapped into an endless reserve of energy. He shouted. He sang. He walked up and down the stage booming into his microphone, spittle flying everywhere, while the congregation clapped and cheered from him. He went on for hours. He was 'carried by the Spirit', he said, and Solomon was carried with him.

'You know, my brothers and sisters, I really pity rich men,' he said, pausing as he watched congregants' eyes turn wide in disbelief. 'That's right, I pity them! Do you know why? Because those who have wealth in their bank accounts suffer from a poverty of spirit. That's right, they suffer from the most terrible form of poverty in existence and that is a poverty of spirit.

'Our Lord and Savior Jesus Christ himself tells us in Mark 10:4 'It is easier for a camel to go through the eye of a needle than for a rich man to enter the kingdom of God.' Do you know how small the eye of a needle is?'

Right on cue, he reached into his blazer pocket and produced a needle, holding it up for the whole congregation to see. 'There is the eye of the needle,' he said, pointing to its top. Solomon craned his neck to see but couldn't make out the eye at all.

'Now, imagine a camel trying to walk through here.' Some congregants laughed at the image. 'It's impossible, no? Now, for Jesus to tell us that it is easier for a camel to walk through here than for a rich man to enter heaven, you must know that Jay-Z will be shaking in their Louis Vuitton loafers when Judgement Day comes!' He paused while the congregation laughed.

'But that's not all, my brothers and sisters. Our Lord tells us in 1 Timothy 6:9, 'Those who desire to be rich fall into temptation, into a snare, into many senseless and harmful desires that plunge people into ruin and destruction. For the love of money is the root of all kinds of evil.' Did you hear that? The love of money is the root of all evil!

'And don't we see this every day?' He paused while people murmured in agreement.

'Look at that businessman Kenny Kunene, who every day flaunts his sin. He eats sushi off the bodies of naked women, he keeps a harem of young girls around him who he buys with Brazilian weaves, designer clothes, and lavish lifestyles. Do you think this is the type of life that the Lord looks at favourably? Of course not! Money has corrupted his soul!

'And perhaps, there is no better example of the corrupting power of money than that billionaire Cyril Ramaphosa. Mind you, Ramaphosa started his career as a trade union leader, advocating for the rights and fair working conditions of miners. He established the first ever trade unions for miners!

'And now we fast forward 20 years and he is in bed with the very same white businessmen he was fighting against! When miners protested against him and his colleagues at Marikana, it was him who called for them to be shot! He abandoned all his principles for money!'

The congregation clapped and shouted in agreement with some leaping to their feet. The video footage of miners being gunned down by police as they ran away was still fresh in their memories. The video had played repeatedly on the news since the massacre happened only a few weeks ago, until it was imprinted on the brain of every South African rich and poor, black and white. He allowed them time to settle down before continuing, 'Oh brothers and sisters, believe me when I say I pity these rich men. They are so poor and they do not even realise it. These rich men are slaves to their master, and that master is money.

'And Jesus tells us clearly that you cannot serve two masters, for you will hate the one and be devoted to the other. Those who serve money will fall into temptation and be plunged into ruin. But those who serve God will have a multitude of blessings. Truly there is no greater happiness than the joy that comes with serving a living God!'

Solomon was transformed. He felt as though his eyes had been opened and for the first time he was seeing clearly. He returned to the church the next week and in all the weeks that followed. He emerged from the church a new man. He was reborn.

TEN

The Holy Children of God Ministries had become Solomon's new home. He became so resolute in his faith that neighbours back in Alex who had once only seen his father in him joked that he had finally become his mother's child.

The more he tried to live his life in accordance with God's word, the more he noticed how far Nobuhle had strayed from it. The skimpy clothes that he once found sexy became distasteful in his eyes and he urged her to wear skirts and tops that covered her up more. He started to hate the tattoos on her arms that he once found fascinating and argued with her when she spoke about getting more. A few days later she broke up with him, accusing him of trying to manipulate her into becoming someone she wasn't. He viewed this as irrefutable evidence that Nobuhle was a Jezebel spirit in disguise, sent to lead him astray.

Over the next five years he would attend church every Wednesday night for worship, Friday night for prayers, and Sunday morning for service. He spent every New Year's Eve there to pray in the new year. He ensured that he paid at least ten per cent of every paycheck in tithes. He convinced his childhood friend Bongani to start attending the church as well. He helped organise church fundraisers. Eventually after three years of service to the church, he was tasked with teaching the youth services each Sunday morning. The additional income that he earned from the church allowed him to move into his own one-bedroom apartment in a quieter part of Randburg. It was the first time in his life he had so much space to himself, so much quiet gave him room to truly think, and he thanked God every morning for leading him into his good fortune.

One day, in the spring of 2018 he began to notice the pastor looking at him with new eyes. Pastor Mkhize had been preaching at Holy Children of God for the past 20 years. Solomon heard whispers that Mkhize was retiring soon to live out his final years resting in his hometown, Pietermaritzburg.

He had approached Solomon after a service and put a hand on his shoulder. 'You have a way with people,' he said.

Solomon chuckled nervously, 'Who, me? I don't think so.'

'Yes, you! Come, walk with me to my office.'

Before Solomon could say anything he was already being led away by the powerful sweep of the pastor's arm.

'I've been watching you, Solomon,' the pastor continued. 'You have a natural way with people. They gravitate towards you. I've been watching the church mothers fight over who gets to introduce their daughter to you,' he said with a wink.

Solomon looked down humbly, 'I didn't notice.'

The pastor stopped to greet two people as they walked past before returning to Solomon. 'Now, what was I saying? Oh yes, you've become a valuable member of this community. And I've been hearing good things about your youth services. You have a lot of potential.'

They stopped in front of his office. Pastor Mkhize looked him square in the eyes. 'Solomon, have you ever considered becoming a pastor? And not just a youth pastor but, doing what I do?'

Solomon was shocked. For months he had dreamt of standing up in front of that congregation. He had imagined what it would be like to step into Pastor Mkhize's skin. To command the attention and adoration he did. He began to feel hope forming in his chest, stretching it wider until it became tight under the strain.

'I... me?'

Pastor Mkhize laughed, 'Yes Solomon, you. I've been thinking I could take you under my wing. Show you how it's done.'

'Mfundisi I… I don't know what to say.'

'I'll let you think about it. But don't take too long,' he said with a playful wink before walking away. Solomon stared after him, still stunned. He felt like he was floating. He was going to be a pastor.

It didn't feel real until he was removed from the youth service and assigned to deliver readings during the main services. Under Pastor Mkhize's wing he became a member of the church committee and would sit in during meetings. He was invited into the pastor's office to help him prepare for the next week's sermon. It was one such Saturday morning when the pastor had decided to share some news with Solomon. He was preparing a sermon to deliver that week on godly women. He told Solomon that he had been particularly disturbed when his granddaughter had told him about Instagram. He'd gone onto the site only to find countless photographs of half-naked young women posing seductively for the camera while followers openly lusted for them in the comments. He had banned his granddaughter from the site and resolved to address it with the congregation.

'You should see these girls, Solomon,' he complained. 'They're practically naked! No modesty at all. And these same ones will be the first ones to cry 'men are trash' when they attract low hanging fruit, when really this is the image they put out! They are telling men, 'I am a common whore, so treat me accordingly!''

'Yes pastor, I agree,' Solomon said. He did not tell the pastor that he had his own Instagram account which he used primarily to follow accounts full of half-naked beautiful women like the ones the pastor described. He was also only half-listening. His full attention was on scanning through the Bible to find the most appropriate verses the pastor could use to bolster his message.

'Mfundisi, what about 1 Timothy 2:9? 'Women should adorn themselves in respectable apparel, with modesty and self-control, not with braided hair and gold or pearls or costly attire, but with what is proper for women who profess godliness – with good works.''

'I'd considered that one,' Pastor Mkhize said, sitting back. 'The only problem is, some of the women get very upset when we point out that the Bible says they mustn't braid their hair. They complain and say 'But Mfundisi how are we supposed to manage our hair if you tell us we can't braid it?'

'Then we must waste time explaining that no, it was the time and the context, and by the time you're done with that everyone has forgotten the point. Rather find another one.'

Solomon paged through the Bible diligently once again. There was another verse on his mind.

'Before you continue with that Solly, there's something I wanted to discuss with you.'

Solomon looked up at him and closed the Bible. 'Yes?'

'I don't know if you're aware but I am retiring. I am leaving Gauteng for good and going back to Pietermaritzburg.'

Solomon tried to feign surprise. 'Oh?'

'Yes. I am an old man now, Solly. I must spend what time I have left on this earth with my family. Which means it's time for me to choose a successor. And I think that successor should be you.'

Solomon was taken aback, his eyes widening in surprise. A smile crept across his face. 'Me? Mfundisi, are you sure?'

'Yes, I'm quite sure,' he took off his glasses and began cleaning them. 'You're very dedicated in this church, diligent in your Bible studies, and you were good at the youth service. Yes, I think it's time you were given a bit more responsibility around here.'

He put his now-clean glasses back on and looked at Solomon. 'What do you think?'

Solomon could hardly contain his excitement. He would be standing on that stage in front of an auditorium packed to capacity, guiding people through the word of God. He could picture them laughing at his jokes, nodding their heads in agreement throughout his sermon, leaping from their seats to applaud him as he said something that resonated deeply within their souls.

And why stop at the church? Solomon dreamed of his star rising, joining the ranks of world famous pastors like TD Jakes. In his dreams he filled stadiums with faithful Christians eager to watch him at the pulpit. His sermons were filmed and broadcast to millions of viewers on the other side of the world. His written meditations on the Bible soared to the top of bestseller lists. He would look down at his congregation and watch as the most beautiful, pious women threw themselves at his feet, begging for a chance to become Mrs Khumalo. He saw himself driving to his mother's home in a shining Bentley to pluck her out of Alex and move her into a beautiful Sandton home where she would live safely and comfortably away from his father. It was the first time in Solomon's life that he felt that everything was possible. He was taking the very first step to seeing his dreams become true.

Saying yes meant that he would have to quit his job to be a full-time pastor. He was due to take over from Pastor Mkhize at the beginning of the next year. He thought it would be a shame to say goodbye to Mr Ife and Abiola, who he had come to consider not just as boss and colleague but as brothers. Mr Ife had even helped him buy a car in installments without needing a loan from the bank. Abiola stood back stoically as always while Mr Ife gave Solomon a big hug. 'I see you're doing big things for yourself eh? You're moving up in life,' he'd said with a laugh. But he was proud. He promised he would stop by the church one weekend to watch him at the pulpit.

Bongani had been shocked when he told him. 'Since when did you want to be a pastor? And the way you used to hate going to church!'

'What can I say,' Solomon responded, 'I'm a changed man now.'

Bongani laughed at him, slapping him on the back. 'I'm proud of you, my brother. I'll make sure I come every week!'

Solomon raised an eyebrow at him but said nothing. He had gotten used to his friend occasionally missing a service because his head was still heavy from the previous night's party. It was one of the things Solomon never understood about drinkers. Why partake in something that you know will make you weak and sick the next morning? It was all the more reason not to drink.

His mother was less pleased with his news, for the simple reason that he had decided to become a pastor for one of these 'new age happy clappy churches' (her words, not his) rather than stay within the Anglican faith.

'Those ones don't do anything properly,' she complained. 'They're lazy Christians. Sacrificing the real, hard work so they can sing and clap their hands all day.'

He didn't have the heart to remind her that the only reason the Anglican Church existed was because an English king wanted to sacrifice real Christianity so he could divorce his wife and marry his mistress. His father had also scoffed at him. 'Congratulations, my boy. Now you'll spend your life preaching colonial nonsense to the black masses.' He had been expecting it but the words still stung. He told himself his father was simply jealous that he was going to do what he had never had the guts to do himself. He was going to lead hundreds if not thousands of black people to a better life through his words. He had expected his family to be a hurdle. He had not expected the church committee to be one. They argued bitterly over Pastor Mkhize's decision.

'The boy is too young,' Mrs Vilakazi, who headed the women's ordination, said. She was a woman in her late 50s who had once tried to push her eldest daughter on Solomon, despite the fact that said daughter was an out and proud lesbian in a committed relationship with a woman.

She continued, 'What about Peter? Peter has been at the church for over 15 years. He was saved, baptised, and confirmed here and he even studied theology in varsity! This one,' she pointed at Solomon, 'has never even set foot on a varsity campus in his life!'

'Peter is too old,' Pastor Mkhize replied. 'What we need is youthful energy. More young people than ever are turning away from the church. We need someone young, relatable, who will show them that church isn't just for their mothers and grandmothers. It's for them too. I believe Solomon is the best fit.'

They argued for some time but ultimately, owing to his seniority, Pastor Mkhize had the final say. The committee decided they would give Solomon a trial run for a few months and if he failed to perform they would have to look for someone else. Solomon was ecstatic. He was determined to prove he was a worthy successor. He spent December poring over his Bible trying to determine what his maiden sermon would be. Would he preach about forgiveness? Resisting temptation? The options were endless and each verse he read brought new inspiration. He settled at last on a sermon about living a life in accordance with God's will. He arrived at church early that first Sunday of the year and practiced preaching his sermon to an empty auditorium.

He left the church offices approximately 15 minutes before the service was to begin. He looked at the auditorium and felt his excitement evaporating, replaced by a bubbling sense of shock and then dismay. The auditorium was mostly empty. There was no one in the gallery. At this time it was ordinarily almost at capacity with more people pouring in through the doors. He stepped back and looked over the auditorium once again. Maybe more people will come, he thought. Was there a taxi strike happening? Had people not returned yet from their festive holidays? He waited another ten minutes to start his sermon. He was prepared to wait another until Mrs Vilakazi poked him from behind and hissed at him to get out there. He knew there had been more Sundays than he could count where Pastor Mkhize had started his sermons significantly late. But he was not Pastor Mkhize. Mrs Vilakazi reminded him of this.

He delivered his sermon with clipped wings. He attempted to feign the enthusiasm he had felt only a few hours before but instead of laughter and heads nodding in agreement he was met with stony faces. Only Bongani sat in the front row smiling broadly, holding a thumbs up in encouragement. He was not Pastor Mkhize. The congregation reminded him of this. It went on like this for six more weeks. 'I'm sorry, Mfundisi,' a kindly congregant said to him one day. 'A lot of people left after Mkhize retired. They used to come just for him, and now he's gone they don't see the point in coming back here.' Solomon was heartbroken. Despite Bongani's reassurances, he knew the situation was dire. If attendance didn't improve he would likely be relegated to being a youth pastor and the church would find someone else. He tried his best with his sermons but he realised that people didn't want boring sermons about forgiveness anymore. They wanted a spark. They wanted something special. And he had nothing.

He went to a second-hand bookstore he'd heard good things about in Melville and decided to pick up some books written by pastors. He deliberately picked a bookstore far away from the church in Randburg so there was little chance of the any church committee members bumping into him and disturbing him with their questions. Besides, Melville was the sort of picturesque place that seemed artistic enough to inspire him when he needed creativity the most. He had hoped that reading one of the books would give him inspiration for his own sermons. Fate, karma and destiny were concepts Solomon didn't believe in. They were rooted in satanic pagan rituals rather than the word of God. But what could not be denied was that him walking out that exact bookstore on that exact day at that exact time was an act that went far beyond pure coincidence.

As he walked into the street, he dropped a pebble into a lake creating ripples that extended beyond himself, shaping the future as he would know it. He crossed the doorway with his books in hand. As he looked up he saw a little girl with a round face, wide curious eyes, ashy knees and head of hair half untangled from its plaits. She kneeled on the ground to reach a ginger stray cat with an open sore on its forehead whining in pain, its leg twisted at a crooked angle. She stroked the cat and, Solomon couldn't believe it, with each touch the wound became smaller and smaller until it disappeared. The cat stood up, distributing its weight evenly on all legs. It was cured! It glanced at her as if in disbelief before darting off. Solomon dropped his books. His mouth hung so wide open his jaw almost dislocated itself from his skull. The little girl looked up at him. The moment their eyes met he knew he had found it. He had found that Special Thing. He ignored the books scattered at his feet and walked towards her.

PART THREE

THE PROPHET

ELEVEN

July 1985
Soweto

'Please explain this again like I'm slow,' Dineo said in an exasperated voice.

Molefi sighed. 'It's the doctrine of common purpose, Neo. It basically means that if you're part of a group that committed a crime like, in this case, murder. You can be convicted for murder even if you weren't the one who actually killed the guy, as long as the state can prove that you were there when the murder took place and you somehow associated yourself with it.'

They were sitting outside a small strip of shops a few streets away from their home. Between them was a generous helping of thick slap chips so oily they turned the paper they were wrapped in see-through, moist Russian sausages, and a cold glass bottle of Coca-Cola. Molefi put a chip in his mouth and felt the acidic salt and vinegar burn his lips with pleasure. Dineo had found them a spot in the weak sunshine, hoping its warmth would keep the crisp winter air's chill at bay. Across the road they saw a group of men sitting on crates playing amadice on the pavement. Approaching them were two women who had decided to involve the whole street in their conversation as they yelled out the details of the latest neighborhood scandal.

They had come back from the High Court in Johannesburg. A protest the day before had meant that school that day was cancelled, leaving Molefi with unexpected free time on his hands. Dineo had told him she was going to watch a court case that day he begged her to let him come. They had spent the morning squished into the dark oak pews of the court room and watched as a young man named Ernest Magubane was tried for murder.

Molefi had a dark fascination with courts. His interest in law had developed slowly. He would sit at the dining table doing his homework while eavesdropping on the evening news his parents listened to over the radio. The snippets of courtroom reports and legal jargon piqued his interest enough for him to steal the newspapers his father left lying in the living room area just so he could read the full stories. He would become completely absorbed reading or listening to court reports until his mother yelled at him to tidy up the living room.

The High Court in particular had an air of reverence with its brownstone walls, large Grecian columns, and greenish dome. He loved listening to the lawyers in long black robes present their arguments, imagining the arguments he would make if he were in their shoes. Magubane's case was of special interest not just to him but a number of his neighbours. The man was being accused of having been part of a group of men who had armed themselves with knives, boarded a train and stabbed several passengers who they believed to be part of the IFP.

'My Lord, the state has obtained substantial evidence which proves that not only was Magubane present at the time the murders took place, he had knives in his possession and was overheard identifying potential victims by witnesses,' a white lawyer with tortoiseshell, wide rimmed glasses had said.

'We intend to prove that the accused shared a common purpose with those who committed the murders and as such, should be found guilty of murder by the court.'

Molefi looked from the judge, an elderly imposing man, to Magubane who seemed meek in comparison. He had seen Magubane's face as he walked in. He looked no older than Dineo. Molefi sat at the edge of the pew in anticipation. How would his lawyer argue his defense? Well the lawyer said they had evidence Magubane had knives in his possession, but that wouldn't prove he had actually stabbed or intended to stab any of the victims in the train. Then again, the common purpose principle made this so much trickier.

'But what I'm not getting is wouldn't they have to prove that guy actually stabbed someone to convict him of murder?' Dineo said in frustration. 'He could have just been there?'

'They found knives on him, Neo.'

'Ja but that doesn't mean he was involved. He could have been taking those knives somewhere,' she took a swig of the Coca-Cola before continuing. 'And even if the knives he had were the knives they used, wouldn't that just make him an accomplice? Why are they charging him with murder if he wasn't the one who actually did it?'

Molefi sighed. 'Because the way our courts see it if you agree to be directly involved in a crime then you're just as guilty as the person who actually did it. It's this principle—'

'It's kak that's what it is,' Dineo interrupted. 'This is the same 'principle' they used to execute Solomon Mahlangu. And he didn't even kill anyone. They're going to hang this man over something he didn't even do Molefi, and you're defending it.'

Molefi was wounded. 'I'm not defending it. I'm just explaining!'

'Ja but that's the problem,' she said looking away from him. 'You shouldn't be explaining this like it makes sense because nothing about this country makes sense. I bet you you'll never see a white man get charged with a murder he didn't commit because of some common purpose nton nton. Because the courts and the government in this country see white people as individuals, as human beings. But with us we're just faceless black beasts. They can execute one black for a crime another one committed because we don't matter. A black is a black is a black to them.'

He went silent. He hated it when Dineo became like this. All dark and brooding and political. Most of all it scared him. The political was dangerous, especially when spoken out loud. There had been something off about her the whole day. Usually she sat in the pews languidly, making the odd private joke to him. But that day there had been no jokes. She had been on high alert, drinking in every word the lawyers and judge had said while staring at Magubane. Molefi had never seen the man before but he saw him glance in Dineo's direction and the two of them had briefly locked eyes as though they recognised one another.

'I can tell this is making you upset,' he said. 'We can talk about something else.'

She shook her head and gave him a small smile. 'I almost forgot that you're the future lawyer around here.' She straightened up. 'Have you applied to Fort Hare yet?'

'Uh...' he paused for a moment, trying to figure out the best way to say what he had been hiding from her for weeks. He felt a lump in his throat. Dineo could be so opinionated. How would she react when he told her he favored a white university over a black one? 'There are some bursary programs for black kids that I wanted to apply for. I've decided that I want to go to Wits.'

She leaned back and twisted her face in surprise. 'Wits? Why? You want white people to come tell you their nonsense to your face every day?'

He had expected that. 'It's a really good university, Neo. And their law school is the best.'

'Fort Hare is good too.'

'But not like Wits. Plus this way you get to come visit me in Braamfontein instead of having to go on a bus for god knows how long to go all the way to Alice.'

She laughed. 'Come now Molefi. You know I love you but there's no ways I'd board a bus to Alice. Can you imagine me in the Ciskei? I can't even speak Xhosa.'

'See? So then why are you complaining about me going to Wits?'

'I just don't want you to end up losing yourself there in that privileged little bubble. Don't let the pretty buildings in Braamfontein and all the rich people you're going to meet make you forget that this is where you come from. You must come visit us here.'

'Obviously I will.' An airplane flew overhead and they stopped to watch it pass by.

'Man, I wish I was on that plane,' Dineo said.

'But you don't even know where it's going,' Molefi said through a mouthful of chips.

'Doesn't matter. If it's leaving this country that's good enough for me. I just want to go somewhere else, you know? Away from all these fights between the hostel men and these stupid laws and all of...' she gestured around. 'This. I swear if I ever get the chance I'm getting on the first plane I can and leaving this country.'

'Me too,' Molefi said quietly. 'Who knows, maybe one day when I'm a lawyer I'll be able to buy us plane tickets and we'll go together.'

She laughed at him and looked down. She reached down and plucked a dandelion with a translucent white mane. She twirled it around in her fingers for a moment. 'I know Mahlatse hates these things but I love them,' she said. 'I don't even care that they're weeds. They're pretty.'

She held it out to him. 'Here, make a wish.' He focused on the flower, mouthed 'I wish I get into Wits' and watched as Dineo gently blew on it, sending the white petals dancing in the air.

* * *

They were walking towards the house when they heard a voice yelling 'Eh, sisi! Dineo!' They turned around and saw the short, round figure of Aus' Rosalia walking towards them. Molefi instantly felt annoyed. He hated interacting with this woman. She was always walking up to people and telling them about her 'prophetic' dreams unannounced. He often joked that the reason her nose was so big was because she was always sticking it in everyone else's business. And here she was with sweat dripping off that same nose, coming to stick it in theirs.

'Dumela, Mme,' Dineo said politely. He mumbled a 'Dumela' as well.

'Dumelang, dumelang,' she responded while panting. She looked up at Dineo, 'Sisi, I'm so happy I'm seeing you. I saw your mother earlier and she told me you were in Joburg.'

'Me and Molefi just got back,' Dineo said. 'Is something wrong?'

'Yes,' she said, quite loudly to Molefi's annoyance. 'Yes, I need to talk to you. I had a dream about you two nights ago and I thought it would be best if I shared it with you.'

Molefi had to fight the urge to roll his eyes. Dineo managed a small, tight smile. 'A dream about me? Really?'

'Yes, sisi,' Aus' Rosalia looked at her gravely. 'I saw you wearing a beautiful white wedding dress with a big skirt. I saw your mother and your sister and some of our neighbours standing around you dressed in black. Now Dineo, I'm sure I don't have to explain to you what that means. And wena, you like playing with fire.'

She lowered her voice and said, 'You must be careful, my girl.'

Dineo let out a hollow chuckle. 'Hhayi, don't worry about me, mme! Who knows, maybe you were having a vision about my wedding day! I think I'll tell I'll my guests they must come wearing black so I can stand out even more in my white!'

Dineo was full of smiles with Aus' Rosalia but the moment they walked away her smile disappeared. They fell into silence. Aus' Rosalia didn't have to explain the dream. Everyone knew that dreaming of a person on their wedding day meant that soon they would die.

Two weeks later Molefi walked into the living room and found his parents, Dineo, and even Mahlatse bent over the radio in silence. A radio host was announcing that following protest action and civil unrest, President Botha had declared a state of emergency. SADF soldiers were soon to be deployed onto the streets.

TWELVE

Mahlatse dreamt about her sister. In her dreams she was in the front yard of her childhood home. She stood there with a plastic green watering can tending to her mother's vegetable garden. The tomatoes were an unusually vivid red, growing bigger as Mahlatse watered them. Dineo walked into the yard wearing a mustard yellow dress and holding a lit cigarette in one hand. Odd. Dineo never smoked near home in case the neighbours or worse, their parents saw her.

'Papa will kill you if he sees you smoking,' Mahlatse said.

Dineo shrugged. 'There are worse things,' she replied.

Mahlatse finished watering the tomatoes and moved to the spinach. 'Worse than death?'

'Worse than Papa,' she stood for a moment finishing her cigarette and then moved towards Mahlatse.

'Listen Hlatse,' she said. 'I need to leave for a couple of hours. If Mama asks where I am can you tell her I went to the bioscope with Mbali? Tell her I went to watch that new Sylvester Stallone movie if she asks.'

By this point the vegetables had risen up to Mahlatse's knees. A steady stream of water continued to pour out her watering can. The overpowering stench of ripe vegetables sat heavy in her lungs. 'Can I come with?' She said.

'No,' Dineo replied. 'I'll see you later, okay?'

As Dineo left Mahlatse felt a gnawing in her stomach. Something was horribly wrong. She could barely see Dineo through the twisting leaves and stems before her eyes. Just as Dineo turned a corner a big, beige casspir appeared. A white police officer leapt out the car, grabbed her, and pulled her in kicking and screaming. Mahlatse tried to run after her but the heavy tomato vines wrapped themselves around her, pulling her back, covering her mouth to muffle her screams. Mahlatse always woke up from her dreams in a cold sweat. The last time she had dreamed about her sister this vividly was after her memorial service. She dreamt that Dineo arrived at their house in a powder blue car.

'Hlatse let's go!' She'd shouted out the window. Mahlatse always wanted to, but she would feel doubt creeping inside her and a force telling her to stay back.

Her mother panicked when she told her about the dreams. She called in a priest to cleanse the bedroom Mahlatse had shared with her sister.

'No matter what, Hlatse, you must never, ever get in the car,' her mother warned her.

Her mother's logic was that the dreams meant one of two things. Either it was Dineo herself trying to fetch her and take her to the other side. Or worse, the person who was trying to take her was not Dineo at all. After all, Dineo had never gotten a driver's license, so why would she be driving a car? At times when life seemed impossible, Mahlatse wished she had gotten into the car. She'd wonder if Dineo had found a happier life and had come to take Mahlatse with her. When Mahlatse's mother died she willed herself to dream of the blue car. When she was in the final throes of her marriage and felt herself sinking she closed her eyes and imagined the car, her sister in her mustard dress with her hand sticking out the driver's seat yelling, 'Hlatse let's go!' But the car never came back.

The blue car clouded her thinking. It joined the persistent tick-tick-tick from the clock, the sound of nails scratching against skin, the smell of tobacco from nearby smokers filling her nose, the buzzing from flies and mosquitoes, as another irritation, more stuff filling up her head, stealing precious space. She had always had stuff in her head. Daydreams, long conflicted streams of thoughts, the incessant tick-tock from the wall clocks, the bleating of neighbourhood goats, the clicking noises of pens, the scraping of a knife against a cutting board, the need to cross her legs, uncross, shift in her seat, change seats. When she was younger she couldn't get past it all long enough to finish her homework. Or hear the teacher explain the past tense in Afrikaans. Or hear the last third of her father's jokes so that when the punchline came and the roar of laughter jolted her back to reality she had no idea what had been so funny. Once while out shopping with her mother she had been so distracted by the smell of a floral perfume and the type of woman who would wear it that when she snapped back she realised she was standing in the middle of Hillbrow alone.

'Here,' her mother said to her one day, handing her a ball of yarn and a pair of grey plastic knitting needles. 'I'm getting tired of you always wandering off, so today I'm going to teach you how to knit.' Once her mother had taught her how to knit a simple square, she turned back to Mahlatse and said, 'Now every time we go somewhere I want you to sit in a corner and knit until it's time to go.' So she knit in shops. When her mother visited a neighbour on the weekend, Mahlatse would sit on a couch and knit. To the horror of the elders, she even knit in church. 'She's not paying attention anyway and it's better than seeing her fidget the whole time,' her mother would say in her defense. The knitting gave her something to do with her hands. If she was moving her hands the white noise in her head calmed down. She became absorbed in her knitting. Her brother and sister received new winter scarves before it got cold. She relished creating the loops and stitches. She knitted enough squares to make a blanket in a month.

One weekend when her mother wasn't on duty at the clinic, she took Mahlatse outside to their small yard. 'I'm starting a vegetable garden and I want you to help me,' she said. Her mother had already bought seeds and saved up old vegetable skins for mulch. They spent Saturday readying the soil and the second day planting the seeds. Over time Mahlatse would tend the garden, watering the plants, mulching the soil, and carefully ripping out the weeds. She had been gardening the day her sister went missing.

She woke up from her dreams shaking, her heart beating loud and fast against her chest. She could smell the smoke of her sister's tobacco mixed with the scent of the ripening and growing tomatoes. The sharp scents clung to her clothes. Why was she dreaming about that day again? It had been decades since but she dreamt about it as clearly as she had during that awful first year of Dineo's disappearance. She tried to dismiss it as a once off, as unsettling as it was. But the dream persisted. After two days of smelling tobacco on her clothes she asked her daughter, 'Are you smoking in my house, Kgethi?'

To which Kgethi gave her a strange look and said, 'No. I don't even smoke.'

It was a lie of course. Mahlatse had often smelled tobacco on Kgethi's clothes, hair, and car long before the dreams. The smell and the lies both drove her crazy. She would often feel the anger in the lining of her stomach begin to grow as it often did when her daughter got under her skin. She did what she'd often done to quell her rising temper in those moments. She shut her bedroom door and knit to calm herself down. She had decided in the months following her divorce when she was particularly cash strapped to take her knitting and turn it into a side-hustle. She made custom knitwear which she sold online. Although she offered a range of items, jerseys, beanies, scarves, and gloves, blankets were her bread and butter and the simplicity of knitting a blanket made it the best thing to lose herself in. She tried to lose herself in the final stitches of a queen-size blanket she had been busy with for three weeks. But her mind was stuck on the dream. She could swear she smelled the vine-ripened tomatoes on the blanket. Am I going crazy? She thought to herself. She was on edge when she went to meet with her client, the dream clouding her mind, until the client snapped her back to Earth.

'Sisi, that's much too expensive,' he bluntly informed her. It would have been one thing if he told her this when she first sent him a quote after he contacted her through her Facebook page. It was quite another after she had already bought the expensive thick cream wool he requested and spent three weeks of her precious time knitting a queen-size blanket.

'What do you mean,' she snapped, feeling lashes of anger begin to whip up inside her. 'We agreed on this price when you first contacted me!'

She was trying to restrain herself. The client had insisted that she deliver the blanket to his house and then had been rude enough to not even invite her into his home. They were standing in the reception area of an Illovo apartment building. She should have charged him more for the petrol but she had thought that since he was spending so much, she could deliver it for free.

'I know but I've been asking around. My girlfriend told me that she saw a blanket just like this one at Mr Price for R300.'

'Hhayi no bhuti. R300 won't even cover the cost of the wool! And I must also be compensated for my time and labour.'

He shrugged his shoulders. 'I'm just letting you know that I can get this very same blanket for R300 at Mr Price. Look, let's negotiate. How about you give it to me for… let's say… R450?'

His offer shortchanged her so much it could not be described as anything other than insulting. She felt the urge to pick up the potted plant sitting in the corner and throw it at him. 'Mamela bhuti, that's more than a thousand rand less than what I quoted you! We had an agreement and for you to do this now is really unacceptable!'

'I think you're being unprofessional now,' he said in a cutting voice. 'If you want to remain competitive you need to be willing to negotiate. How do you think you're going to last if you keep ripping off your clients? Because really, this blanket isn't worth almost two thousand rand I can guarantee that! Like I said, Mr Price sells the same one for 300.'

'Then go buy it at Mr Price!' She yelled before storming off. She heard him yelling after her and used every spare ounce of energy not to turn around and slap him. She breathed in and out in and out to calm herself down. She stepped out of the building and went straight to her car. Once inside, she hit her steering wheel, breathed for a few minutes, and drove home.

THIRTEEN

Kgethi was enough now. She was tired of her mother. That woman has serious issues, she thought. She'd been needing to get out of Mom's house for years now. She was nearly thirty. But with the cost of rent, the cost of Thato's school fees, and the cost of Thato full stop, her plans had always been delayed. Until now. Look, it wasn't actually her fault, she kept telling herself. She was just being honest and it wasn't her fault Mom couldn't handle the truth. Mom had stormed into the house earlier that day, banging everything she came in contact with. Her medium brown skin had adopted a familiar reddish undertone. Kgethi hadn't seen her this pissed off in a long time. She didn't want to ask. Her mother had offered the information without invitation, force-feeding Kgethi her thoughts and feelings until they overwhelmed her. She felt like her mother had plugged right into her emotional reserves and the more she spoke, the more drained Kgethi felt. She had some sob story about a blanket she'd made and a client who refused to pay for it. Kgethi had enough.

'Why didn't you ask for a deposit?' She asked.

Mom sat up. 'What do you mean?'

She sighed. 'I mean, why didn't you ask him to pay for 50 per cent of the blanket upfront so that if this happened you wouldn't be totally screwed over?'

Mom furrowed her brow and stared at her. 'I didn't ask because my clients have always been honest and paid me in full. It's a very small business, Kgethi, and most of my clients are people I know.'

'Doesn't sound like you knew this guy very well.'

'Are you trying to imply something?'

She shrugged her shoulders. 'I mean, it's common sense, Mom, that you ask for a non-refundable 50 per cent deposit upfront before you do anything. So now you've spent all this money on materials and it's your own money. And you're not getting it back.

'Plus, no one is spending two grand on a blanket in this economy, Mom. You were crazy to even charge that much in the first place.'

Her mother exploded. It wasn't about the blanket anymore. It was about what a horrible, cruel child she was. How much Mom had put up with over the past 28 years. How Mom was convinced there was something wrong with her. 'I've never met anyone as cruel and thoughtless as you! You're a sociopath,' Mom had yelled at her.

'You're just pissed off because you know I'm right,' Kgethi yelled back at her. 'You can't handle it when anyone tells you the truth and that's why Dad left you!'

All the air was sucked out the room. Kgethi knew she had gone too far. The words had fought their way out her mouth before she had a chance to stop them piercing her mother. Fuck, I shouldn't have said that, she thought. But it was too late now. Mom looked at her for a long moment as if considering exactly where and how hard she should slap her. She straightened up instead.

'Mamokgethi, I want you out of my house,' she said. 'I'm not putting up with you anymore. I'm done with you. You need to pack up and get out my house right now.'

So Kgethi woke Thato up, packed up her things, and got out. She looked at Thato in the rearview mirror. She had no idea what to do next or where to go. Should she go to her father's house? He had sent her a few messages over the years apologising and asking to meet his granddaughter. Maybe, she thought, she could guilt him into letting her and Thato stay with him? Maybe even cover one of her major bills like school fees or medical aid? There was only one problem. Rachel. God, she hated Rachel. Kgethi was convinced the only reason Rachel shacked up with Dad was because no decent Afrikaner wanted her. She was built like a firetruck, had a face like a pig, and had the wit and personality of a teaspoon.

'You left Mom for that?' She said to her father the first time she met Rachel. It was shortly after her parents divorced. In retrospect, she probably shouldn't have said it but the words came out of her like vomit. Dad hadn't been pleased. That small twinge of guilt she felt melted away when she was forced to interact with Rachel and her family. They often spoke Afrikaans around her, deliberately excluding her from their conversations. Whenever she went to Dad's house, Rachel would snap at her, fussing over small details.

'Don't leave the dishes like that! What did I tell you about how the cushions need to be arranged? Gethi (yes, despite numerous corrections she still could not pronounce Kgethi's name) stop lying around like that and come make yourself useful!' The only people more insufferable than Rachel were her family. Rachel, her mother, and father standing together reminded Kgethi of the three little piggies. They ate like pigs, squealed like pigs, and had a distinctly piggish complexion. Then there was Rachel's son, Marc with a 'c' (God, how pretentious). Rachel would sometimes tell people his name was French because he was conceived in Paris. I bet she means Parys, Kgethi thought. Marc was a pale, weedy child of about 12 when Kgethi met him at 17. He was constantly staring at people, staring at her chest, yet running away and hiding when confronted by actual human interaction. He also played the violin, badly, and despite practicing every day at his mother's insistence he only appeared to get worse.

One morning, when Kgethi was recovering from an awful hangover from the previous night's sneak out to a nearby club, she heard the awful warbling noises of Marc's shrieking violin. He sounded like he was torturing a cat. She seriously considered torturing him. Instead she walked down the stairs to the living room where he was. She arrived to see him awkwardly going at the violin as if they were at odds with each other.

'Marc!' She yelled, leaning against the doorframe. He stopped playing and looked at her.

'Can you please shut the fuck up? Some of us are trying to sleep.'

'It's half past one,' he said with a confused look on his face.

'And so?'

'Mum says I need to practice.'

'And I'm saying you need to stop. Preferably forever. You really suck at that thing and you're not getting better, so you should quit while you're ahead.' She turned around and walked back to her room.

Less than an hour later an irate Rachel came knocking at her bedroom door. When Kgethi opened the door she was met with a bright pink face which exploded, 'Did you swear at my son and tell him to quit violin?'

Kgethi put one hand on her hip. She was about half a head taller than Rachel. 'Someone had to tell him.'

'Well, I don't know where you get off bullying my child. Really, it's disgraceful Gethi and I won't tolerate it! I have a half a mind to tell your father!'

'Rachel, can you relax? I was just being honest with the kid! He sucks at that thing!'

'He doesn't 'suck', Gethi,' she said, pointing a finger in Kgethi's face. 'He is learning and he needs to practice every day! That boy is going to Harvard one day and playing an instrument will help him stand out. Not that I expect you to understand.'

Kgethi laughed. 'Oh please Rachel, I caught him trying to eat a grasshopper the other day. He's not going to Harvard. He's not even getting into UCT. You'll be lucky if he gets into UNISA and they even take prisoners.'

The bright pink deepened dramatically. 'Is jy mal?', she shouted. She began yelling at her in Afrikaans which echoed through Kgethi's ears, worsening her headache, until she finally said, 'Sorry Rachel but I don't speak oppression,' and closed the door.

She meant it and she told Rachel and her father as much when they tried to force her to apologise. 'Rachel is my wife, Kgethi. This is her home and as long as you're under this roof, you need to respect her,' Dad warned. So she resolved never to come back. She swore to her mother she wouldn't when she returned home.

Over ten years later, true to form, she hadn't been back. She paused and parked the car at a well-lit petrol station, drumming her nails against the steering wheel. She had a hard time admitting this to herself, and would never admit this to anyone out loud, but she cringed at the memory of her last interaction with Rachel. A few weeks later she had thought to herself, Kgethi, you shouldn't have done that. Maybe you went a little too far. In a moment of weakness she had considered calling Rachel to apologise. Then she thought about her hateful mauve face screwed up in anger and screaming at her in Afrikaans. She thought about how smug and punchable that face would look if Kgethi ever did apologise. Especially if Kgethi came child in tow to ask them for help. I can't exactly go back now, she thought. What would I even say to them?

She racked her brain over what to do. Uncle Molefi, she thought. Yes, his Parkhurst home was far from work and Thato's school in Parkmore but it wasn't too far and she'd likely be driving against traffic anyway. And where else could she go? She started her car and drove to his house. When he opened his gate and front door for them, she could tell he wasn't pleased. Uncle Molefi was unimpressed by everything as a general rule. He wore condescension like cologne. He closed the door behind them, handed Thato his tablet, and told her to watch Netflix in the guest room while he spoke to her mother. Then he poured himself a glass of red wine, offered Kgethi nothing, and sat her across from him in his living room. After Kgethi explained what happened he looked at her for a long while before sighing deeply.

'Kgethi. I want you to look around my house. Do you see children anywhere?'

It was as though Uncle Molefi had purposefully designed his home to be as child unfriendly as possible. The furniture in his living room was crafted from lush cream suede, a faux mink blanket thrown over the edge of the couch for effect. All around his shelves and in corners were the delicate ornaments he had collected from his travels. On the coffee table was a crystal vase that screamed expensive. The whole room looked as sleek as he did, with smooth sharp edges that mirrored his razor-like cheekbones, strong jawline, and glass smooth, blemish-free skin.

'Really, Uncle Molefi?'

'Well, do you?'

She rolled her eyes and said through gritted teeth, 'No.'

'Exactly. You will notice that I have kept my home child-free. And yet today you have come into my house asking me to let you move in with your child.'

'Oh, come on, Uncle Molefi! You love Thato. You've fetched her and brought her here yourself.'

'For a few hours,' he said, wagging a finger in her face. 'There's a massive difference, young lady, between having a child in your house for a few hours on a Saturday afternoon and having a child living here 24/7.'

'Okay, but Thato isn't like other kids. You even said that! And where else must I take her? To go play Rainbow Nation with my dad and his wife? Rachel would probably complain that Thato will mess up her, I don't know, 'Lorna Jane gravity pilates tights' or whatever white women are into these days.'

He lifted an eyebrow. 'You say things like that and then wonder why they don't want you in their house.'

'Look, Uncle Molefi, please? We have nowhere else to go.

We won't stay forever. I'll… I'll try to find a new place and once I do we'll go.'

He leaned back. 'There's always Ntatemogolo. You could work on your Setswana while you're there.'

She gave him a look. 'Funny.'

Eventually he gave in. 'Alright, you can stay here,' he said, sitting up. 'But you won't try to find a new place, you will. Your mother may have put up with your nonsense for 28 years but I certainly won't. I'm giving you three months and then you need to leave. Talk to me like I'm one of your little friends and you leave earlier. Am I understood?'

She took his words in. She couldn't fight him on this. She had no bargaining power. 'Okay. Got it. Three months and I'm out of here. Thanks, Uncle Molefi.'

There was a strained silence between them. His eyes were burning holes into her. 'Can I have a glass of wine?' She eventually asked.

He laughed. 'Baby girl, you may not have much money or sense but you have audacity in spades! There's a cheap bottle of red wine someone gifted me. One of those awful Robertson ones. You can have that and only that.'

* * *

Later on that night, Kgethi lay on the bed in her uncle's guest bedroom and tried to think of how she would get out of there. She wasn't making enough money to afford a decent two-bedroom place. She knew. She'd looked. She might even have to get a second job. And three months didn't give her a lot of time. She suddenly remembered the pastor. She had been in a boutique in Melville looking at dresses she couldn't afford when she turned around and saw Thato with that ugly stray. She ran out as fast as she could, hoping that no one had seen Thato cure the cat. She was healing everything she could get her hands on these days, and Kgethi wasn't sure she wanted the whole world to know.

She grabbed Thato. 'What did I tell you about doing that in public,' she hissed. She looked up and saw a short man in a button-down shirt with a long face and patchy beard coming towards them.

'Thato, get behind me,' she said. Thato hid behind her while Kgethi cast a protective arm over her.

The man stopped a few metres in front of them and looked from Kgethi to Thato.

'Can I help you?' She asked using her 'fuck off' voice.

'I think so,' he said. 'Do you have any idea of the incredible gift she has on her hands?'

'I don't know what you're talking about,' she said quickly.

'My sister, please. I know what I saw. Your daughter healed that cat with her bare hands. Her bare hands!'

'You sound crazy,' she said grabbing Thato's hand. But the man was determined not to give up that easily and continued walking next to them.

'My sister, please. I am a man of God. I know God's gifts when I see them and your daughter has truly been blessed. Clearly she wants to use her gifts for good otherwise she wouldn't have touched that cat. Why not let her?

She stopped and turned back to him. 'Can you please fuck off? Just leave us alone!'

'Look, my sister,' the man said adamantly. 'If it's compensation you want, arrangements can always be made.'

'Compensation?' She said in disgust. 'Look, I don't know who you are and I think you need to get the fuck away from me and my daughter before I call security.'

He sighed and produced a small business card from his pants pocket. 'Alright my sister, but please take this. Just in case you change your mind.'

He looked one last time at Thato. 'A gift like hers shouldn't be wasted, my sister. Your daughter has truly been blessed. Enjoy the rest of your day, you and your daughter. May God bless you.'

There were three types of people Kgethi hated: Soundcloud

rappers, politicians who made long self-important speeches (especially the university student variety), and pastors. She couldn't remember the last time she had even been in a place of worship. She actively avoided the religious. She remembered how much her religious aunts had judged and pitied her when she fell pregnant, telling her to seek God's mercy and repent for her sins. She hated the lot of them and that pastor was no exception. She'd told herself she would throw away his card. But for some reason she hadn't. She fished it out of her handbag and held it in her hand. Solomon Khumalo, head pastor of the Holy Children of God Ministries. There had been something earnest and admittedly persuasive in his tone. Given her current situation, his offer to compensate her was growing more and more persuasive by the minute.

And look, despite what her uncle thought, hell despite what everyone thought, Kgethi wasn't stupid. She looked at Thato sleeping next to her and knew that she was looking at a ticking time bomb. She couldn't keep Thato's powers a secret forever. The choice to keep them a secret hadn't originally been hers, but the more she thought about it over the years, the more sense her mother made. Despite her privileges, Kgethi had still come to learn that this country was not one interested in protecting black women. It would not protect her. She had to be careful where she walked and could only walk by day. She avoided the CBD. She covered her drinks with her hand at parties and refused to go to the bathroom alone. It would not protect Thato. Not only was Thato endangered by virtue of being a little girl in a country where little girls were routinely violated, she was endangered by virtue of her powers.

Kgethi had read stories of muti killings. Of small children whose corpses were found dumped in bushes, missing eyes, internal organs, and genitals. Some believed that people with albinism held magic powers and because of this, they were hunted and killed. If someone could do that to a person they believed had magic powers, what would they do to a little girl who actually did? She tried to keep Thato's powers hidden.

She told her more times than she could count not to tell people about the visions and for God's sake don't tell anyone about the ghosts. The truth was, whether she liked it or not, Thato liked using her powers. She had seen the excited look in Thato's eyes when she cured that cat. And worst of all, the pastor had seen.

He wouldn't be the last. If she kept going like this, someone else would see Thato's powers and it could be someone much worse. Kgethi didn't like pastors, that was a fact, but one thing she had picked up from the times she had been dragged kicking and screaming into a church service was that Christians did not look kindly on black magic. They regarded chopping people up to create potions as witchcraft. Satanic. And Christians hate Satan more than they hate rapists, she thought cynically. So what if it wasn't just about the money? What if it was about getting Thato to use her powers, like she obviously wanted to, in a safer space? She looked at the card again and resolved to call him in the morning. She wouldn't promise him anything. But maybe she'd hear him out. Maybe he'd have something compelling in mind. Maybe.

FOURTEEN

Thato's powers twisted together like Koko's threads of yarn. She would have dreams of strangers and wake up looking at their see-through bodies. She learned that both the living and the dead had threads. The threads of the living were alive too, curling and waving behind them. But the threads of the dead dragged on the ground behind them withered. They were closer to grey than gold.

Most kids needed a grown up to explain what death meant. But Thato knew death as intimately as the smell of her mother's perfume. Death walked beside her pointing out where it had been and where it would go next. When she saw the injured bird in Uncle Molefi's garden she watched its spirit slowly floating up and up, bit by bit. As its spirit rose up, its wing flaps slowed down. She wanted to do something to help it. Without thinking, she picked the bird up. When its soft feathers touched her skin she felt something flowing out of her into the bird. It didn't feel like air and it didn't feel like water. It felt more like mist. She felt the mist pour out of her and as it did she watched its spirit float back down and settle in its fragile body. The bird stood up in her hand, looked at her for a second, and then flew away towards the clouds.

Her body felt heavy, as if she'd run laps and laps around the field at school and needed to find something to lean against. She stared at the bird in flight and swelled up with pride. She did that. She helped it. It was flying away to its bird friends and family because of her. She wasn't sure how she did it but she knew she wanted to do it again. She wanted to help more animals. She spent her December holidays looking around for things to help. She found a moth trapped in the house one Saturday afternoon. It flung itself against the windows over and over again until it fell against the pane. When she tried to pick it up, she accidentally crushed it in her hand. She felt so awful she looked at it in shock before crying. Okay, so maybe insects were too small. She left them alone and turned to other things. Once she found a thin, brown snake in the garden with a bleeding sore on its tail. She grabbed it excitedly and felt the healing power flowing out of her and into the snake. She watched the sore on the snake's tail get smaller and smaller. She needed a nap afterwards and slept peacefully, knowing she had helped something else.

On the day she cured the cat she felt everything shift. She had been bored in a shop watching Mummy try on dresses when she looked out of the window and saw a ginger cat with sore on its forehead and its leg twisted at a crooked angle. It was limping down the street, whining in pain. She felt so sorry for the poor thing. She knew she could take its pain away so she ran outside.

The cat froze and stared when it first saw her as if figuring out its escape plan. She walked slowly towards it with her hand stretched out. She could see it more clearly now that it was closer. Its fur looked dull and thin between patches of bare pink skin. The sore on its head was oozing yellow pus. Its eyes were a cloudy yellow. She saw it starting to trust her little by little as she inched towards it, bent down, and put her hand on it. She stroked it slowly and felt the mist pouring out of her each time her hand touched its fur. She looked into the cat's eyes and felt connected to it. As the mist poured out of her she saw the sore get smaller and its eyes become clearer and whiter. She could feel herself getting tired but she kept going for the cat. She wanted it to live and it would because of her.

She realised then how much she loved healing even though

it made her tired. She wasn't sure she liked her other powers as much. There were times when she had bad days. Days when the see-through people were everywhere. She would have bright, scary visions when she was asleep. When she was awake she could see so many threads, she was tangled up in a spiderweb she couldn't escape. When the teacher yelled at her for not paying attention or her friends asked her what she was looking at, she couldn't tell them. She hated those days. They always made her feel so alone.

And then were days when everything went quiet. She wouldn't see anything. Not one single thread. Not one see-through person poking their head around a corner. She had fuzzy dreams of her flying instead of the sharp dreams she could still smell when she was awake. Those days were better than the bad ones but she still didn't like them. They made her head feel empty. Boring. She missed her powers. She would look at a shadow for a long time hoping it would turn into a person and when it didn't she felt a little let down. The other kids in school thought she was weird. 'Why are you always staring at nothing?' One kid asked her one day. She just shrugged her shoulders. She never knew what to say. Even the parents thought she was weird. She remembered hearing one mom tell hers, 'Have you ever thought of getting Thato checked out for ADHD? It might be worth a trip to a child psychologist. I know a good one I can recommend.' Thato tried to wrap her tongue around these four letters, ADHD, and wondered if maybe it was another fancy grown-up way of saying something was wrong with her.

I wish I was normal, she'd sometimes think. She'd watch the other kids running and laughing in the playground. I bet they've never seen a see-through person, or gotten tangled up in other people's threads, she'd think. She wished she could be more like them. Being her was hard. Thato learned what she could share and what she couldn't. She could share her gift for finding missing things. That was easy-peasy. All she had to do was pretend to look in some other places first before pointing to where the missing thing actually was. A girl in her class came crying after she lost her jersey, saying, 'I'm gonna be in so much trouble,' between sobs. When Thato helped her fish the jersey out a bush the girl was so happy she'd hugged her tight and said she'd ask her mom if Thato could come over and play. She couldn't share the see-through people. She couldn't share the dreams. The dreams bothered her the most because she didn't always know what they meant. There were three she kept having.

One was at Ntatemogolo's house. Koko was there but she looked way different. Way younger. More like Mummy, except with a big curly hairstyle and weird clothes like the ones they wore on that show Mummy liked, The Fresh Prince of Bel Air. She was watering the garden when another woman with blonde hair as short as a boy's and a yellow dress came out holding a cigarette. The woman talked to Koko for a bit and then walked away. The day turned into night and then right back into day. People walked in and out of the house looking worried or even crying but the woman never came back. The dream ended when Koko, and another lady Thato had seen in the pictures at Ntatemogolo's house walked out with a bunch of people dressed all in black.

Another one was in a big hall, bigger than the one at school where they had assembly. There were lots of people packed in there, men and women, old and young, some in nice smart clothes and some in faded clothes with holes. They were all standing up and singing, clapping and cheering for a short man on stage with a long face and patchy beard. Thato saw herself standing next to him, looking into the crowd. All along the sides were see-through people. All the alive people looked at the man but all the see-through people looked at her. She had the last dream more often than the others. She was standing on a green patch with a lake in front of her and a rocky patch behind her. There was a strong swampy smell coming from the lake that made her want to cover her nose. Far away on the other side she could see big houses and some small boats on the lake.

Between her and the lake was the woman with blonde hair and yellow dress. She was looking at her. She looked faded, like the watercolour paintings they did in arts and crafts. There was a big gust of wind that sent the dress flapping and swirling around the woman. She held out her hand like she wanted Thato to take it. She always woke up before she could. She didn't know who the woman was or why she looked different from all the other see-through people. She had seen the woman before, she just didn't know where. Sometimes Thato looked in the mirror and swore she saw the woman in the yellow dress looking back. When she was out with Mummy or Koko she looked for the woman in the yellow dress. She looked for her in the faces of all the women she saw but couldn't find her. Instead, she found the man on the stage. She knew it was him the second she saw him. He came to her after she cured the cat and then, she felt too tired to say anything. He looked different in real life. He looked normal. On that stage there was something dark in his eyes. She wanted to tell Mummy. And then her life turned upside down.

She couldn't cure everything. She couldn't fix the anger and hurt and ugly words between Mummy and Koko. She couldn't fix their fights. This one had been worse than all the others. She stayed in her bedroom, covering her ears with her hands and wishing they would stop. Mummy came bursting into her room. 'Thato, pack your things,' she ordered.

Thato poked her head up. 'Where are we going?'

'Will you just pack your things! Don't ask me questions.'

So they packed up their things. As she walked to Mummy's car, Koko gave her a big, tight hug and said, 'I'll see you soon, baby.'

Now she was lying next to Mummy in Uncle Molefi's spare bedroom. The last time she had been there was to help him unpack. He'd changed a lot of things. He'd moved around a few tables and all the cardboard boxes were gone. She felt a bit sad when she saw that. She had hoped she could play with some of them. Maybe build her own secret fort that no one could come into except her. She hadn't packed a lot of toys and most of her books were still at Koko's. She sat up. In the corner of the room there was a see-through old woman with her hair pulled up in a bun wearing a flowery dress down to her ankles. She looked like someone had poked a hole in her and let all the colour out. The woman wrinkled her nose at Thato like she smelled bad, whispered, 'Bloody kaffirs', and walked through the wall. Thato had never saw a see-through person that looked so faded before. She looked more like the white ghosts she saw in movies and cartoons than any of the more colourful ones Thato had seen. She thought again of the woman in the yellow dress.

* * *

'We're going to do something and you're going to have to trust me on this,' said Mummy. It had been over a week since they moved in with Uncle Molefi. Mummy had been giving her weird looks the whole time. Thato had seen the man again in her dreams. This time he was walking through a crowd of people. All of them were shouting and cheering, begging to touch him, and bursting into tears when they did.

'Do you remember that man we met? The one who saw you with the cat,' Mummy asked her.

Thato slowly nodded her head. She could feel her tummy twisting in knots.

'Well, today we're going to go pay him a visit. You liked helping that cat you found didn't you?'

Thato nodded again.

'Well, how would you like to do that with people? You could be like a doctor. Wouldn't that be cool?'

Thato wasn't so sure. She wanted to help people. She sometimes saw people limping on the side of the road and wondered if she could take their limp away. If she could make people happy just by finding a missing jersey, imagine how much happier they would be if she helped them get better?

She nodded her head.

'I thought so. So I talked to that man and he said he might be able to help you cure people.'

She didn't know what to think. She didn't want to be near that man. He made her feel funny. Like the creepy men who stared at her sometimes when she was walking in the mall with Mummy. There was something wrong with him. Thato was sure.

'Come on, Thato,' Mummy said, looking annoyed. 'Let's just talk to him and see what he says, okay? If it's so bad then we won't go back.'

Thato was learning how to read Mummy like the books in the school library. She was getting that look in her eye, bringing up her eyebrows the way she only did when she was annoyed. Thato didn't like upsetting her. She didn't like upsetting anyone. So she thought that instead of upsetting Mummy even more by telling her about the dreams, she would go with her to see the man.

That night she dreamt of him. This time it was him, her, and a girl who was older like one of the big kids at school. They were standing in a long, white hall with see-through women everywhere. She saw old faces, young faces, angry faces, sad faces, faces that were half covered by hands clasped over mouths. Every one of them was turned towards them, accusing them of something Thato didn't know. Her stomach twisted into knots and the ground opened below her, swallowing her into a dark pit underneath.

FIFTEEN

The pastor had suggested that they meet. Even though Kgethi had been the one who had called him, she hadn't quite managed to hide her apprehension on the phone.

'I understand you're not sure,' he had said. 'You don't know me and with the things that happen to women in this country, you have every reason not to trust me. Why don't we meet in person so we can have a proper conversation about this? I would be able to answer any questions you have?'

A few days later here she was. She had insisted they meet in Melville, familiar turf. In retrospect it was probably the worst time for her to meet up with a man she ordinarily wouldn't be caught dead with. Valentine's Day had been that Thursday and there were still couples playing catch-up to compensate for their busy schedules. If someone she knew saw her they might get the wrong idea.

I can't believe I'm doing this, Kgethi thought to herself. She wanted to laugh. More than that, she wanted to leave. She was sitting inside her car near the entrance to the coffee shop she was to meet the pastor at. There were a few colourful posters already up in anticipation of the upcoming election and Kgethi found herself staring at the faces of the presidential hopefuls. She didn't particularly care for the upcoming election and wouldn't bother to vote. She looked at Cyril Ramaphosa's face smiling from an ANC poster and knew, just like everyone did, that he would win as the ANC had for the past 25 years. She felt her heart beating against her chest. She hadn't told anyone she was here. If she had what would she even say? She knew how bad the words would sound without having to say them out loud.

She thought about driving home more than once. She looked at the key in her ignition and thought if she just turned it she could leave and pretend she had never had this idea. Pretend that she had never met the pastor. But she never touched it. If she was being honest, she and Thato needed the money. They needed to get out of Uncle Molefi's house. Her mother's house wasn't an option. She was tired of the judgmental stares, prying comments and questions. She needed to be free of her mother for good and the only way she could do that was with money. On top of that, she needed to find a relatively safe outlet for Thato's powers. She couldn't make the pastor unsee Thato healing that cat. So why not spin the situation in their favour?

She finally got out the car and walked into the coffee shop. Melville was one of the few places that still resembled a quaint European street where shops and restaurants existed free from the confines of the monstrous malls that had mushroomed around the city. Here people cycled, walked their dogs, and people watched from tables that sat right on the pavement. She generally preferred to sit outside but today she chose a table inside. The fewer people that saw them the better. She was checking her messages when she heard someone clearing their throat. She looked up and saw him standing in front of her looking sheepish in an ill-fitting faded blazer. He greeted her and sat down.

'I didn't mean to keep you waiting,' he said. 'I hope you haven't been waiting for too long?'

'Not really, no,' she said putting her phone away and straightening up. 'Now I want to make it clear that I'm not promising anything. I just want to get a better idea of who you are and what you're planning here. So who exactly are you?'

He chuckled nervously and then quietened down when he saw her stony face. 'Look, Kgethi… it's Kgethi isn't it?'

'Yes it's Kgethi.'

'Alright, Kgethi,' he said carefully. 'Would you like me to order something for you?'

She shook her head. He called over a waiter and ordered a coffee. After the waiter walked away he turned back to Kgethi. 'As I said on the phone I am just a humble pastor. I was born and raised in Alex. I spent a few years working as a used car salesman—'

'A used car salesman?' She said raising her eyebrow. God could it get any worse? A used car salesman and a pastor rolled into one person?

'Yes a used car salesman. For a Nigerian-owned dealership in Braamfontein. I can give you the contact details of my old boss so you can call him yourself and ask him whatever you want to know about me.'

She nodded her head. Maybe I should call that guy just to check him out, she thought. She felt tension building up in her shoulders and forced herself to drop them.

'So then how did you go from a used car salesman to a pastor?'

He chuckled again. 'I'm afraid that story isn't very interesting. I grew up in the church, the Anglican church. My mother took me and my siblings to a cathedral in town and growing up I wasn't really that invested in religion. Of course I believed in God and His power but I'm embarrassed to say I didn't see the real value in church. That all changed a few years later when I ended up going with a…friend to the Holy Children of God church in Randburg and I found my spiritual home. I've been there ever since, worked hard for the church, and my loyalty was rewarded with a position as the pastor.'

She admittedly wasn't very interested in his story. She was watching him. If he had seemed too nervous or too arrogant she would have walked away that second. But there was an openness about him. When the waiter brought his coffee he thanked him with earnest sincerity. Her own father used to bark orders at waiters in restaurants. The few times she hung out with Luvuyo he would barely even acknowledge a waiter's presence. But something about the way that this pastor looked at the waiter when he accepted his coffee, thanked him with a warm smile, and addressed him as 'my brother' made Kgethi think that maybe he was actually harmless. Potentially annoying as all religious folks were, sure. But harmless.

She felt herself relax more. 'Before we agree to anything, I want to know two things. I want to know how me and my daughter will be compensated for our time and effort. And I want to know how exactly whatever you're planning is going to keep her safe.'

He looked at her and smiled, 'Well, you must understand that paying you directly out of church coffers would be out of the question. At least for now. We have a treasurer who goes through our books with a fine-toothed comb. She would notice immediately.'

'We do, however, have a bursary fund that we use for fees. It's mainly used for university fees but we do take on some cases where we fund high school or even primary school fees. I would be able to list Thato as a recipient.'

'So you're offering us school fees?' She asked tilting her head. That might help lighten the financial load but it wouldn't give her the money she needed for a rental deposit straight away. She was tempted to ask for more but kept quiet. Something about demanding more money for her daughter made her feel uncomfortable. She didn't want to sound as though Thato was for sale when she wasn't.

'To start. You must understand they're watching me very closely at the moment, and if they notice anything dodgy then I'm out. But if things work out like I hope they will, I'll be calling the real shots around there. No one will ask me anything. Then we'll be in a position to renegotiate.'

She nodded. 'I guess it'll have to do. For now. But before we agree to anything, you need to answer my second question.'

'Yes,' he said. 'I have given it a lot of thought and I've come up with what I believe could be a good solution. What if I pretend your daughter's powers are mine? That way I'll be able to root the healings in biblical teachings and if no one suspects the power is actually hers, it'll keep her safe.'

Kgethi recoiled, 'So basically, you want my child to do all the work so you can take all the credit?'

'Don't think of it that way,' he said quickly. 'You yourself said that you wanted your child to be safe, and I agree with you! This is a dangerous country for a little girl, especially one as special as your daughter. It's not as dangerous for a grown man like myself!'

She wasn't convinced and didn't bother to hide it.

'Think of me as your daughter's mask. This way she gets to practice her powers as she wishes while keeping her identity a secret. Then, when she turns 18, she can choose whether or not she wants her identity to be known and if she wants to, we can reveal it.'

She leaned back and sighed. She looked at the man again. A tingling sensation settled on the back of her neck. Negotiating her daughter's powers was admittedly something that felt a little gross. She had thought about it many times over the years, but thinking about it and actually doing it were two different things. A voice in her head whispered, 'Are you really going to do this? Are you really going to sell Thato off to this man.'

No, she thought firmly. I'm not selling her. I'm giving her an outlet where she can practice her powers safely. She can do what she loves and if we manage to get out of Uncle Molefi's house off this then even better. Besides look at this man, she thought, regarding him once again. He looks like he could fight a cockroach and lose. Hell, he was shorter and smaller than her. She could probably slap him around if she ever needed to. If I'm in the room the whole time then what's the worst that could happen?

So she agreed to his deal. 'I'll speak to Thato about it and as long as she's onboard we can try this out,' she told him.

He practically leapt out his chair from excitement. He grabbed her hand and shook it vigorously. 'Oh thank you, thank you my sister, thank you! We're going to do wonderful work together, you'll see!'

She told herself all the way home that she was doing the right thing. Alright, an okay thing. A harmless thing. When she got home she scrubbed at her hands. No matter how many times she washed them, they still felt dirty.

SIXTEEN

It's just another sales pitch, Solomon thought to himself. He had done this before. He had practiced each morning before going to Mr Ife's exactly what he would say to the customer he was expecting. Which car he would try to sell them and what he would say to convince them to buy it. Although Solomon told himself it was a sales pitch to calm his nerves, he knew intuitively that there was far more at stake here than a customer walking out on a sale. If the woman with the magical child walked out on him she would be carrying her handbag and his career away with her .

He felt he had won the mother over, but he couldn't be too sure. He knew that dangling money in front of her would lure her in but if he wanted to secure the deal, the only way to do that was through the child. So he invited one of the remaining members of the congregation there that day. She was a single mother from Zimbabwe with a rail thin son of about six who was half-dead from tuberculosis. Solomon had specifically wanted someone who was ill rather than injured. If the little girl could not cure the sick, she would not be useful to him. The boy made a pathetic sight, wheezing and shivering in his mother's arms. Solomon knew she had come because she was desperate. She was in the country illegally and the nursing staff at the public clinic were reluctant to help her.

'You lot are clogging up the system for everyone else. You

should go back to Zimbabwe and get treatment there,' a nurse had apparently hissed at her.

Admittedly, Solomon hadn't originally thought of her until she came begging for help after one of his services. The moment he saw the frail child inching closer to death by the second he had an idea. 'Why don't you bring your daughter to my office? There's a woman here with a very sick child,' he had told the mother when she phoned him. What was her name again? Mokgethi or something like that. He continued, 'When she sees how much of a difference she can make to other people's lives she might decide that she actually wants to keep doing this.' The woman had sounded reluctant. Solomon imagined her internal conflict, her brain working out the pros and cons of accepting his money in exchange for her child. He had looked at her in her wavy, shoulder length wig and too tight dress and knew immediately he was dealing with one of those immoral women with no self-worth who loved money more than her own dignity.

He wasn't too enthusiastic about having to appeal to such a woman. She hadn't mentioned anything of the girl's father so he could only assume that she, like most of her ilk, was a single mother. 'She probably has even more children she's shoved off on her mother to raise,' he thought to himself. Unfortunately, to get to the girl he would have to go through the mother. And the girl was essential. She was the miracle that hundreds would fill the pews to watch. She was proof that God's power was living and breathing everywhere; that miracles were not just written in the Bible but could be recreated by ordinary people if they believed in and were faithful to Christ.

He spent sleepless nights that week planning that moment in detail. He would keep it small. It would only be him, the mother and child, and the Zimbabwean woman and her sick boy. He hadn't even wanted Bongani to know. He told the Zimbabwean woman that it was important she not tell anyone about the meeting until he gave her permission. If he failed, the last thing he needed to see was Mrs Vilakazi's cruel, judgmental stare before she sentenced him to serve as a youth pastor once again.

He was waiting for the woman inside his office. He assessed it with a frown. It was much simpler than he had wanted it to be. It had a dark oak desk, two wobbly chairs with threadbare upholstery that was somewhere between yellow and green, a flaky pleather couch in the corner with a deep impression in the centre, a wall clock that was five minutes behind and a half-empty cabinet. Pastor Mkhize had taken most of the decor, books, and life out the office with him. He would have to work harder to make a good impression given his surroundings. He looked at the clock on the wall and saw the woman was ten minutes late. Typical. He instructed the Zimbabwean woman to wait outside. He couldn't risk contracting tuberculosis in the event that the experiment failed. He was beginning to grow impatient when he heard a knock at his door.

'Come in,' he said.

The door opened and the woman entered, the girl trailing in after her. She wasn't as young as he had remembered. He had sworn she had been on the cusp of full womanhood but he saw now that she was in her mid to late 20s, perhaps only a few years younger than him. He noted with contempt and arousal the tightness of her pants which showed off her figure, the makeup on her face, and the tops of her breasts bulging out of her shirt. She was clearly one of those women who decided every detail of her curves needed to be presented for the world to see.

'Dumelang. I see you've made it,' he said standing up.

Well, at least she'd bothered to moisturise her child and comb her hair, he thought. The child looked much smaller than he remembered, quite skinny too for her age. Her mother greeted back but the child said nothing. She had a particularly bulbous pair of eyes that she used to study him closely, as though she were an antelope deciding whether or not to take off.

'Come on Thato, greet him. Don't be rude,' the woman said impatiently.

The girl managed a half-whispered hello.

He performed the usual pleasantries he had perfected at Mr Ife's. He offered them seats, offered them tea, coffee, or water, and tried to make good-natured conversation before the woman cut him off with a curt, 'Yeah, why don't we just get to the reason we're all here?'

He sat up straight. He was dealing with a no-nonsense woman. 'Alright. I don't know how much you've told her,' he said while looking at Thato.

'I've told her everything we talked about,' the woman said. 'But like I said at coffee, whether or not we go through with this all depends on how she feels about it. Hey, Thato?' She said looking at the little girl.

The little girl didn't say anything, choosing to stare at him instead. She had the roundest, biggest eyes Solomon had ever seen. The type of eyes he would feel watching him no matter which part of the room he was standing in. He smiled at her but she was unresponsive even to that. Not that it mattered, Solomon thought. He was fairly certain all his mother actually cared about was the money and her daughter's feelings were only being barely considered out of courtesy. She seemed like the type.

'And if she does this you'll pay her school fees, right?' The mother asked. 'That's your offer?'

'Of course,' he responded. 'I'll see to it personally that she is added to the church bursary scheme. If she agrees to go ahead with this, of course.

He had thought long and hard about this. He lay awake at night debating how a man of God who had spent so much time decrying the evils of corruption in his sermons could himself be complicit in corruption? What he suggested was corruption and, worst of all, what he proposed would not be stealing from the state but from God himself. But, he thought, surely this is what God's plan dictated? After all, He had placed the child in Solomon's path. He had given the child the gift of healing. Surely, God meant to use Solomon as the vessel that would allow the child to serve His purpose, to heal the multitudes? And surely, curing a thousand of God's loyal followers outweighed the wrong of deceiving the church treasurer? And it wasn't really stealing, when he thought of it. He would be paying the child's school fees, which was precisely what the fund was for!

And surely, he thought, working himself up, the very least they could do for the child who used her incredible gift to heal was to pay her school fees? Doctors charged a small fortune for a mere consultation. People bankrupted themselves paying for treatments that were not guaranteed to work and that was not considered immoral. How could it possibly be immoral for a child who healed with a touch, whose treatment was guaranteed to work, to be paid back in the form of a good education? He tried to remain calm as he looked at the mother who in turn looked at the child. His heartbeat faster. It really was the best he could offer but what if it wasn't enough? She looked back and considered him. He felt her eyes sizing him up. They were playing a game of chicken. Whoever spoke first was the loser.

'As long as we renegotiate once you're in a better position then yeah, I'm still happy with it.'

He breathed a sigh of relief.

'Also you said you'd pretend her powers are yours? How exactly do you plan to do that?'

He had thought long and hard about this. Lying in bed, he imagined himself at the pulpit, his congregation leaning forward in suspense and a sickly man laying at his feet. The little girl stood at his side. He leaned forward to touch the child and at the same time, the little girl leaned forward too. The man gasped and seconds later, he stood up. He was cured. The congregation burst into a frenzy, whooping and singing his and God's praises. The more he thought about it, the more he realised that no other way could work. She didn't have the biblical knowledge to address the important questions regarding miracles. Jesus Christ himself said His true followers would be able to replicate the very same miracles He had performed. So why not him? He could see the hall filling with bodies, snaking into a long queue that spilled out of the auditorium, all of whom had gathered to witness God's power in action and listen to His word. No, it had to be him. Any other arrangement wouldn't work.

'I don't how familiar you are with the Bible, Kgethi—'

'Never read it.'

He tried not to flinch . 'Okay, well Jesus Christ considered children to be pure and innocent. There is a passage in the Bible where Jesus sees that there are children who want to come to him but adults are holding them back. You see, the adults think the children are disruptive, but Jesus doesn't feel the same way. In fact he tells them to let the little children come to him and that no child should be kept away from God. Well I was thinking what if we used that?'

'What do you mean?'

He straightened up and told her his plan. It was the first time he had said it out loud and he was both excited that he had thought of it and nervous at how she might take it. She looked at him for a long moment. She then turned to her daughter, 'Well, Thato, what do you think?'

The little girl looked from her to him and said nothing. She seemed to get even smaller behind his desk. After a protracted silence he became impatient.

'Come on my girl, don't you want to heal people?' He said, plastering a fake smile on his face. She continued to give him a long stony stare.

He stared at her, trying to mask his rising annoyance, and then turned back to her mother. 'Why don't we try it out? Then Thato here can decide whether or not she wants to do it?'

This was the moment he had been waiting for. He told them about the Zimbabwean woman and her child sitting outside. He looked away from the mother and focused on the child.

'Well, Thato, what do you think? Do you want to do it?' She asked her. The little girl remained silent. 'Come on Thato, say something! Yes or no?'

He was glad he wasn't the only one becoming annoyed. 'Maybe if she sees them, she'll be able to make up her mind,' he said. He opened the office door and allowed the Zimbabwean woman carrying her ailing child into the room. The woman and the Zimbabwean mother exchanged greetings. The little girl fixed her stare on the little boy, her stony stare transforming into one of pity. Even the woman avoided looking at the sick child. He turned to the Zimbabwean mother and explained why he had invited the child. 'I always feel it's important for children to participate in prayer sessions and witness God's power in action,' he explained.

The Zimbabwean mother looked at him with empty eyes, as though she did not care whether he invited along an entire classroom of children or even the whole of parliament as long as her child was cured. He told her to place the sick boy on the floor. He looked towards the little girl, stretched out his hand, and urged her to come towards him. The girl would not come. The woman had to nudge her forward before she stepped tentatively towards him, not taking her eyes off the sick boy. He told everyone to bow their heads in prayer. Everyone except the woman, who never took her eyes off her daughter, did. He gently placed the girl's hand on the child and whispered to her in a barely audible voice, 'I need you to cure this child.'

He began a prayer. He prayed in a loud, booming voice. He asked the Lord to take away the boy's illness and grant him his strength once again. Five minutes passed and then another as he called on God to use him as a vessel of his power. 'In the name of the Father, the Son, and the Holy Spirit, we pray this in your Holy name. Amen.'

'Amen,' said the Zimbabwean woman.

They all opened their eyes and looked at the boy. He was staring wide-eyed at the ceiling. The grey pallor he had was gone. His once laboured breathing had returned to a normal, steady rhythm. Solomon put his hand on the boy's forehead and smiled once he realised the hot fever had cooled to a normal temperature. The boy was cured! The Zimbabwean woman shrieked with joy and burst into tears. She hugged her child, kissed him on his cheeks and forehead, and thanked God between kisses. She thanked everyone in the room, Solomon whose hand she shook vigorously, the little girl who she hugged tightly, and even the woman who she hugged as well. Solomon smiled and glanced at the woman. Not only was the experiment a success, but he knew when he saw the look in the little girl's eyes as she watched the Zimbabwean mother hug her child that she would not say no now.

SEVENTEEN

Thato was getting sick of the lady in the flowery dress. She was like a baby. She was like one of the girls in Thato's class who always stuck her bottom lip out and yelled, 'That's not fair' when someone ran out during break and took her favorite swing. She sulked around the house and moaned. 'This neighbourhood has gone to the dogs', she would say.

The lady in the flowery dress had a number of thin dried up threads coming out of her but there was one that looked bigger than all the others. This thread looked like it had been cut by a sharp pair of scissors. The edges of it were frayed like a rope. Thato had only met a couple of see-through people like her before. They were so angry and sad, floating around looking for something they'd never find. Not like some of the others, who laughed among each other or drifted to the other side carrying peaceful expressions on their faces. She wondered why the lady never disappeared forever like a lot of the others did, why she kept coming back.

One day she asked the lady, 'Why are you still here?'

The lady sniffed at her. 'This is my home,' she snapped. 'Why are you here, you filthy little monkey? If you don't leave my son will come back and when he does you'll be in trouble. He's a military man, you know. He kills your kind for a living!'

Thato couldn't say why but the woman made her really sad. She'd hear her muttering about her son named Greg. He was in some place called South West Africa. At least that's what the lady said. The lady didn't know it but Thato knew Greg wasn't coming back. She figured out that the big thread was Greg. It was frayed at the edge because he was gone. She hadn't told anyone else about the lady in the flowery dress. Uncle Molefi loved the house so much that she didn't want to ruin it by telling him he had a someone else living there too and she wasn't very nice. She also didn't tell Mummy. Thato could see her getting sick of all her stories. She was tired of hearing about people she couldn't see, hear, or touch. She didn't even shudder anymore when Thato told her there was a see-through person standing right behind her.

Thato didn't really like the see-through people anymore. For people who would walk through walls, their presence felt heavy. She could feel their sadness that their lives were over. They were mad life had been so unfair. They were scared because they didn't know what happened next. Their whole lives they were told dying was the end but it wasn't. There was a new life, one they didn't know, and one where no one could see them but a little girl who could hear what they were saying but didn't understand. She liked healing more. She liked touching things and feeling their bodies get warm. She enjoyed feeling their insides come together, patching themselves up, mending the tears, taking away the ickiness until they were better again. She looked at the healed things and knew she'd saved them from spending forever drifting down hallways looking sad, mad, and scared like the lady in the flowery dress.

She saw it with the little boy at the church. She had never seen a child so thin and grey before, who looked so weak it seemed that every breath he took knocked whatever energy he had left out of him. She was half scared he would snap in half if someone moved him too suddenly. When they put him on the floor she could see him slowly coming out of his body, his spirit rising up while his body got greyer and greyer. He reminded her of the bird in Uncle Molefi's garden, and like the bird she knew that once his spirit left completely he would be dead. When she put her hand on him he felt almost empty. Hollow. She didn't know if she could heal him. She had never tried to heal a person before. What if it didn't work? She felt so nervous she started shivering all over. She looked at the boy and felt so sorry for him she wanted to cry with his mother. I have to try, she thought. I have to try help him. So she used her power. She put her hand on him and felt his chest heave, her mist pouring into him. She watched his face slowly turn from grey to a warm brown. When she was done she saw he was whole. He felt full again under her hand.

Knowing he was alive and healed felt better than hearing his mom's hugs and thank yous. Thato looked at the little boy's face and felt proud of herself. So proud that later when Mummy asked her 'Are you sure you want to do this?' she had nodded her head and said yes. That night she dreamed about a long line of people, some sick, some carrying sick kids or helping sick old people walk, and knew they were coming to see her. She was going to make all of them better. Starting that Sunday. She had only ever been to church once or twice and couldn't remember it very well. She remembered hearing stories about a man named Noah who built a big ark and filled it with animals. She remembered hearing about Jesus being put on a cross. Mummy didn't like church so they didn't go unless they had to. She didn't even have any good church dresses. Mummy took her to Woolworths and Cotton On to buy her a few. 'We need to make you look normal,' Mummy told her. 'When you're there just act normal.' She was confused. She didn't know how else to act.

Mummy warned her that was that she wasn't allowed to tell Koko or Uncle Molefi or anyone at school what she was doing. Koko still phoned her on most days and every time she talked to her, her throat got dry like there was something stuck in the there. She'd never kept secrets from Koko before. She was excited and scared at the same time. She wanted to help more people like the little boy. But there was something about the Pastor's face. Something about it that scared her. If she told Mummy what she felt she wouldn't be able to help sick people at all. But if she told someone else, Mummy would get in a lot of trouble. She felt stuck. The closer Sunday got, the heavier the secret weighed on her.

After the week had dragged on and on, she woke up one morning and realised it was Sunday. Mummy woke her up. She whispered, 'Come on, we have to go.' When she was washed and dressed she looked up at Mummy and saw she was in fancy clothes too. She was in a long skirt and button up shirt that Thato had never seen her wear before. They drove there in silence. Thato's head was buzzing, thinking of the visions she'd had last night. She'd had the vision of the long line of people snaking in front of her again. But just as she was about to step forward, the pastor had stepped in front of her, blocking her view of the line. Then she heard people cheering and knew they were cheering for him, not her.

Thato was surprised when she got to the church. She had looked up pictures of churches in the books at school and saw pretty buildings with long pointy roofs like witches' hats and windows made up of all the colours of the rainbow. She was disappointed when she looked up and saw an ugly, pointy brown building instead.

'I need you to go in there and do your best,' Mummy told her in the car. 'These people are going to be paying for your school fees. So the least you can do is be a good girl and help those people. You like helping people, right?'

Thato nodded her head.

'Good,' Kgethi looked up at the church. 'Alright, let's get this over with.'

Thato wasn't sure what expect. She hadn't expected to be hit with the smell of musty air, dim sunlight coming in from the high windows, and the sight of peeling paint on the walls when she walked in. She had thought she would see rows of wooden benches like in the pictures, not plastic maroon chairs put into skew rows. The room wasn't even halfway full. She had thought the choir would be wearing gold and white robes singing loudly and clapping like in the Tyler Perry movies she'd watched with Mummy and Koko. Instead she saw less than 20 people dressed in mismatching black clothes and singing songs badly with words she couldn't really understand. She hadn't expected all the see-through people in and around the church, both bright new ones and dull, gray old ones. The church had more of them than living people. They were all squished together, on top of each other, standing inside the church and waiting outside in the halls. None of them spoke to her or even looked at her. Some of them looked forward, some of them looked up, all of them looked like they were waiting for something. The living were singing inside, reading from the Bible over the microphone, and shouting back in agreement.

She sat backstage with the pastor who was a ball of energy, bouncing up and down like one of the boys in her class. He was wearing a shiny suit and kept asking her, 'Are you ready? It'll be just like it was with the boy.' She felt like she could hardly breathe. There were so many eyes in that room all looking at the stage. They would all be looking at her. She held on tight to Mummy's hand and felt it get sweaty. Mummy pulled her hand away and wiped it against her pants. Thato looked at her and saw she had a frown glued to her face.

She stood and watched as the pastor bounced on stage full of energy. The audience looked bored, tired of him even. Thato watched their faces as the pastor talked to them about miracles, telling them about all the miracles that Jesus performed and how everyone who really, really believed in God hard enough could perform miracles too. The more the pastor spoke the more time slowed down. She could hear her heartbeat echoing in her ears. She looked at the audience and remembered last year when during their class play a boy in her class wet himself on stage. She got scared she might wet herself on stage too and almost thought she could feel her bladder filling up.

'It's true!' He said, bringing her attention away from her bladder and back to him. 'God tells us repeatedly, that all things are possible through God. That even true believers, those who are strong of faith, will be able to perform the same miracles Jesus Christ himself did!

'Jesus tells us in Mark 16:17, 'And these signs will accompany those who believe: in my name they will cast out demons; they will speak in new tongues; they will pick up serpents with their hands; and if they drink any deadly poison, it will not hurt them; they will lay their hands on the sick and they will recover!''

He paused, like he was expecting something from them. They gave him nothing back. 'People make the mistake of thinking Jesus was speaking figuratively but he was being very literal. I say to you today that those who truly believe in God's power will be able to perform those very same miracles.

'And if anyone doesn't believe me, I am here to offer myself as an example. I am going to stand before you today, and heal someone in this room the same way that God healed the sick through the hands of Jesus Christ and through Paul!

'All I need is a volunteer. Is there anyone who wants to witness the power of faith in action?'

There was a long moment of silence. The congregation looked at each other and then at the Pastor like he'd gone mad. They were all wondering who would go up first. Even the see-through people turned to look at the Pastor with confused eyes.

'Does no one want to witness God's power in action?' The Pastor boomed.

Finally, an old man stood up. He propped himself up with a cane and moved to the stage.

'So we have our first volunteer! Let's all give him a hand,' the Pastor said, jumping up to go meet him. Everyone clapped, slowly, awkwardly. Thato saw they were all looking at the Pastor like he'd grown a new eye on his forehead. The old man came forward and was helped by two people onto the stage. He walked towards the Pastor with an annoyed look.

'Thank you for coming up, Baba,' the Pastor said, shaking his hand. The man looked at him with an empty stare. 'I've had a limp for 20 years. No doctor has been able to help me and I know you won't. I just want to get this over with so we can all go home,' he responded.

The Pastor asked him to lie down and he did. Then he asked Thato to step forward.

'Jesus once said, 'Let the children come to me; do not hinder them, for to such belongs the kingdom of God', he said to the audience. 'Therefore, let all the little children come forward now, so they may be part of and witness the miracle we are about to perform here. I have one child with me. Do we have any others?'

He looked out at the crowd expectantly. Only two mothers nudged their children forward. One of them was the Zimbabwean woman. The little boy Thato had cured a week before stepped up shyly and took his place beside her.

'Do we have any others?' The pastor looked to the audience again. No other child stepped up. 'Very well then.'

He told the children to kneel and Thato knelt beside him. Then he told everyone to bow their heads in prayer. Thato could hear people whispering around her. It felt like she was on stage at one of her school plays and all the grown-ups in the audience were looking at them, waiting for them to do something. Thato knew what to do but a part of her was still scared she wouldn't manage to do it. What if the mist didn't come out? What if she couldn't cure the old man? Don't mess up, don't mess up, don't mess up she kept thinking. She put her hand on the old man and felt the mist flowing out of her. After the pastor had given a long, booming prayer filled with energy he said, 'Amen,' and everyone said the same back. When Thato opened her eyes she saw a shocked look on the old man's face. He was touching his leg as if he'd noticed it for the first time. 'No,' he said. 'It can't be.'

'Come Baba,' the Pastor said, holding the man's arm. 'Stand for the congregation so they can see you've been cured.'

He helped the man up and, to the shock of the congregation, he stood on his own!

The whole room went quiet. Thato saw jaws hanging wide open and eyes ready to pop out of their sockets.

'Ngabe ngiyaphupha na?' the old man stuttered.

'Now walk, Baba,' the Pastor said. The old man hesitated and slowly took a step forward. And then another. And then another. His steps got faster with each one he took. He walked across the stage and aged backwards ten years.

Everyone started shouting and cheering the old man on. When he reached the edge of the stage without help, he let out a loud whoop. 'I can walk! I can walk!' He said, with tears streaming down his cheeks.

'And Jesus said to him, 'Go on your way, your faith has made you well!' The Pastor shouted after him with a giant smile swallowing up his face.

The whole church began to clap and sing and cheer. Their voices made a loud ringing sound, filling the whole room. Thato saw the see-through people cheering too and heard their echoey voices join in the song. The dead were looking at her, singing for her, but when she looked at the sea of living eyes, they were looking straight at the Pastor's face.

EIGHTEEN

The day after the little boy had been cured in his office, Solomon told Bongani about the little girl. For the first time he could remember, he had responded to Solomon's plan with shocked, wide-eyed silence.

'Are you sure about this?' He asked Solomon after a few moments. 'Won't people notice if the girl is always next to you?' They were sitting in Solomon's living room. As always, Bongani was sipping his beer while Solomon explained his latest big idea over a bottle of Coke.

'As long as I have other children there no one will know anything,' Solomon responded excitedly. 'Think about it Bonga, think about how many people will come to church just to see this! Think about all the people we could heal? All the people we could touch with the word?'

Solomon had expected his friend to be excited for him. He could hardly believe his good fortune. Instead, Bongani looked at him with an expression Solomon had never seen before. Doubt. When he had suggested Bongani apply to fill his old position at the Nigerian-owned car dealership after he got promoted, he did. When Solomon insisted on him switching churches and attending Holy Children of God Ministries instead, he happily went. Now the same Bongani who had gone along with all of Solomon's plans before was actually doubting him. Solomon could hardly believe it.

'I don't know about this Solo,' he'd responded, reluctantly.

'Just trust me on this, Bonga. I know this sounds crazy but this is going to work.'

'And what if it doesn't?' Bongani interjected. 'Angizwa ukuthi why are you so comfortable with this child? A little girl comes along with magic powers and you just go along with it as if witchcraft doesn't exist?'

'Now, Bonga,'

'Where does she get this power from? Why does she have it? What if she or her mother are witches sent to destroy you? You don't think it's suspicious that she shows up now with this 'miraculous power' right when you're desperate?'

Solomon sucked in his breath. He was becoming annoyed. 'God has clearly given her this power and sent her here,' he said in an icy voice. 'This is a miracle, and I'm not going to sit here and question it!'

Bongani opened and closed his mouth. He leaned back. 'If you say so.'

'Look,' Solomon said. 'We're having our first healing session this Sunday. Why don't you watch it and then if you still think it's a bad idea then we can talk about it?'

Bongani shrugged. 'Whatever you say.'

* * *

After the old man was cured in front of the whole church, Solomon's whole world changed overnight. He was elevated onto a platform no one else could touch. Even Mrs Vilakazi looked at him with newfound respect. All threats of him returning to his former role as a youth pastor disappeared instantly. He walked with a new sense of purpose, basking in the praise and wonder people showered on him. Even Bongani apologised to him. 'You were right, Solo,' he said after the sermon. 'That was a miracle! I never should have doubted you.'

He didn't mention witchcraft again, which was a relief to Solomon. He hadn't wanted to admit that Bongani's concerns worried him as well. But after how well that first sermon had gone, Solomon's concerns had melted away, confidence hardening in its place. The success of the sermon was a final affirmation that the little girl had been sent by God himself. The two of them had crossed paths as part of God's Plan and they were carrying out his will together. One of the congregants (he hadn't figured out who) had recorded the old man's healing and posted it online. After that it had mushroomed, spreading into every corner of the country touched by the Internet and even further north into neighbouring countries. There were those disbelievers who called it fake, of course. But so many people knew it was real that Solomon received a frantic phone call from one of the ushers at the church during the week. 'Mfundisi,' she said, 'There is a long line of people here. They want to see you.'

'Who are they? Are they members of the church?'

'No, Mfundisi,' she said. 'I've never seen any of these people before. Some of them say they don't even live close. They've come from far just to see you. They all have sick people with them. They say the clinics keep turning them away because they're not South African. They've all come here to be cured by you.'

Solomon had a conundrum on his hands. The way he saw it, there were two immediate problems. The first was that if these people had come then surely more would be on their way. While he wanted more people to come to his church, he had no desire to turn it into some sort of free clinic for the masses. The whole point of doing this was to attract more congregants to listen to the word of the Lord, but he had no way of knowing whether or not these people were Christians. After all, there were many Africans who were Muslim or who still believed in ancestral worship, which Solomon considered demonic. I won't have it, he thought to himself. The second problem was that he couldn't exactly haul Thato out of school to cure people every day. After all, the church couldn't on the one hand offer to pay for her school fees and then on the other drag her out of school altogether. Yet he would need a sensible excuse to delay them.

'Mfundisi, are you going to come?'

He thought about it for a moment and then said, 'No. I can't possible see all those people today. Tell them I can't make it. And I'll only see those who are congregants of the church.'

The usher protested but he hung up before she was finished. He poured himself a cold glass of ginger beer, sat in his living room, and considered his situation. He thought back to the girl. She had been tired after curing the old man. He saw it in the sleepy look on her face. When he spoke to her mother about it afterwards she'd said, 'Yeah, healing makes her tired. So you'll just have to limit the amount of people she sees.'

This would be a problem. If there was already a sizable crowd waiting to see him on a weekday, that crowd would surely triple in size by the weekend. Thato wouldn't be able to cure them all. He needed to find a way to sort those she'd cure from those she wouldn't. Then it came to him. Why not make it a requirement for those who wanted to be cured to donate money to the church? That way he could kill two birds with one stone: he would increase the church's revenue, which had suffered ever since Pastor Mkhize retired, and he would be sorting out those who were serious about making a commitment to God from the opportunists. He got up in excitement and started pacing his room. It wasn't a bad idea. He didn't see what the problem would be. After all, a donation to the church would still be significantly less than what they could expect to pay if they went to a doctor. Those people charged a small fortune to prescribe medicines that were little more effective than a Panado.

He paused. Jesus had never charged any of the people he had cured. He hadn't charged the blind man or the leper a cent. Not even Lazarus – and he'd raised him from the dead! How would Jesus feel about Solomon taking money from people who were desperate to be cured? He suddenly wasn't so sure anymore. An uncomfortable feeling settled in his stomach.

Jesus was never tired after healing people, he thought. The Son of God hadn't had to deal with Thato's little problem, nor with modern-day social media. As much as the idea made him uneasy, the way Solomon saw it, it was a necessary evil. So that was that. He phoned the usher back and told her that from now on, he would only heal people on Sunday and that not only did they need to attend the Sunday service, they needed to make a donation to the church. 'And a proper donation,' he added. 'We won't be accepting any brown coins, please. People must show a serious commitment.' The plan worked. The prayer and Bible study sessions that week were full. Solomon noticed people sitting up straighter. The glazed looks he had come to expect were replaced by looks of wonder. They drank up his words and by the time he finished, they held on, hungry for more.

'Mfundisi,' one member said to him. 'How do you do it? How do you heal people just by touching them?'

Solomon chuckled. 'You don't understand. I'm not doing anything. It's all God. I'm just acting as a vessel for His power. If you read the Bible, pray to God, and remain strong in your faith, he may choose you to be a vessel as well.'

That Sunday people showed up in droves. They packed into cars, buses, and taxis and filled the auditorium until it was packed with people in the gallery and along the aisles. Solomon was shocked. He hadn't seen this many people in the church since Pastor Mkhize had left. And all the congregants had come to see him. They all started cheering wildly as he stepped on the stage. From the moment he started speaking a hush fell over the room. The congregants looked at him with new, wide eyes, filled with awe. They hung onto his every word, laughed at all his jokes, and shouted in agreement with him. He fed off their energy. With every song, with every cheer, he felt himself become stronger. He felt alive. And for the first time in his life he stood on that stage and felt himself inhabiting his father's skin, becoming the man he could have been if he had put down the drink for good. The sight of the congregation staring at him in adoration, each pair of eyes saying, 'I'm listening, please continue,' was intoxicating. After he had given his sermon, he announced that all those who had come forward to witness God's power in action should stand in a line. He called the ushers to stand near the stage with the offering basket.

'All those who wish to be cured,' he announced, 'must line up in a single file and first show your commitment to God and the church by making an offering. For Jesus tells us in Luke 6:38 'give, and it will be given to you. Good measure, pressed down, shaken together, running over, will be put into your lap. For the measure you use will be measured back to you.''

People scrambled to the front. Some were carrying young children in tow who were crying out in sickness. Others were helping up adults who had grown frail or had a limp. All lined up in a single file, with some digging through their bags and pockets for money. There was a long line of people snaking out the door looking up at him expectantly. Solomon turned and found Thato standing behind him in her place, eyes wide and mouth hanging open. Then he called for more little children to come forward and join the prayers. This time a dozen children came up, some pushed forward by their parents, while others gleefully leapt up and ran to the stage. He had to call one of the ushers to come up and help him keep all the children under control. Then he stood forward and took his place. He called for the first person to come up. A young shivering woman came forward carrying a small child. She said the child had played in the water from the stream that ran near their home and was now very sick. She placed the small child on the floor in front of Solomon.

'Now come children, put your hands on this child and let's call God to heal him together,' he said. The little hands all shot out and laid claim to a body part so enthusiastically the usher had to swat at them. 'Hhayi, hhayi, be gentle! Don't grab her like that!' She said.

Once they all settled down with one hand on the child, he told everyone to bow their heads in prayer. When he ended his prayer the child was cured, and the mother fainted from relief. That day, Solomon learnt two things about the child who lent him her power. The first was that she was unable to regrow missing limbs. A rather embarrassing incident happened when after praying for a long time, the man seated on the floor remained with a missing right leg. There was a long, uncomfortable silence.

'It is God's will, bhut' wami,' Solomon quickly said. 'Isn't it that the Lord doesn't give any of us a burden that is too heavy to carry? The Lord has given you this burden to test your resolve. He has a plan for you, my brother, and that plan does not include a right leg.'

'Can't you ask God to grow it back?' The man pleaded.

Solomon shook his head solemnly. 'I'm afraid these things are not up to me. Remember, I am just a humble servant of the Lord. I do His bidding. If He bids you not to have a right leg then who am I to question Him?' He turned to the congregation and boomed, 'Who are any of us to question God's will?'

When he saw the congregation nodding in agreement he knew the crisis had been averted. He turned to Thato and gave her a look. She squirmed under his stare, looking as though at any moment she'd burst into tears. The second thing he learned was that her endurance was far shorter than he realised. After curing no more than ten people she collapsed against him. Her mother rushed forward and picked her up.

'You need to stop now,' she hissed at him in a low voice. Her child tried to open her eyes but it was as though a heavy weight had been placed on each of her eyelids. The moment her eyes were halfway open, they closed once again. Solomon stood there awkwardly. There was still a long line of people waiting to be cured and he had no way of doing it. He looked back at the little girl, at all the children staring up at him expectantly, and turned back to the congregation.

'I'm afraid that's all we can do today,' he said sadly. 'The Lord has sent us a sign that it's time to stop.

The people still in the line gasped. 'No!' Someone else cried. 'Can't you just replace her with some other child?'

Solomon shook his head sadly. 'I'm afraid not. We have been incredibly blessed today, and when you are blessed, it is not your place to demand more than what you have been given. After all, are we not grateful to the Lord for what he has done for us today?'

Some congregants looked uneasy while others answered firmly, 'Yes!'

'Then we must show Him we are grateful by thanking Him and not asking for more than what we have been given. Come, let's bow our heads in prayer. Let us thank the Lord for what he has done for us today, and ask that He see fit to bless us again in this manner.'

The uncured shuffled back to their seats wearing disappointment on their faces. Solomon commanded them to all bow their heads and once they did, he said a long prayer of gratitude. By the time he dismissed the congregation it was late afternoon. His excitement had turned to annoyance and embarrassment that felt white hot on his skin at the memory of the amputee. As he turned to walk off the stage he grabbed the mother's shoulder. 'Into my office now,' he hissed. She followed him there with the sleeping child in her arms. He closed the door behind her with a loud bang.

'I don't know what you were expecting,' she started, placing the child on the sofa in his office. 'I told you she gets tired. Did you really think she was going to cure all those people? There were at least, like, fifty!'

He stood in front of his desk with his arms folded. 'I was expecting more than ten! And I thought she could cure everything?'

'Curing someone and growing a new leg are two completely different things!' The woman turned to him placing an arm on a hip. 'Mind you, we had a deal! Don't think this changes anything. Thato will cure ten people for you each week and you will pay her school fees, end of story!'

He took a moment to collect himself. He had expected a more robust performance than this. If things were going to continue in this manner it would only be a matter of time before people figured out the truth. He needed to go about this differently.

'If I were you,' the woman said, 'I'd find a better way to filter through the people that need to be healed. Because this isn't gonna work. Fifty people will line up every week and only five or ten will be cured?'

'So what do you suggest I do?' He said. His patience was beginning to run thin.

She shrugged her shoulders. 'I don't know. You're the priest here.'

'Pastor'

'Whatever.'

The child began to stir behind her. She looked at her daughter for a moment and then back to Solomon. 'All I'm saying, is I better start seeing that school fee money. And if you're gonna start charging people to get cured you might as well give me a cut of that too. After all, it is my daughter's labour they're paying for.'

He glared at her. She was insufferable! If there was some way he could keep the child and get rid of her he would frog march her to the church entrance and shove her out into the street that minute. But unfortunately for him, she was the mother. Whether he liked it or not his future was chained to her.

'Fine then,' he said. 'Fine, fine, fine. Just give me some time to figure it out.'

She turned and picked up her stirring child. 'If I were you, I wouldn't wait too long,' she said. She walked out the door, leaving a seething pastor behind her.

NINETEEN

Kgethi thought she knew what desperation was. She'd felt it when she was pregnant with Thato. She'd never admitted this to anyone, not even her mother, but when both the government hospitals and Marie Stopes hadn't been able to help her, she had considered an illegal late-term abortion. Abortion flyers were plastered on the walls, traffic lights, and streetlights of Braamfontein like wallpaper. The words 'Quick, Easy, Painless ABORTION,' followed by a cell number jumped out at her like neon letters. And look, she wasn't stupid. She knew that some women died from backstreet abortions. But there were also women who survived them. She wanted her pregnancy to go away and the closer and closer her due date came, the more and more desperate she felt.

'You can't fucking get a backstreet abortion! You'll die!' her friends told her. They were right of course, and eventually she backed out of it when her fear of death overrode her fear of motherhood. She always looked back on that as the darkest period of her life. She had known what it meant for desperation override your mind and body until it consumed you. Or so she thought. Then she spent more time at the pastor's church. As word and viral video footage of 'his' powers spread, more people poured into the church. They came on foot, in bicycles, buses, taxis, BMWs, and Range Rovers, every one of them shrouded in desperation. It was on their faces, compelling their hands to dig further into their pockets in search of more money, heavy in their voices as they pled for the Pastor to heal them, and clouding their eyes as they watched another person being healed.

The church was making so much money in collections they were able to buy proper uniforms for the choir, replace the plastic maroon chairs with proper wooden pews, repaint the walls, fix leaks in the roof, and buy a proper sound system so the pastor could speak in a normal voice into a small microphone pinned on his lapel instead of booming across the room. He boomed anyway. Rather than shrink back from the noise of his shouting through the speakers nailed to the walls, people leaned in closer, allowing his testimony to wash over them.

He started to give her a cut, as promised. She was shocked at first by the size of the crisp wad of cash he handed her each week. She had already started spending the cash first on clothes and school supplies for Thato and then on hair products, makeup, and clothing for herself. His genius plan of ensuring that Thato healed people without collapsing on stage was by making people donate at least R500 at first and then R1,000 and now R2,000 to the church. And even then, they still needed to get on a waiting list which was growing longer by the day.

'Is there a way we can make Thato heal people faster?' The Pastor asked her. 'More and more people keep coming. They're coming from all over the place.'

'I can't force her to do anything,' Kgethi said, shrugging her shoulders. The best she could manage was to bring Thato in to heal people during the prayer sessions (which now required a separate list and deposit due to high demand) twice a week. Kgethi would look at her daughter and see her dropping off to sleep in the car. She would have to carry her sleeping body into the house and hope Uncle Molefi wouldn't notice.

But of course, he did. 'Why is Thato tired all the time? And where do you keep taking her?' He asked Kgethi one evening. He was cooking pasta in the kitchen and had ordered her to help him chop up the onions and tomatoes.

She was midway through an onion when he began questioning her. She could already feel her eyes watering and her nose becoming stuffy at the onion's sting. She shrugged her shoulders and continued. 'She's started some new sports at school. They make her tired.'

'Oh really? What kind of sports?' Without looking up she could tell that he had stopped spicing the meat and was looking square at her.

'You know, the usual. She has netball practice in the afternoons and I've signed her up for gymnastics which is in the evenings.'

'So then where do you two go every Sunday morning? You're not the churchgoing kind.'

She put down her knife and looked at him. 'How would you know?'

'Because I know you.' He folded his arms. 'I've also noticed all the new clothes and toys you've bought. They seem a little lavish for someone on a secretary's salary, no?'

She didn't say anything. After a moment she gave a barely convincing shrug.

'Kgethi, is there something I need to know about?'

'No, there isn't Uncle Molefi. And since when are you in my business?'

'Since you moved into my house, Kgethi, if something is going on you need to tell me. Especially if it concerns Thato. I have half a mind to call your mother.'

'Don't!' She yelled. Her voice echoed through the kitchen and hallway. She paused. She hadn't meant to be that loud. Uncle Molefi stood for a moment in shock. Then, he moved towards her.

'Kgethi,' he said, standing in front of her. 'What's going on?'

She had taken it for granted that her uncle didn't really care about what she was doing. He had been a welcome change from her mother whose prying eyes and questions had followed her from room to room. But as she looked into his eyes, she realised that he hadn't been as indifferent as he'd made himself out to be. He was watching her. Or, at the very least, he was watching Thato.

'Nothing,' she insisted. 'I just don't want Mom to know my business.'

'She's your mother. And Thato's grandmother.'

'She kicked me out! She can't just kick me out and then still expect to know my life! I thought you of all people would understand that with your situation.'

'Mamokgethi,' he snapped, a cloud of anger darkening his eyes. 'Do not ever compare your situation to mine.'

'Or else what, you're gonna kick me out too? Well, you don't have to worry about that because I'll be moving out with Thato soon anyway!'

She left the room before he had a chance to respond. She walked into her bedroom and locked the door behind her. Thato was fast asleep on the bed. Kgethi knew she wouldn't wake up until morning. She opened Thato's school bag and searched for the new iPad she had bought Thato for school. She was only in Grade 3 so at least the homework was still so easy it took about ten minutes. She knew to make a few mistakes here and there. Not too many that Thato would get a bad mark, but just enough that her homework wouldn't arouse suspicion.

Kgethi had gotten a nasty surprise the first week she started taking Thato to prayer sessions. She had completely forgotten that such a thing as homework existed until she got a call from the school telling her that Thato had failed to complete her homework for both Wednesday and Thursday. She assured them it wouldn't happen again. She squatted on the floor with the iPad in her lap doing the eight times table. Am I doing the right thing? The thought caught her by surprise. It crept up every so often, especially when she saw Thato passed out on the backseat. It crept up whenever she looked at the way the people in the church hung on the

Pastor's every word. The way they talked about him when he wasn't there. 'He's a prophet you know. I'm convinced. That's why he can perform these miracles,' she'd heard someone say. She sometimes looked at Bongani, the Pastor's chubby, dark-skinned companion, to see if she was the only one who was seeing this. He was the only other person who knew the truth.

'Don't worry, we're helping these people,' he'd said to her once. 'The Pastor knows what he's doing.'

Are we doing the right thing?

The thought had come to her more than once when she looked into the eyes of the congregants and saw the hunger of desperation staring back. They had somehow been convinced, or perhaps they had been told, that the Pastor could cure absolutely everything. Earlier that night a man in a dishevelled suit had come walking, head bent into the prayer session. 'Please Mfundisi,' the man said. 'I've been looking for a job for the past year. I've spent so much money on printing and sending CVs, getting taxi fare to go to interviews, but nothing. Please Mfundisi, please ask God to grant me a job.'

The Pastor made everyone in the room form a circle around the man and pray loudly that he would find a job. That he would be able to feed his family, who were forced to survive off his wife's small salary that couldn't stretch to month end. He was not the only one. The shrinking economy was bleeding out jobs. Every week there were announcements of more retrenchments, another company going under, another company implementing a hiring freeze, another industry barely hanging by a thread. Meanwhile the cost of living went up. Petrol went up. Electricity went up. Kgethi may have hated her job where she'd worked in the same position for almost nine years, but at that point she felt grateful just to have a job. Many of her former varsity friends, who were much smarter than her and had two or three degrees to their names, were struggling to find work. The whole country was in a state of despair and the only glimmer of hope that seemed to exist was the Pastor.

Am I doing the right thing?

She tried to push it from her mind. They had money now. She could afford Thato's school iPad, new clothes for them, and most importantly, rent for a new apartment. She was freer than she had ever been since she first became pregnant and didn't it feel good? She'd loved the fact that she could finally afford the things she wanted. The clothes, shoes, hair. Sure she felt a little empty inside after she bought them but so what? At least she had them. She finished Thato's homework and felt vaguely numb. Then she opened her laptop and started looking for two-bedroom apartments.

TWENTY

Solomon liked to think of the first healing as the moment he struck a staff on the banks of the Red Sea and parted the waves. The people came behind him first as a trickle and then as a stream, following his footsteps enraptured by the proof of God's power he had laid before them, journeying closer to the promised land by way of his church. There were so many people flowing into his pews and gallery, pressing against the sides of the church and eventually pouring out into the makeshift pews the church had been forced to place new rows using the remaining maroon plastic chairs on the hard gravel of the church grounds. More still came each week. With the new cash injection from the healings he was able to start making improvements first around the church and then in his office. He was able to replace the oak desk, chairs, and couch with a more modern one. He found a few prints he liked online and put those up on his wall. He bought his first iPad to prepare his sermons and took it with him when he stood at the pulpit. One day he walked past a jewelry store and saw a watch with a price tag that a few months ago would have been unattainable. He bought it on the spot.

While he enjoyed the new perks the healings brought with them, he had to confront the the practical problems that came with the swelling crowds. 'Either we will have to consider having multiple services each day like most other churches or we will have to find a new space,' Mrs Vilakazi protested during a church committee meeting. She was one of the few remaining members of the original committee. Solomon had added Bongani to the committee, and swapped out the old treasurer with someone more agreeable. With his new ability to perform miracles, he had the rest of the committee eating out his hand. 'We need new voices and energy here,' he had explained. It was only Mrs Vilakazi who insisted on being difficult by being even more vocal during meetings. This time around committee members nodded their heads in agreement.

Solomon had to concede she had a point. The church had become overcrowded, with people practically sitting on top of one another. The litter from abandoned pew leaflets, plastic water bottles and food packaging was starting to build up on the church grounds. Long queues had started snaking outside the bathrooms where toilet paper disappeared at an astonishing rate and the toilets themselves became clogged on an almost weekly basis. He could no longer ignore the stench of sweating human bodies pressed close together as he preached inside the church. He had considered doing morning and evening mass, but the problem was Thato.

'No man, you can't give her energy drinks. She's nine,' her mother had said when he proposed it to her.

There was of course the proposal that they keep the healing for the main 12 o'clock mass and have morning and evening mass without the theatrics. When they rolled out this solution they found out that the morning and evening masses were poorly attended while the 12 o'clock service remained overcrowded. Solomon had always known that people came to his church for the healing, but he still found himself feeling wounded by the congregations' lack of interest in him. He had foolishly allowed himself to believe that the healings would be the hook that piqued everyone's interest but his sermons were what would ultimately win their attention. The image of Pastor Mkhize came to his mind. He remembered how people had adored him as he was without theatrics, and memory stung him. He stubbornly pushed it back. There was nothing wrong with people coming for the healings, he told himself. In a time where people had nothing but bad news greeting them at every corner, the healings were the miracle they needed to witness to keep the spark of hope alive.

He had proposed as one temporary solution that they build outdoor speakers and set up chairs outside the church in the gravel courtyard there so that latecomers would still be able to hear the Word. Not even these proved enough. There was still a crowd of people forced to stand outside during mass when the chairs filled up, each straining to listen to his message. As the last of the summer rains poured down they squished together, taking shelter under the awnings, umbrellas, and plastic bags held over heads to listen to his message. But he thought more and more of what Mrs Vilakazi said. And then it came to him. What if they built a new church? What if they built the largest church in the city? The more he thought about it, the more it seemed like the only viable solution to their problem. They could find a vacant plot of land somewhere big enough to accommodate a church that could rival the Rhema churches. He had driven passed Fourways a number of times and noted how much empty land was in that area stretching further than the eye could see. He would write up a proposal for the church committee, maybe get one of the church ushers to help him with research. And with all this money coming in, they would be able to afford it.

He was floating on air. He could do whatever he wanted, say whatever he wanted, and people would listen. They would probably only be too happy to help him fund a new church. The church's rising success was a rare opportunity. What if he used his growing platform to show his followers a greater, purer Christianity than the one they had been practicing? In his opinion, Christians had become too complacent. Every weekend he saw self-professed Christians drink until they no longer remembered their own names. He was approached by self-professed serially divorced church members wanting him to officiate their second or even third marriage. Such things were explicitly forbidden by the Bible, both in the Old Testament and the New.

Even worse were the churches that accepted them. The Bible itself said 'whoever relaxes one of the least of these commandments and teaches others to do the same will be called least in the kingdom of heaven, but whoever does them and teaches them will be called great in the kingdom of heaven.' Yet everywhere he looked, he saw pastors relaxing the commandments, resigning themselves to be condemned as least for eternity just be liked. Just to ensure there would be bottoms in the pew seats each week. Solomon refused to be like them. He reached a resolution. He would be the one to usher his followers from the darkness into the light. It was the purpose that God had set out for his life. He felt like Jesus must have when after being baptised he saw the spirit of God descending like a dove to rest on him. In his church, his followers would have to live in accordance with the word of God. The first thing he decided was that alcohol must be banned. Whenever he thought of that awful, satanic substance he saw his father's face as clearly as though he were standing in front of him. He was such an intelligent man, he'd think to himself. Yet he squandered his life and his money on booze.

Solomon could still picture him stumbling home in stained clothes smelling strongly of vomit and urine. He could remember how his father's hands would shake until he'd had his first drink of the day. He could remember the pungent smell of alcohol that seeped through his skin. He remembered his mother's face, the way she would look at him with eyes heavy from disappointment and rage. The way she swore under her breath when she saw he was drunk again. One day he came home from school early the day term ended and overheard her arguing in the kitchen with a friend she had over for tea. 'I must divorce him with what money?' He heard his mother say. 'I can barely afford to feed the kids and now you think I can afford to divorce him?'

'He makes you so miserable, Patricia. He's not the man

he used to be and we can all see it. Maybe it would be for the best,' her friend said to her.

'No, I can't divorce him. He's the father of my children. Do you know how many children here don't have fathers? I can't do that to my kids. And besides, Jesus said what God has joined together man cannot separate. I can't divorce him. It's a sin.'

The memories pained him. Every time he smelt the previous night's drink on a congregant's breath he became angry. He would not entertain people like his father in his church. No, all alcohol consumption had to be banned. Yes, the Bible permitted drinking in moderation, but South Africans didn't know what drinking in moderation meant. His people were incapable of such. So rather than chance fate, no one would drink at all and anyone who did would be banned from the church. When he preached this at mass he saw a number of faces stare back at him in shock as though he had slapped them. Some people who stood up and walked out. Probably to the nearest bar, he thought. When he saw that he laughed.

'You see how the devil has infiltrated? Those people have been so blinded by their alcoholism that they can't even imagine living their lives without it! Jesus says to us that we cannot serve both God and money, and the same can be said for alcohol!

'Indeed, Proverbs 20:1 tells us, 'Wine is a mocker, strong drink a brawler, and whoever is led astray by it is not wise.' And is this not the truth? Just last week, another young man was killed fighting in a bar. I even saw on the news that over 50 people were killed in car accidents caused by drunk drivers over Easter weekend! 50 innocent lives gone! Every day you open the newspaper or watch TV and see another woman was killed by her drunk husband. Another one raped while she was too drunk to remember her own name. Must your daughter be raped too for you to realise that alcohol is the problem? Must your husband come home stinking of beer and kill you too?

He paused for effect before continuing, 'Alcoholism is the

biggest evil we see in this country. The murders and rapes we see today are directly caused by alcoholism. Corrupt officials steal tax money meant for the poor so they can go to the nearest restaurant and spend it on expensive imported liquor. Go into your community today and count how many families have been torn apart by alcohol. How many breadwinners let their children starve so they can drink away their wages. You will spend days, months, years even counting them all! Adverts on television teach our children to believe that drinking is cool, that it is fashionable. Well, I say there is nothing cool about slowly poisoning one's body, a temple of God. We can see from all the sinful behavior drunk people partake in that alcohol is indeed a satanic drink.'

He pointed his finger at the congregation and continued, 'So listen to me carefully when I say that to be a member of this church means to give up drink. In Ephesians 5:18 we are told, 'Do not get drunk on wine, which leads to debauchery. Instead, be filled with the Spirit.'

He explained that the reason he was able to heal people right before their eyes was because he had been filled with the Spirit. The Spirit had allowed him to carry out the same miracles as Jesus in the Bible. And that if they allowed themselves to be filled by the Spirit, they would be able to perform miracles through the grace of God in their own lives as well. Solomon made the whole congregation stand up and swear before him and God that they would give up drink so they would be filled with the Spirit instead. There were members who looked uneasy but as they watched more and more people leap to their feet, they reluctantly stood up. Even those who weren't entirely pleased at having to give up alcohol were hungry for the Spirit to fill them as well.

TWENTY-ONE

Molefi was convinced the world was divided into dinner people and party people. Party people were happy to go to nightclubs and bars, down shot after shot of tequila until the backs of their throats burned, stumble home drunk out of their minds in the early hours of the morning and be greeted by a head-splitting, earth-shattering hangover when they woke up. Party people were the good time people; full of energy, determined to enjoy their youth, and never let a little hangover get in the way of a good story.

Dinner people, however, preferred the intimacy of conversation. Their idea of drinking was sharing a bottle from a winery that didn't also offer a five litre option in a box. They shared food, they listened to music released 20 years ago 'back when music was still music' and were home in their beds by midnight. Like most students, Molefi had been a party person in his undergraduate years. At that point only a few bars like Ratz in Melville were willing to provide refuge for (admittedly, mostly white) gay men, and they patronised them well. Then one day he turned 25 and the hangovers started lasting two days instead of one. By his late twenties he walked into clubs and wondered why the music was so damn loud he couldn't have a conversation with someone right next to him. When he turned 30 his body officially turned on him and he turned his back on the party scene when the only other alternative to keep going was by resorting to cocaine.

Now that he was in his mid-50s, most of his age-mates felt the same. Dinner parties were far more common today than they had been 30 years ago and for that, he was grateful. He attended a couple a month hosted by his old friends who he had loved since his undergrad days at Wits. Molefi was in desperate need of a dinner party escape after dealing with his niece (who had grown infuriatingly secretive) for a few weeks. The next one took place at his best friend Mabel's house. Mabel had started off studying law with him but while he had 'sold his soul to capitalism' as she put it by studying commercial law, she had gone on to specialise in human rights law. She now worked for a socio-economic rights non-profit where she spent most of her time getting poor people who had been illegally evicted back into their homes and grassroots activists out of jail cells. More than that, she was one of the kindest, most empathetic people Molefi knew, in addition to being one of the smartest. 'You won't believe who's back,' she teased him when he walked in.

'Who?' He said, regarding her with suspicion.

She looked around the corner into her living room. He could hear smooth jazz playing and the background and the sound of his friends' laughter echoing into the kitchen. When she was sure no one was listening she turned back to him with a fat smile on her face.

'Okay, spill,' he said. 'Who is it?'

She moved closer to him. 'It's Emile! He's back from Paris!'

Molefi's eyes widened. Butterflies fluttered in his stomach. Emile Mutombo. Or rather , Professor Emile Mutombo. Professor of African Philosophy at the Sorbonne and visiting professor at UCT, Oxford, SOAS, and Yale. Author of seven books (five of them award-winning), and the chair of various French and English academic councils Molefi couldn't remember the names of. The first time Molefi had seen him he had been a fresh-faced undergraduate with broad shoulders and sinewy arms making up one of the few black faces on campus. The last time he saw him he was offering Molefi a plane ticket to a new life in London. Molefi never got on that plane. That was over ten years go.

'What is he doing back in the country?'

'He's back at Wits. He's a visiting professor at, what's that place called again? The Wits Institute for Social and Economic Research. I think he calls it WISER.'

He took a deep breath. He could feel himself becoming annoyed. 'Mabel, why didn't you tell me he was coming?' He did not leave one unnecessarily tense situation at home to come here and be faced with another one.

'Come now, don't be angry,' she replied. 'I didn't know for sure he was coming. His plane only landed a couple hours ago and he wasn't sure if he'd be able to make it through immigration on time.'

'Well, you still should have warned me,' Molefi said, picking up his jacket again. 'I really don't appreciate being ambushed like this.'

Mabel checked the living room once again before putting her arm on his shoulder and dropping her voice. 'Eish Molefi, I'm sorry I didn't warn you. But it's been over ten years. Don't you think it's time you spoke to him again?'

* * *

Molefi's least favorite phrase in the English language was 'blood is thicker than water'. It was a phrase that had been sharpened and weaponised against him, used by people who believed family was entitled to forgiveness, was inherently deserving of being prioritised, because the fabric of society itself rested in the existence of the strong family structure. However, these people were entirely wrong, and Molefi never let an opportunity to remind them of this. The full phrase was 'the blood of the covenant is thicker than the water of the womb' meaning that the bonds one chooses to create through companionship are stronger than the bonds created through familial ties.

Molefi thought about this often. For him, the incorrect

version had been used in an attempt to shame him into forgiving someone who wasn't sorry. The first time he heard it was shortly after he had been kicked out of his father's house after a neighbour told him of a rumor that Molefi couldn't deny.

His father, always the proud traditionalist, had told him that no son of his was going to be gay. Except he hadn't used the word gay. He had used a word which to this day made the hairs on Molefi's neck stand up and his blood turn cold. He could still hear his father's voice shouting, 'Get out of my house! Leave and don't come back!' The two institutions he had been taught to find solace in, the family and the church, were no sanctuary for a man like him.

His father told him he was unAfrican. The church told him he was an abomination. Church halls conjured memories of pastors at pulpits who spat out the story of Sodom and Gomorrah through curled lips. The city of sin destroyed in a hail of fire by a God that considered it too far gone to save. They called men like him Sodomites, a term that stripped away the richness of intimacy between two men and distorted it into an act of animalistic perversion. Molefi had never understood the story. How could the men who had consensual sex with other men be the villains while Lot who offered up his virgin daughters to a crowd of rapists be the hero? For him, a rejection of both was necessary for survival.

He was relatively lucky. He was in his first year at Wits on a full bursary staying at a campus residence which gave him with a roof over his head for most of the year. But having a place to stay is not the same as having a home. Molefi felt isolated in his residence, surrounded by straight white men, their blinding privilege, and their violent entitlement. It wasn't until he found the few other black students on campus that he found a place where he belonged. They became his new family. They were the ones he laughed with, cried with, fought and made up with. Mabel would invite him home with her for the holidays, telling her family he was an orphan (which he supposed, he was). When the university's first queer society, the Gay and Lesbian Organization of the Witswatersrand, was started in his third year, he threw himself into the space, donning a paper bag on his head when two years later they hosted the first Pride march through the Johannesburg inner city.

Aside from the occasional letter and phone call to Dineo, he wouldn't speak to his family. Until one day, just as his first academic year was entering its final exams period, Mahlatse phoned him to tell him that Dineo was missing. She had been gone for nearly three weeks. He had almost laughed at the absurdity. Dizzy, daydreaming, forgetful Mahlatse who almost never remembered the reason she walked into a room had been the only one who bothered to remember him. So he had Mahlatse. He had his new friends and his old chosen family. And for a short time he had his first love, Emile.

Now the presence of his spoilt, 20-something year old niece and her child had upended the peace in his house. Kgethi was Kgethi, and as annoyed as he was he had anticipated her. But what he had not anticipated was Thato. He was used to her sweet, gentle temperament but was unnerved by the startling way she moved without making a sound, making him jump when he turned around and saw her standing there. When she was awake, he often saw her staring at nothing. Molefi brushed it aside until he once stepped in front of her and felt the patch of air grow colder. Something unsettling had moved into his house along with Thato and Kgethi, and Molefi could feel its eyes watching him. One of the reasons he had left his house that night was to escape it and in the process he had collided headfirst with his past.

Emile's presence took up all the space in the room. Molefi couldn't avoid him even if he wanted to. His silhouette was always in the corner of Molefi's eye. He would see a flash of Emile's smile and remembered how Emile would reserve that smile just for him when he walked into a room. He heard the deep, hearty laugh of Emile's voice on the other side of the room carrying over, interrupting his thoughts. He was pouring himself another glass of red wine when he felt a hand on his shoulder. He turned around felt his heart stop. It was the very man he had been hoping to avoid.

'Emile,' he said weakly. He hated that looking at Emile's face still sent his stomach into knots. He felt like a schoolboy with his first crush.

'Hi Molefi. Long time,' he said, pouring a glass of wine.

There was an awkward silence between them. Was Emile still angry? Of course, he had every right to be cold. But it had been ten years...

'So you're back from Paris,' Molefi said.

'Just for six months. I'll probably fly back there in December.' He turned to face Molefi. 'How have you been?'

Their conversation started in short awkward stops and starts before flowing into full sentences, lengthy descriptions, and light-hearted jokes. Molefi stood in front of him and felt as though no time had passed.

'It sounds as though Paris suits you,' Molefi said.

Emile paused and wouldn't meet his eyes. 'I guess so. I always felt that it would have suited you. And London.'

Molefi's heart sank. 'I'm sorry I did that. I... I know I messed it up.'

'You never did say why.'

He sighed. 'It's...it's complicated. I'm not entirely sure I understand it myself.'

'I've been thinking about it a lot,' Emile said. He looked at Molefi again, this time holding his gaze. 'I've been wondering if maybe I pushed you too much.'

'You didn't. It wasn't your fault. It had nothing to do with you. It was me. I had some things I needed to work through.'

'We all have things we need to work through. But... you could have called. You had me standing there at the airport waiting for you. I nearly missed my plane,' he said with a sad smile.

Molefi looked at him and realised that all these years later the hurt was still etched across his face. His heart broke all over again. There was nothing he could say to make what happened okay. He wanted to reach over to Emile and say… what exactly? That the night before he was supposed to leave he felt a heavy stone crushing him, holding him back? That when he went to bed that night he saw Dineo's face? How could he explain something that even he couldn't understand?

He opened his mouth to speak but before he could say anything, they heard a commotion happening on the other side of the room. A large group of people were gathered around a phone.

'No man! These pastors!' Someone said in disbelief.

'These are definitely paid actors. You know these guys will come up with the most ridiculous schemes to scam people,' another said.

'What's going on?' Molefi asked.

'Oh, just ignore them,' Emile responded. 'Sbu has a video of one of these mega church pastors apparently curing a man's limp.'

'Another one?' Molefi said in disbelief. He was sick of reading about these stories. He swore there was a new one every week.

'This one is even more gimmicky than the others. He gets a group of kids to stand around him while he 'heals' people,' he shook his head. 'Really, these guys are shameless.'

He gets a group of kids. There was something…unsettling about that statement. Molefi looked at him. A group of kids.

'I'll be back now,' he said before turning from Emile and towards the huddled group.

'Hey, can I see this?' He asked.

The person holding the phone turned it to Molefi and played the video over. He watched the video and gasped.. There was a short man with a long face praying over someone on the floor. A group of kids was huddled around him. One of them was Thato.

TWENTY-TWO

Mahlatse felt guilt clawing into her chest. At the young age of 21 she had gone from her father's house to her husband's but for the first time in her adult life she was living completely and utterly on her own. Her house was eerily empty. She felt like she was in a horror movie. The doors made thudding noises from the wind, the wooden floorboards she was once proud of creaked under her step, and for a split second the long, dark shadows that formed in her hallways took the shape of a person. At first, she tried to convince herself this was liberation. She had sold the blanket at full price to a bottle-blonde suburban housewife. 'Ugh, my daughter has been begging me for one of these. This should keep her nice and warm down in Grahamstown,' she'd beamed when she saw the blanket.

'She's starting at Rhodes this year and you know how cold that place gets! Me and my husband practically froze to death when we went there for the Arts Festival a few years back.'

Mahlatse didn't know. She had never been. The annual National Arts Festival in Grahamstown was something she and Itumeleng had talked about going to when they were still married. Then as Kgethi grew older the two of them drifted further apart until their marriage existed on paper alone. His affair destroyed it. She had gotten the house in the divorce. It had been over twelve years and their memories still lingered in the walls. 'Why won't you sell this place and move?'

Molefi often asked her. 'It's probably worth a fortune now that everyone wants to live near Sandton.'

Initially she'd stayed for Kgethi. It was a pretty three-bedroom house with a garden and a swimming pool. A mulberry tree grew in the back and she remembered picking the ripe red-black fruits in spring first with Itumeleng and then with Thato. Kgethi never came around to the taste. The house was in Parkmore, a quiet, safe neighbourhood near enough to work and good former model C schools with a park in walking distance. Not that she ever let Kgethi walk there alone; shady characters liked to hang around the jungle gyms. She'd decided she would sell the house and move somewhere else once Kgethi went to varsity. Then, after less than a year at Wits her daughter came back home with a pregnant belly and no degree. So they'd stayed for Thato.

Selling the blanket had been her up yours to her ungrateful daughter. But as the days went on, and the reality of being one person living in a double storey three-bedroom house hit her, she was forced to concede that maybe, just maybe her daughter had a point. She'd taken on a new job and demanded 50 per cent upfront as a deposit, which her client sent her immediately. The deposit alone covered the supplies. She considered phoning Kgethi to apologise for her outburst. The truth was the memory of it made her cheeks burn in shame. She replayed the fight so often in her head that her boss had already told her off for not paying attention to her work. She became so distracted she forgot important details of the houses she showed and had more than once shown a potential buyer the same room twice.

She also thought of everything else. The years and years of fighting, of frustrations, of her efforts being greeted with rolled eyes and disrespect, of being called into a principal's office because Kgethi somehow snuck alcohol into class, of being forced to phone and apologise to that awful Rachel for whatever inexcusable thing Kgethi had said. She thought of all the lectures she'd received from her father and brother about her daughter's behaviour. 'Your daughter has too much white in her,' Mahlatse's father would say. 'She behaves like a white child. Look at how she talks to you! If you or your brother or sister ever spoke to me that way I would have given you a good beating with the belt!' She had to concede that he had a point. Kgethi was impossible. Mahlatse had lost count of the amount of screaming matches they'd had. It's not as if she'd never tried corporal punishment. She had smacked Kgethi and smacked her often. But her child always found new ways of digging under her skin and opening fresh wounds.

And that was the thing. Itumeleng had been able to just walk away. He held his hands up, said, 'I'm done with this child,' and washed them of Kgethi. He'd washed them every time he refused to get up in the night when she cried, every time he made up an excuse not to watch her, not to take her to the doctor, not to help her with her homework, not to discipline her. Then he turned around and blamed Mahlatse. 'You've let this child run wild,' he'd say, as if it were entirely her fault. As if he hadn't been there the whole time. And she supposed he hadn't. He'd been drinking beer with his friends and watching soccer while she was stuck raising their child. When Kgethi had Thato, Mahlatse was often stuck raising her as well. She thought about Thato often. She worried constantly whether she was eating well. Coping with her schoolwork. Stressed about the upheaval between mother and grandmother. And most importantly, whether anyone had found out about her.

'We shouldn't have let anyone know she can find missing things, and we can't let anyone know about these other powers,' she'd told Kgethi. For a time she thought that perhaps on this one issue, her daughter had actually listened to her. Until one day, she got a call from Molefi. 'Have you heard about a pastor named Solomon Khumalo? From the Holy Children of God Ministries?' His voice sounded strained. Something was wrong.

'No, I haven't,' Mahlatse said. 'Don't tell me you've turned Christian on me.'

'Me? Never. But it looks like your daughter might have.'

She sat up. Kgethi didn't have a Christian bone in her body. She treated religion as though she was allergic to it. 'That's impossible. What do you mean?'

'It looks like there's a certain Pastor Solomon who claims to be able to cure people by the power of Jesus. He's already managed to attract quite a following. He's even started charging people to cure them.'

Mahlatse's heart sank into her stomach. She could see where this was going. I really hope I'm wrong, she thought.

'Are you listening?' Her brother's voice snapped at her.

'Ja. Yes I am. And I'm really hoping you're not going to tell me Thato's involved in this.'

'Hlatse,' he said sharply. 'I was at a dinner party last night and a friend of mine showed me a video of this man praying over a disabled person. He had a bunch of kids on stage with him. Thato was one of them.'

She felt the oxygen squeeze out of her lungs. 'What? Molefi, are you sure it was Thato? As in our Thato?'

'I wouldn't be phoning you if I wasn't.'

Mahlatse felt the ground shift under her. It seemed that every other month a new report would come out about another megachurch where pastors were convincing their congregation to drink cleaning products, spray pesticides in their faces, and even eat snakes. The reports had all been unbelievable to her. Who would actually fall for that, she'd asked herself. It looked like Kgethi had. Why Kgethi, a girl who refused to listen to any authority figure, would suddenly listen to this pastor was something Mahlatse couldn't understand.

'Hlatse, it gets worse,' Molefi continued. 'Kgethi has been taking Thato somewhere every Sunday morning and a couple nights a week. Every time they get back Thato is tired tired. She's almost always asleep. I tried to confront Kgethi about it but she was very defensive. And now that I've seen this video, I know Kgethi is taking Thato there. And I don't know why.'

She closed her eyes and breathed in deeply. A million

thoughts ran through her mind, playing and replaying the worst possible scenarios. She could feel her heart pounding against her chest.

'Where is Kgethi now?'

'She hasn't come back yet. She probably went to that church with Thato. They usually get back here just after eight.'

Just after eight! Thato's bedtime was eight o'clock sharp! Mahlatse could feel herself turning hot, her anger searing through her body.

'I'm coming there now. I'll wait for them with you,' she said. She dropped the call and headed straight for her brother's house.

She was shaking. She had always known Kgethi was irresponsible, but she couldn't believe she would involve her own daughter in whatever mess she'd gotten mixed up in. She thought of Thato who was so shy she would hide behind her whenever a stranger came near. What the hell has Kgethi done now, she kept thinking. When she arrived at Molefi's house she was so worked up he made her a cup of tea to try calm her down. But that wasn't enough. She paced the room, feeling the anger bubbling up inside her. When Kgethi walked through the door it burst out, sending her flying into a rage.

'Have you lost your mind? Sending your daughter to a cult? Your own daughter?' She thundered.

Kgethi looked from Molefi to her, betrayal written on her face. 'It's not a cult, Mom, it's a church! And Thato likes it there! Shouldn't you be happy we're going to church?'

The two argued for some time with both Molefi and Thato trapped in the middle. Thato's eyes filled with tears. Mahlatse saw her clasping her hands over her ears, trying to block their noise out.

It was Molefi who intervened. 'Why doesn't Thato tell us exactly what goes on at this place?' He proposed.

They looked at her with expectantly. Her eyes darted between the three of them before she finally burst into tears. Mahlatse's anger dissipated as she watched the crying child.

She hadn't seen her since they left her house and now her first visit had reduced her to tears. She wanted to cry along with her.

'You see? Now look what you've done!' Kgethi said angrily. She bent over and tried to get Thato to stop but instead she cried harder. Mahlatse walked towards her and crouched down.

'I'm sorry to make you cry, baby girl,' she said, wiping away her granddaughter's tears. 'I've just been very, very worried about you and this new church your mom's been taking you to.'

Thato's sobs began to slow down. She looked up at Mahlatse.

'Why don't you tell Koko what happens there? Did you go there today?'

Thato rubbed her eyes. 'No, Mummy took me to see a new house. She says we're going to live there.'

'You see, I told you we're getting out of here,' Kgethi said to Molefi. Mahlatse ignored her. 'Why don't you tell me about the church?'

'I get to help people there.'

'And do you like it?'

Thato nodded.

'They're not making you do anything you don't want to are they?'

Thato shook her head.

'You know,' Kgethi butted in. 'If you're so worried you could always just come yourself.'

'I wasn't talking to you, Kgethi.'

'No,' Molefi interrupted. 'I actually agree with her.'

They both turned to face him. Mahlatse was taken aback. Molefi never agreed with Kgethi on anything.

'Why don't you go and see it for yourself? Then you can see exactly what we're dealing with here.'

She stood up and thought about it for a moment. Everyone was looking at her, expecting an answer. 'I don't know about this.'

Kgethi rolled her eyes. 'Honestly, Mom, if you're going

to make such a big deal out of this you might as well come. There's a prayer session on Thursday night. You can see what happens there.'

If anyone had told Mahlatse that her daughter would one day invite her to a prayer session at an actual church she would have laughed at them. But there was nothing funny about the situation she found herself in. She looked from her daughter to her granddaughter and felt an incalculable level of rage towards the former. She resented Kgethi for putting any of them in this situation. But she owed it to Thato to do due diligence. It was the only way she could ultimately protect her from Kgethi's worst impulses. So for that reason, and that reason alone, she said yes.

Two days later she found herself facing an ugly brown building. It was the tail end of sunset and just behind the church she saw a great orange disk against a sky with strips of pink, purple, and blue. She'd seldom stepped inside a church since reaching adulthood. She only really went these days for weddings, funerals, and christenings. She looked up at the building and felt a heaviness inside her. Then she pictured Thato's face. It was Thato who gave her the strength to step out the car and into the building. She was shown by a female usher inside what looked like a seminar room. There were already people inside holding Bibles and speaking to one another. She looked around and saw Kgethi standing with an unfamiliar short man with a long face. Mahlatse looked at his clothing and noted the tailoring of his suit and his soft leather shoes. This pastor had expensive taste. She walked towards them.

'Hey, Mom,' Kgethi said waving her over. When Mahlatse reached them, Kgethi introduced her to the man. So, this was Pastor Solomon Khumalo, Mahlatse thought. She knew the minute she looked at him that he wasn't to be trusted. There was something about the way that he looked over her body as if she were a piece of meat he were examining at the butcher that made her skin crawl.

'You must be Koko,' he said to her with a smile on his face. 'I've heard many good things about you.' Mahlatse still felt uncomfortable when anyone other than Thato called her Koko or Grandma. At the age of 51, she still didn't feel old enough to be a Koko.

'Yes, I've heard a lot about you too,' she said with a tight smile.

'I'm so glad you could join us tonight. Please, please take a seat. Make yourself comfortable.' He excused himself to go greet someone else.

She took a seat next to Kgethi. 'You're lucky I managed to talk him into letting you come here for free,' Kgethi hissed at her. Mahlatse was confused but didn't have the energy at that moment to ask her what she meant. She was disturbed to see Thato sitting next to the Pastor but then she noticed all the children were seated near his feet. She didn't know if that made it better or worse. A few minutes later, the Pastor called everyone to attention. The room quietened immediately. All eyes lay on him.

'Sanibonani, dumelang, good evening,' he said. The congregants greeted him in return.

'Kumnandi ukuba apha!'

'Ukuba apha kumnandi!' The congregants said in unison.

'Thank you all for joining us for this evening's prayer session. Let's begin with worship. Lucille,' he said gesturing towards a thin woman with light skin and big almond eyes. She stood up and began singing in a light, high pitched voice, which the others joined in unison.

> Siyakudumisa,
> Siyakudumisa,
> Siyakudumisa,
> Nkosi yama khosi

The familiar song triggered something in Mahlatse. She felt herself suspended in time and then pulling back, years and years, until she heard her own mother's voice sing:

Akekho fana nawe,
Akekho fana nawe,
Akekho fana nawe,
Nkosi yama khosi

Her mother was standing next to her dressed in black. Mahlatse looked down and saw she was also wearing a black dress. When she looked around they were in a different church filled with people all dressed in black as well. They were in a church she recognised as the one in Soweto she had attended with her family as a child. In front of her on the altar was a blown up framed photograph of her sister smiling, her relaxed, pre-peroxide blonde hair tightly pulled back. Dineo hated that photo. She'd insisted her smile in it was lopsided. Yet here it was, her lopsided smile facing a church full of people who had given up on her. Who were choosing to believe she was dead because it was easier.

The people around her were singing in a sad, mournful tone. Standing next to the podium was Dineo's best friend Mbali, who was wiping away a tear as she looked over her notes. It was a memorial service. Dineo's memorial service. Mahlatse sat down frozen as the service went on around her. Then when it was over, everyone stood up. Her mother shook her shoulder. 'It's time to go,' she said. But Mahlatse's legs refused to move. Her mother walked away, leaving Mahlatse sitting in an empty pew. She didn't want to get up. She didn't want to believe her sister was dead. She wanted to scream at them all, 'You're wasting time with this! You should be out there looking for her!' Instead she sat in silence with her hands balled into fists. The pastor sat down next to her. She had long forgotten his name but she would never forget his face. It was dried up and wrinkled as a prune, hidden behind a pair of too-big, square shaped tortoiseshell glasses.

'Why aren't you with your family, child?' He asked her in a soft voice.

She didn't want to speak to him but knew it was rude not

to respond when addressed by elders. 'I just want to sit here a little longer,' she finally said.

'You seem angry.'

She wanted to laugh. What a brilliant observation! Pastors were so good at taking the obvious and wrapping it up as soul-tapping wisdom, she thought. Of course, she didn't say that. 'I am angry.'

'And why is that?'

She breathed in. She just wanted him to leave her alone. 'Because we're having a memorial service for my sister like she'd dead. But she's not dead. She's alive somewhere out there. The police took her. I know they did. And we're sitting here giving up on her when we should be doing something to bring her back.'

'And how do you know the police took her? Did you see them?'

She wanted to punch him in the face. 'No. But I know they did. Everyone thinks she's part of the ANC. I know they took her because of that.'

The pastor leaned back as though digesting her words. 'Mahlatse,' he eventually said. 'You can't be certain the police took her. The same way we can't be certain she was part of the ANC. But what we do know is that she has been missing for over a year now. Your parents have hosted this memorial service to try to move on. And perhaps you should try to as well.'

She didn't want to listen to him. She didn't want to move on. In any case he was lying. The memorial service had been all her mother's doing. Her father had refused to attend. 'My daughter is not dead and I won't go to that church to pretend she is!' He'd shouted at them when they told him about the service.

The Pastor put a hand on her shoulder. She flinched under his touch, fighting the impulse to slap him off. 'Mahlatse, you cannot live with this anger in your heart. The Bible tells us that everyone who hates his brother is a murderer, and that no murderer has eternal life abiding in him.

'If you truly believe that police officers have taken your sister, then you must forgive them. Because God tells us, 'Love your enemies and pray for those who persecute you'. Forgive them, my child, and pray for them that God will show them the light.'

That was the first time Mahlatse remembered feeling the lashes of anger whipping against her insides. She felt hot tears come to her eyes at the memory. She left the room, running down the hallway until she reached the bathroom. She bent over the sink and started dry heaving tears. The memory had been so visceral. She could still smell the incense lingering in her nose. Over 30 years later the memory still made her blood boil. She had watched the TRC hearings. She had heard of the horrific things the police had done to those they had taken. And not a single one of those former police officers who took the stand and cried their way out of accountability had mentioned Dineo's name. How could she possibly forgive people who were not sorry?

When she composed herself she left the bathroom and returned to the prayer session. Her daughter glared at her as she walked in. 'What the hell, Mom?' Kgethi hissed. Mahlatse didn't answer her. Instead she watched as the pastor kneeled next to the sickly person lying on the floor. He called all the children to gather around him and 'help him pray'. He told them to bow their heads and gave a long-winded prayer. By the time he was done and Mahlatse looked up, the sick person was cured. Everyone in the room rejoiced at the 'miracle'. But Mahlatse knew it was no miracle. She looked at Thato's drained face. She couldn't tell if she was happy.

TWENTY-THREE

Thato was tired all the time. She felt like someone plugged into her and sucked her dry. She walked slower than the other kids. She didn't run out and play on the jungle gym during break like she used to. She started sitting with a group of girls who didn't mind her even though she was quiet most of the time. She kept falling asleep during class. When the teacher told Mummy, she started making Thato take energy boosters in the morning and packed more juice and sweets in her lunchbox. 'These should wake you up more,' Mummy said. They moved out of Uncle Molefi's house into a two-bedroom flat with a small balcony. Thato had her own room again but she was too exhausted to feel excited. All she ever did was sleep. Mummy would wake her up to eat or do homework or go to church. When she was done she would go back to sleep again.

The energy boosters were no good when it came to healing people. Thato didn't want to take them anymore. The Pastor kept changing things. He was getting rid of nice people in the church committee and bringing in new people who just did everything he said. He'd just gotten rid of Mrs Vilakazi. He was making people pay more and more money for a healing. Some visitors to the church came in wearing faded clothes and shoes with holes and handed over piles of cash. 'Please, this is all the money we have,' they'd say. Sometimes the church people took it, sometimes they didn't and said the waiting list was too long and the money was too little. Thato always felt sorry for them. She could see the sadness in their eyes. There were a few times when a sick person would come in and their soul was already leaving their body bit by bit. When the Pastor didn't let her help them she'd sometimes see them walking around the church later completely see-through. They always looked at her asking with their eyes, 'Why didn't you help me?' When she saw them she wanted to cry but she felt too tired.

People didn't just come in to get their sores and sickness healed. One lady came in saying her son had something called epilepsy. When Thato asked Mummy what epilepsy was she said it meant the boy had something in his brain that caused shaking fits he couldn't control. The woman wanted the Pastor to heal him. Thato didn't know how to heal brains but she tried her best. A few weeks later the lady came back to say that the healing didn't work. The Pastor looked at her and said, 'If it didn't work, it means your faith is not strong enough.' It was like everyone in the church was playing a game of 'Simon Says'. The Pastor said no more drinking, so no one drank alcohol. He said no more pork so no one ate any pork. He said all the ladies must cover themselves so they did. He said no one who had gotten divorced and married someone else could be part of the church any more so they got kicked out. Anyone who broke the rules got told on and kicked out. Except for one man with a big belly and fancy clothes who drove a Bentley. He was on his third wife and was getting ready to marry another lady.

'How come the Pastor hasn't kicked him out?' Thato asked Mummy.

'It's because he gives lots and lots of money to the church,' Mummy said.

The pastor also told the men that they must do something called circumcision. He said that in the Old Testament, Abraham had been told by God to circumcise all his sons and if men today wanted to be filled by the Spirit, they had to do it too. When Thato tried to ask Mummy what circumcision meant she said, 'Don't worry about that.' Thato also heard her tell the Pastor that she didn't want Thato going anywhere near circumcisions.

Healings were the part everyone came for. The energy in the room always picked up when the pastor announced the healings were about to start. Thato would watch as the living grew bright smiles on their faces and fought over each other craning their necks to watch the healings for themselves. The dead didn't care anymore. They used to cheer too but now they turned away from the Pastor, looking at him like they smelled something disgusting. The healings brought new hope to people's hearts, she could see it in their eyes, the light in them changed. If the Pastor could heal people with his faith maybe they could too. Thato heard people say that if they stayed in his church then they would never get sick again. That if more people listened to the Pastor then fewer and fewer people would get sick until one day, no one would ever get sick again. More and more people were beginning to say the Pastor wasn't just a pastor at all. That he was a prophet sent by God to bring them closer to Jesus.

'Don't you see,' one of the Pastor's new committee members said. 'God has gotten tired of all the sin we commit. The world has gone mad! Now two men can get married! A woman can kill her baby as it sleeps in her womb! A man can wake up one day thinking he's a woman and the government will chop his member off and give him breasts! God has sent Pastor Solomon to us as a new prophet to stop all that nonsense!' When she heard people speak like this about the Pastor, she felt bad. She felt like they were lying. The Pastor told her that what they were doing was not really lying, because everyone knew that the healing powers came from God. The details were not important. He told her it was all part of God's plan. 'The fatigue you are feeling is coming from Satan. He is trying to stop you from carrying out God's plan. You mustn't let him win,' he'd say, before urging her to take more energy supplements.

Thato was hearing so much about God but she still didn't understand who or what God was. If He was sending her to heal people then why did He make her so tired? She had never heard of Jesus being tired when he healed people. She started to wonder why God gave her the power to heal at all? Why let her heal if she felt so tired after? Why let her see ghosts and have visions if she could never tell anyone about them? One day she closed her eyes and bowed her head like the Pastor always told the church members to. 'God, why did you give me my powers?' She asked. She waited and waited but no voice answered her. She asked again. Maybe God didn't hear me, she thought. But the Pastor said that God heard everything. Still, no one answered her. She opened her eyes and felt like she was talking to nothing.

If God did answer her, what would He sound like, she wondered. Would he have a big booming voice or a soft gentle one? She wondered what he looked like. 'We're all made in God's image,' she'd heard the Pastor say, but that confused her. She didn't look anything like her teacher who was a middle-aged plump Indian woman, and neither of them looked anything like the P.E. teacher, who was a tall, broad white man with pale skin, blue eyes, and thick hair covering his arms and legs. How could God look like all three of them at the same time? Maybe he can change faces whenever he wants, she'd thought. But even if He could, she still didn't understand what He really was or where He came from. Who were God's parents? What happened to them? When she tried to ask the Pastor he looked at her strangely. 'Those kinds of questions come straight from the devil,' he said. 'You shouldn't question God, child.'

One day they arrived early for the service and she was standing in the halls when she turned and saw a dog. It was a white dog with grey spots and its ribs poking through its skin. She looked at it for a long time until she realised she'd seen it before. It had been there ages and ages ago when she first dreamed about the boy who got killed in the sunflower field. The dog glanced at her before walking away. She followed after it. It led her into the courtyard. It looked at her one more time before it disappeared around a corner. There were lots of see-through people standing around. Some were as faded as the flowery dress lady. Others were still brightly coloured. They confused her. The Pastor said that when you died you went to Heaven if you were good and Hell if you were bad. He said when you died your body stayed on Earth while your soul went up to heaven. But if that was true, why were there still so many ghosts hanging around? Some of them had been around for years and years but didn't go anywhere.

Then Thato remembered the time she had to go with Mummy to the Home Affairs office to get her a new ID card. They had waited for a very long time. Thato thought that maybe the entrance to heaven was like a Home Affairs office and you had to wait ages and ages to find out whether your new ID card said you belonged in Heaven or in Hell. Maybe, she thought, the line was really, really long because there was only one Home Affairs office that people all over the world had to go to. Maybe, she thought, that's why there were so many dead people around the church. Maybe churches were the entrances to the office. But these ghosts weren't waiting in line on hard plastic chairs like she and Mummy had to. She decided the best way to get to the bottom of this whole God and Heaven thing was to ask one of them.

'What are you looking at?' Someone barked at her. She saw a man glaring at her. The man was see-through like all the other dead people, but his skin was a weird, shiny pink. His hands were tied together by what looked like rope. He had a big rubber tyre hanging around his shoulders like a necklace. She didn't say anything. 'Why don't you just go away?' He yelled at her. 'You're making enough trouble in there. Now you want to make trouble out here too?'

'Oh, leave her alone,' another voice said. This one was

much kinder, more soothing. She turned and saw a lady sitting on a half-wall that had a small patch of garden on the other side. She was wearing a wide straw hat and overalls. She had red patches all over her clothes. By now Thato had learned to look at bullet holes the same way she looked at pimples on the big kids' faces; something to be ignored unless she wanted to upset the other person.

'Come over here, sweetie,' she said, gesturing to her with a big smile on her face. 'Ignore him. He's just sour.' The tyre-neck man mumbled something Thato couldn't hear before walking off. She went to the straw hat lady and sat down next to her.

'Why does that man have a tyre around his neck?' She whispered.

She knew it wasn't very polite to ask questions about the other dead people. She thought the woman would scold her. But the woman looked over at the man to make sure he was gone before turning back to Thato. 'Because he's a thief,' the woman whispered back. 'He broke into a couple of houses. Robbed some people. Every time the community called the police, they'd come and arrest him and then let him out after a couple of hours. So one day the people got tired and they went to his house, dragged him out, put a tyre around his neck and set him on fire.' When the woman saw the shocked look on Thato's face she laughed. 'Oh sweetie, I thought you'd be used to this kind of thing by now! That's how they sort out criminals these days, and if you ask me they deserve it. Funny, when I was growing up they used to do that to snitches. You know what a snitch is don't you?'

Thato nodded her head.

The woman looked her up and down. 'My God, you're small! How old are you anyway?'

'Nine,' she mumbled.

'Nine! You're small for nine aren't you? And you've already caused such a mess! But don't worry,' the woman said with a wink. 'I'm on your side.'

Thato bent her neck in confusion. She didn't know there were sides. 'My… side?'

'Yes. God, I wish I could smoke!' The woman exclaimed. 'Not being able to smoke has been the worst part of being dead! But yes, like I was saying, we haven't really known what to make of you, my dear. You've really shaken things up around here! All these new people coming in and spending all this money to see that pastor, when really, they're here to see you.'

Thato felt her face turning hot. 'I… I'm helping people.'

The straw hat lady laughed. She laughed so hard she leaned backwards, almost collapsing into – or rather, through – the greenery behind her. 'Oh, my dear sweet child! You're helping the pastor more than anyone else, my darling! But I think you already know that.'

She looked into the distance and pointed. 'Do you see that little boy over there?'

Thato followed her finger until her eyes landed on a thin little boy leaning against a wall. He was staring at the clouds. There was something about his face that looked familiar. Suddenly, it came to her. She saw the boy lying in his mother's arms, his soul inching out of his body. 'Please, Pastor,' his mother had begged. 'He's very sick and this is all I have!' But the Pastor shook his head. 'I'm sorry but it's not enough. I have lots of people with sick kids who've contributed more than this. I'm afraid I must cure them first.' Thato looked at the boy again. Sadness crept into her chest, wrapped around her lungs and started squeezing. She wondered how many other people were like the boy? How many people had come to be helped by her only to die instead?

'If it makes you feel better, sweetie,' the straw hat lady said. 'He doesn't blame you. I don't blame you. You should have been protected, you know. If you were my kid, I would have done a much better job keeping you away from that man than your mother has.'

'But the Pastor said we'd be helping people together,'

Thato said with tears welling in her eyes. 'He said it's part of God's plan!'

The lady chuckled again. 'And just how would he know? Sweetie, I'm dead and I can't even tell you what God's plan is. Spent my whole life being told there was a Heaven and a Hell only to get here and find neither. Trust me, we don't know what God's thinking or even if He's up there. I promise you, that pastor doesn't know either.'

Thato blinked back in surprise. 'But if God's not up there then where is He?'

The woman smiled. 'I can't tell you where He is. But I can tell you where He came from.'

Thato leaned in, listening eagerly. Finally, someone would answer her questions!

'My dear, God came on a boat. He travelled on a ship from Europe. Brought here by a man named Jan van Riebeeck and his Dutch brothers and then later by English people who wanted to come here, set up churches, and make everybody already living here become Christians too.'

Now Thato was more confused than ever. 'But... why? Why would they do that?'

The straw hat lady shrugged. 'They wanted the same thing your pastor wants. They wanted money. They wanted power. They wanted all of this,' she said gesturing around. 'And they figured the best way to do it was by convincing us to give it to them.'

'But how?'

The straw hat lady looked straight in front of her, like she was looking through Thato and not at her. 'It's quite clever, when you think about it. They told us our gods who look like us were evil, so they gave us their God who looks like them. They told us to forgive everyone who hurts us, to turn the other cheek so we would when they hit us. They told us that He,' she said, pointing up, 'hated the rich and loved the poor, so we wouldn't complain when they became rich by making us poor. And they told us that there was a beautiful shining kingdom, a home up there, waiting for us when we die so we'd think of that when they took our homes away.'

The woman was quiet for a long time. The smile was gone from her face. She looked up at the sky. 'You know,' she continued. 'There was once a man, I think he was a president or an activist, I don't remember. He once said, 'When the missionaries arrived, they had the Bible and we had the land. So they taught us to pray with our eyes closed. And when we opened our eyes, we had the Bible and they had the land!' She chuckled, but it was dry. The kind of laugh you gave when you didn't find anything funny, but when you didn't know what else to do.

'I remember the first time I heard it I thought 'No! How disrespectful to God!'' The woman looked at her, 'But now I'm here. I've been sitting here for five years begging God to take me and no one has answered. And I'm starting to wonder, what was the point? I think we all are now. We look at all the people in there and we laugh. Not because it's funny, but because we were all once there. And now look at us.'

Thato looked at the woman and felt sick. There was something about what she said or the look on her face that made the sadness suffocate her. She couldn't breathe. She needed to get away. She got up and walked away from the straw hat lady and the little boy she couldn't save and the tyre neck man and all the other dead people in that courtyard, waiting for something she didn't think would ever come. When she ran into the church she bumped into one of the new church committee members. 'Where have you been?' He asked her. 'The Prophet is looking for you.' The Prophet? Thato was confused. She slowly moved through the church and saw that while she was outside everything had changed. There wasn't a Pastor anymore. Now he was called the Prophet. 'From now on, that's how you will address me,' he said to the congregation who cheered and chanted, 'Prophet, Prophet,' after him. Thato looked at the dead. She looked at the straw hat lady standing at the back, staring at her, and she felt herself turn numb.

TWENTY-FOUR

The birth of the internet had been both a blessing and a curse to Mahlatse. She remembered the first time she and Itumeleng got internet in their home in 1999. She still remembered the loud whining noise the dial-up connection made as it started up and how it hogged the phone lines, rendering the other person incapable of using the landline. The beauty of the internet was that it exposed her to a new (albeit, Americanised) world. She had all the information she could ever need at her fingertips. She could use it to explore the volcanoes in Hawaii or the stars in space. She used it to read about horrific regimes from the Khmer Rouge in Cambodia to Pinochet in Chile. She used it for mundane things, like knitting tips, and more urgent things, like disciplinary techniques.

Years ago, when there was a gap between Kgethi first starting school and Mahlatse finding a job she would chase away the boredom by going on the internet as soon as she tired of the Generations repeats on SABC. The internet became her sanctuary. It was also a black hole, sucking up precious minutes until she was snapped back by a phone call and realised she'd lost half a day. Her internet obsession worsened when she was anxious. In the weeks following her visit to the Holy Children of God Ministries, anxiety moved into her home and settled permanently in her body. The church noises mingled with the sound of her mother's voice and Dineo's memorial service swirled together, taking their place among the stuff in her head. She kept thinking of Thato kneeling next to the Pastor. How drained her little face looked after healed people. She kept thinking of the energy in that room. Like the Pastor was the sun all his followers fought over each other to soak up what light they could. She hated that church. In her hatred she turned to the internet for answers and read the search results with horror.

In one story, a self-professed prophet in Mpumalanga was caught on video feeding his followers snakes, rats, cockroaches, and dog meat. He claimed the Bible never limited communion to bread and wine. That when Jesus called upon his followers to partake in his body and blood anything, literally anything, could be used as a substitute. He commanded his congregates to strip naked and rode them like horses. He said that anyone who questioned him was questioning God. In another story, a pastor in Gauteng fed his congregants rat poison mixed in water. He drank it himself before turning it over to his congregants and demanding they drink it too to 'show forth their faith'. In a third story, more chilling than the others, a church in the Eastern Cape was the scene of a massacre. Police clashed with armed church members who were believed to be acting under the church's commands. An estimated 13 people were killed while congregants cheered on, believing that the armed shooters were protecting them by carrying out God's will.

These stories and many others like them chilled Mahlatse to the bone. But she was addicted. The more she read, the more disgusted she became, and the more compelled she was to read more. Where is the Holy Children of God in all this, she would ask herself. Where did they straddle the line? She didn't wait long to find out. A few weeks after her visit to the church, when the winter chill had set into her house, she tuned into Checkpoint, an investigative journalism program she had been faithful to for years. 'On this week's edition of Checkpoint, we talk to the pastor who claims he can cure HIV,' the pretty presenter said straight to the camera.

Mahlatse recognised the ugly brown building behind her and sat up. 'This church, the Holy Children of God Ministries, was founded 15 years ago by Pastor Reginald Mkhize. It was by all accounts, an ordinary church,' the journalist continued. 'That was until this year when a mysterious man named Solomon Khumalo took to the helm eight months ago.'

Images of the church service flashed on the screen. Mahlatse saw congregants singing, cheering, crying, convulsing, falling over themselves to get closer to the man she hated. He was standing on a stage in front of them soaking up their adoration, spreading out his arms as if calling for more. Mahlatse sat back aghast as the journalist dissected the church on camera, holding up its innards for the viewers to see. A middle-aged woman who was beaming outside the church appeared on screen. She was looking just off camera, speaking animatedly to a journalist who wasn't visible.

'I threw my medicine away,' the woman said gesturing with her arm. 'I had some blood pressure pills and some medicine for my diabetes and I got rid of it all.

'It was useless because, you know, we don't get sick here. Because here, in this church, we are filled with the Spirit of the Lord. And when you are filled with the Spirit, you can't get sick. As long as I am here I will not get sick! And if anything happens I will be cured by the Prophet. I have seen people being cured here with my own eyes!

'There was even a woman here, just last week a woman came, and asked the Prophet to cure her HIV and he did! Not even the government can cure HIV but the Prophet can!'

The program switched scenes from the church to a small, dilapidated one room house in Vosloorus. A man with arthritic hands and a blue circle outlining one of his pupils was shifting through papers slowly. He began speaking in isiZulu before his voice faded and was replaced with a robotic voice reading in English, 'This is all I have left of my daughter. These are all bills she owed when she was alive. She sold everything she had. She believed that the pastor could cure her. She was HIV positive and she had pneumonia. I tried to warn her not to go but she did.' There were tears welling in his eyes, 'She went. She gave him everything she had and it wasn't even enough to move her to the front of the waiting list. She passed three weeks ago.' Pictures of a lovely, tall woman in a white dress were shown before the camera cut back to him. 'People need to know that man, that so-called Prophet is not a prophet,' he started shaking from anger. 'He's not a man of God. He's a scam artist, and he's taking advantage of vulnerable people. He's playing with people's lives, that one. And he needs to be stopped!'

Then the details came. He had bought a plot of land just outside of Fourways worth over R30 million. The house he was building for himself, another R10 million. The luxury cars that he owned. The messages he spread to his followers which were little more than a laundry list of dos and don'ts. Don't drink alcohol, it was the devil's drink. Don't go on social media, it was the devil's playground. Do give the church every last cent, including the ones you couldn't spare, for God commanded his followers embrace Him by giving up their wealth. The Pastor's smug face appeared. Mahlatse turned off the TV. She looked at her hands and realised they were shaking. She felt the lashes of rage whip up against her stomach, pushing themselves up further and further until they forced their way out of her throat as a loud Fuuuuuuuuck! She picked up a cushion and threw it against the wall. When this outburst did nothing to calm her shaking, she began pacing up and down, up and down her living room. Her heart was pounding against her chest. She was restless. She wanted to punch something. She felt like a caged animal, equal parts angry and hopeless.

She was stuck. She had pleaded with Kgethi to take Thato out of the church. So had Molefi. But Kgethi had insisted that Thato was fine. 'Jesus Mom, it's not like they're abusing her!' She'd yelled. One of the worst unintended consequences of kicking Kgethi out was that she had become accountable to no one but herself. Mahlatse felt the guilt gnawing at her again. If she hadn't kicked Kgethi out she could have escalated things. She could physically prevent her from taking Thato to that church. If she hadn't kicked Kgethi out, maybe she never would have taken Thato there in the first place. Mahlatse didn't know what to do. She leaned against her wall and sunk onto the floor. She could feel the tears coming. Her hands were balled into tight fists. She took a deep breath and started counting to ten.

One… two… three…

Thato was in danger. Mahlatse had been aware of it before but the TV show had thrown it into her face.

Four… five… six…

Mahlatse didn't have a lot of options. She could call child protective services but she didn't want to see Thato sent away to a children's home. She'd heard stories of kids hardly older than Thato hooked on drugs, pimped out by their foster parents, being taken in and then spat out with nowhere to go once they aged out. The government would likely give Thato to Mahlatse. The state prioritised family reunifications. But how long would that take? How long would Thato have to sit in the system?

Seven… eight… nine… ten

Mahlatse opened her eyes. It came to her. She was holding a losing hand but had no other choice than to play it. If she didn't she would likely never forgive herself. She walked back to the couch and dug out her cellphone. She waited a few rings before she heard her ex-husband's irritated voice answer, 'Yes?'

'We need to talk about Kgethi,' she replied.

TWENTY-FIVE

Solomon was livid. He should never have agreed to that interview. He had half a mind to report that journalist to BCCSA. Why stop there? I should sue her for defamation, he thought. He could contact the church lawyers to sue her on his behalf. The way he saw it, by defaming him she had defamed his church and twisted the work he was doing to make it sound evil! In fact, it wasn't just defamation, he thought. It was racism. Yes, that's what it was! It was White Monopoly Capital controlled STRATCOM determined not to see a black church outside the clutches of white ownership. He felt himself getting worked up. These journalists never go after the white churches, he thought. There was a big church in Sandton that kept getting bigger. Every week, lines of German cars and SUVs trailed in and out of the church grounds so long the church had to hire their own traffic marshals just to avoid a jam. Every year they expanded, took on new projects, displayed their grotesque, untaxed wealth. But no one came after them. No one called them a cult, not even after a white pastor had delivered a sermon claiming that whites had never taken anything from blacks and colonialism had been God's gift to South Africa. Even after that, there were no journalists doing TV specials on how evil they supposedly were. But they were doing it to him.

Solomon had been tricked into trusting the journalist. He was sure of that now. She had come to his office looking pretty in a conservative knee-length dress and a blouse covering her shoulders and no hint of cleavage. The softness in her voice put him at ease. She wasn't like other women, he thought. This one had morals. This one didn't try to act like a man, as so many in her generation did, but rather embraced her place as a woman.

'Your church has been getting a lot of attention, Mfundisi, and I think it's important to hear your side,' she'd said to him. And he thought, sure. Why not? After all, he was launching his YouTube channel soon to reach believers who couldn't cram into the church. And there was the new monument-sized church they were in the process of building. He thought a TV special would be the perfect platform to launch the church. A week later the cameras started rolling, and it all went pear-shaped.

'There have been allegations that you encourage your congregants to stop taking chronic medications for serious diseases. How true are they?' The softness evaporated from her voice, leaving a cold, calculating interrogator in its place. She leaned forward and stared bullets into him. The camera with its accusing stared focused on the changing expression of his face.

He let out a nervous chuckle. 'My goodness!' Then he realised that neither the camera man nor the interviewer were laughing with him and straightened up.

'I am of the opinion,' he began slowly, 'that in these times we are overmedicated. You come in with the slightest discomfort and the doctor prescribes a pill for you! When half the time, what people need isn't pills, it's to deal with whatever issue is disturbing their spirit.

'Did you know, for example, that high levels of stress can often cause stomach pains? A doctor will prescribe, say, Buscopan, when what that patient really needs is to deal with the stress in their lives.'

'With all due respect Pastor—'

'Please, my title is Prophet,' he interrupted. 'I must ask that you show me respect by using my proper title.'

She sighed and gave him a small, tight smile. 'Alright… Prophet, you have not answered the question. Are you or are you not encouraging your congregants to stop taking chronic medications?'

The journalist transformed before his eyes. She was no longer the pretty, demure woman who had lured him in. She was a cold, calculating snake, ensnaring him in her trap. She may very well have even been a feminist. His neck turned cold. He looked at her and felt as Samson must have when he looked up, saw Delilah dangling his freshly cut hair before his eyes and felt his strength draining away. He tried to evade her questions but she held them over his head like a whip, striking him again and again. Are you encouraging your congregants to stop taking life-saving chronic medications? Are you aware of the medical risk you are putting your congregants in? Are you charging people thousands of rands to be 'healed' by you? Is it true you have plans to build a megachurch and a private house for yourself worth millions while telling your congregants to give up their own wealth? We have papers to prove it right here, Pastor. Is that not your signature? Each question hit him in the chest. He felt naked in front of her. Worst of all was the camera and the microphone pinned to his button-down shirt, capturing every stutter, every um, every nervous side-glance. At the end for his own sanity he cut the interview short. 'I'm afraid you really must go now,' he said to them. 'I'm a very busy man and I've given you enough of my time.'

They left with little protest. They had gotten what they came for. He saw it in full that weekend. They'd gone to town on him and the church. They had gotten that stupid, grinning woman and made her look pathetic. They had dug up a clearly disgruntled man and tried to blame Solomon (Solomon!) for his daughter's death. They called him corrupt, accusing him of taking advantage of the very poor people he was helping. Of enriching himself with church funds. He had gotten so angry at the flagrant misrepresentations that he turned off the TV in a fit of rage. He railed against the show in his prayer sessions.

He pronounced that the show and the journalist had been sent by the devil to mislead the masses. 'And anyone who agrees with them, is agreeing with Satan himself!' He boomed.

He decided to dedicate his upcoming sermon to her. It would be the very first he uploaded to his YouTube channel. He would spend the first few minutes speaking out against her and all the other STRATCOM journalists like her, sent by their white masters and Satan to discredit black churches and bring down black men. Then, he would make sure someone recorded the healings to prove to all the viewers that her words were meaningless, that he served a living God and that here, right here, was evidence of God's power. As he sat down to write his sermon he heard a knock at his office door. 'Come in!' He shouted. Bongani entered the room with a worried expression on his face. Solomon had been meaning to speak with him. As the new youth pastor Bongani had been spending a fair amount of time with Lucille, the sweet-voiced young woman who drove Solomon mad. He hadn't been able to stop thinking about her. Every time he saw her he wanted to find an excuse to be near her. If only he could be alone with her…

'Mfethu, did you see that news special?' Bongani said, interrupting his thoughts.

Solomon sighed. 'Yes! I'm writing a sermon about it as we speak. I can't believe that witch tricked us!'

Bongani moved towards the desk, saying nothing. He seemed to hover around the chair, opening and closing his mouth as if he had something to say. Solomon looked up at him.

'Yes? Do you have something to say?'

Bongani hesitated before sitting down. He didn't meet Solomon's eye. 'It's just… I've been thinking.'

Well, there was a surprise. Solomon put down his pen and looked at him. 'Thinking… what?'

'Solo do you… do you ever think that maybe we've gone too far?'

Solomon was taken aback. 'Too far? Too far with what?'

'It's just… I know you said we needed to charge people

more to make the list shorter. You know, because the girl can't heal a lot of people at once. But… isn't it too much, now? I mean there are people who have died. And now we're going to use that money to build this church worth millions?'

'We need a bigger space,' Solomon said curtly.

'I know but does it really need to cost, what, R60 million? Couldn't we maybe use that money to send kids to university or something?'

'Expanding the church is our top priority right now. We're overflowing every week. Once we've fixed that problem we can worry about university kids.' He was becoming annoyed. Where was this coming from?

'Okay but also, now people aren't taking their medicine. There are people that are going to die, mfethu. And they're going to get sick quicker and need us to heal them—'

'Those people decided to throw away their medicine after they saw that we can heal them better than any doctor can,' Solomon insisted. 'Bongani where is all of this coming from?'

'Solomon,' Bongani said, looking up at him. 'Please my brother, I didn't come here to fight.'

'Then what did you come here to do?'

Bongani paused and took a deep breath. 'I've been thinking… you know… maybe we should just tell people the truth? Tell people who's really doing the healing here? That way they'll see they must still take their medicine until the girl—'

'Have you lost your mind?' Solomon shouted, standing up. He couldn't believe Bongani would say something so stupid! 'If we tell people they'll go after the girl! They'll forget all about everything we've taught here—'

'No, but—'

'But nothing!' Solomon slammed his desk. 'You want to tell people? Don't you see what a stupid idea that is? If I didn't know better, I would think that maybe you want to bring this church down. Maybe you want to destroy everything we've built.'

Bongani looked at him in wide-eyed shock. 'I could never do that! You're taking this the wrong way!'

'I don't see how else I can take it,' Solomon said, glowering at him. 'You must know that if we tell people the truth they will stop listening to the word of God and start worshipping the girl instead. Maybe that's what you want.'

Bongani stood up, 'No that's not what I want! I don't want to fight with you Solomon. I was just thinking. We can forget all about it.'

'You were thinking. That's the entire problem. You should think less.'

Bongani put his hands up in surrender. 'Okay, I'm sorry. If I knew I never would have… just forget about it.' He turned around and left the room.

Solomon stared after him, still reeling from anger. His heart was pounding against his chest. He felt something he had never felt in relation to Bongani before. Threatened. As though Bongani had morphed into Judas Iscariot right in front of his eyes. For the first time he became aware that Bongani held the power to destroy him, and he was stupid enough to do it unthinkingly.

He jumped when he felt his cellphone vibrating in his pocket. He looked at it and saw his mother calling. The anger turned to guilt and worry. He used to be diligent about sending money home every month. Initially he'd only kept enough to pay his own bills while sending the rest home. But over time, he sent less and less. At first he tried to justify it. While he was still selling cars for Mr Ife his sister had struck it big, getting a scholarship to study a degree in computer science at the University of Cape Town. A few months ago she had been employed as a software developer for one of the big banks, making outrageous amounts of money while being buffered by the security of knowing that as a black woman with a scarce skill in a white male dominated industry she was virtually unfireable. She had since taken over the family black tax. So yes, Solomon had become somewhat complacent. He thought hard but couldn't remember the last time he had even been home. So when he answered the phone and heard his mother's voice say, 'Solly, we need you at the house. Come for dinner tomorrow,' he knew he had no choice but to say yes.

The next day, as he drove through Alex he looked at it with new eyes. He was struck by how much things had simultaneously stayed the same and drastically changed since his childhood. He still saw the same busy street where he and his friends would buy vetkoeks stuffed with mince from an old woman who sold ANC doeks on the side. Except now, instead of the green and yellow of the ruling party he saw the brilliant red of the EFF. He saw the same school he had attended, played at, and matriculated from, but now there were large piles of rubbish outside. Rows of corrugated iron shacks had sprung up like mushrooms in the schoolyard he used to play soccer in, casting long, eerie shadows in the dimming light of the setting sun. He saw the same tavern where his father would stumble out, drunk out of his mind, in the afternoon when the sun still shone brightly. Except now a new shack had been erected right up next to the entrance. The informal dwellings had sprouted up all over the pavements and in every spare bit of space since he'd left, leaning right up against the roads.

He was reminded that just a few months prior the township had been up in arms. Angry protesters threatened to bring the neighbouring Sandton CBD to a grinding halt unless the rampant overcrowding, lack of sanitation, and lack of service delivery was immediately addressed. Solomon heard his father's voice on radio and switched it off. But he could see it. The filth on the streets, the smell of sewerage, and the rats that had grown three times larger. Seeing Alex in this state made him angry. Soweto didn't look like this. The streets were cleaner there. Neat bicycle lanes had even been painted onto the pavements in Orlando West. Of course Soweto gets preferential treatment, he thought bitterly. That's where all the tourists went. That's where Nelson Mandela and Desmond Tutu used to live. The government couldn't let their precious anti-Apartheid heroes look like they lived in filth to the white fat-pocketed foreigners now could they?

No one cared about Alex but the people who lived there. So the government sat back, ate up the money it had allocated for the township's development, and did nothing as it rotted into decay. This was precisely why Solomon hadn't bothered voting at all in the election earlier that year. The only person he could put his faith in was God, and not this useless government. Guilt slowly settled into him. He was supposed to have taken his mother out of there. It was clear his sister had no real interest in doing so and as for his brother, well, the fact that he hadn't heard many updates about him forced Solomon to conclude that he may very well have followed in their father's footsteps.

He saw the children watching his car as he drove past. He used to be one of them, watching the fancy German cars that had made a wrong turn in Alex on their way to more affluent areas, and fantasised about one day driving one. Now that day had come. When he looked at the children's faces he recognised the same look of admiration he had worn on his own face all those years ago.

He stopped in front of his childhood home. The house had deteriorated since he left. Somehow the walls looked even dirtier, the patches of gray had gotten larger, and when he peeked through the gate he saw the weeds had taken over what little bit of soil had remained. I was supposed to take her out of here, he thought. He parked his BMW on the pavement and walked past the children who had gathered to stare at it with open mouths. When he walked into his childhood home, he immediately knew something was wrong. The kitchen which was ordinarily neat and orderly had dirty pots and dishes strewn about the counter and in the sinks. There was dust on the floor. Curtains were drawn, leaving the room unusually dark except for the light from the oven. He could smell chicken cooking inside and saw pots of rice and spinach gently bubbling on the stove.

'Ma?' He said, walking into the house. He heard footsteps coming towards him. He looked up and saw his mother entering the kitchen wearing slippers, faded clothes, and a doek. She was smaller, frailer, and looked like she had aged a good 20 years. He felt a stab of guilt when he saw her. He should have taken better care of her.

He greeted her but was met with an inaudible mumble. 'How are you, Mama?' He asked her.

'It's been tough, Solomon,' she replied. 'Your father is very sick.'

'Is it his liver?' He asked. She nodded. So the old man's years of heavy drinking had finally caught up with him.

'Come in and greet your father,' she said. He followed her into the master bedroom. The whole house had taken on a musty, medicinal smell. His father was lying in a heap under the bedcovers. When Mama lit a bedside table lamp he almost fell over from shock. If Mama had aged 20 years his father had aged 50. He was painfully thin and shaking. He had bumps on his skin from eczema. Mama propped him up and as he shifted, Solomon could see his belly protruding through his shirt.

'Mthobisi, look, Solomon is here,' she said as she propped him up. When his father looked up at him, Solomon could see that his eyes had taken on a yellow tint.

'Sawubona, Baba,' Solomon mumbled.

His father stared at him blankly. Solomon felt as though those yellow eyes were sucking up all the air in the room.

'Solomon,' he finally said. 'Where have you been?'

'I've been working, Baba. At church.'

'At church?' His father looked confused. 'What happened to your computer job?'

'No, Mthobisi,' Mama said. 'It's Mary who has the computer job. Solomon used to work at a car dealership before he became a pastor.'

'Oh?' Mthobisi looked at him again. 'Oh yes, you are the pastor. You're busy feeding people Jik at your church and telling them it'll take them to Heaven.'

Solomon felt a kick in his chest. 'What? No.'

'Dinner should be ready now,' Mama said. 'Solomon, come help me in the kitchen.'

He glanced one last time at his father before following her to the kitchen. He noticed how she barely looked at him. His once-affectionate mother hadn't touched him once since he arrived. His chest tightened every time she looked at him with a blank expression. He took out plates while she checked the food to see if it was done. 'What are the doctors saying?' He said.

'They say he has severe liver damage. I think they called it… cirrhosis… or something like that,' she replied. 'There's something wrong with his brain as well. I can't remember the proper name but they called it wet brain. He has problems with his memory and gets confused sometimes.'

She held out her hand and he passed a plate to her. She began dishing up.

'Is there anything they can do?'

She shook her head. 'They've given him some medicine but they say he needs a liver transplant. But the waiting list is long. And they probably won't give him one because of his drinking. They'd rather give livers to people who don't drink than let heavy drinkers ruin another one.'

He watched her dish up in silence. Then she took out a tray and cutlery, filled a glass with water, and set the food on the tray. 'You can dish up for yourself. I'm going to give this to your father.'

He dished up in silence, went to the living room, and waited for her. He switched on the living room light and for the first time saw how dirty the house was. A thin film of dust covered surfaces. There were papers scattered on the floor. He remembered the times he was woken up by Joyous Celebration at 7am to help clean the house and wondered what had happened. Mama walked back in and sat opposite from him.

'Mama, aren't you going to eat?' He asked.

She shook her head. 'I'm not hungry now. I'll eat a bit later.'

She looked at the switched off old TV. 'So the doctors say he might not have much time left. Maybe a couple of weeks. I'm doing my best to make things comfortable for him.'

'But how are you coping with this?'

She shrugged. 'I've been keeping up as well as I can. Between taking care of your father and going to work I haven't been able to take care of the house. That's why it's such a mess.'

'But where are Isaac and Mary?'

'I don't know where Isaac is. Last I saw him he'd gotten into a bad crowd. Now he comes and goes. He hasn't been back in months now and no one's heard from him.

'Mary took that job in Cape Town, remember? She sends back money and she's flown back here when she can but there's not much else she can do. She tried to put your father on medical aid but no company would cover him because of his drinking. She's actually getting married soon. To some Xhosa man she's apparently been seeing since she was at UCT.'

He was surprised. 'Mary's getting married? How come I never heard about this?'

Mama looked him in the eyes. 'Because she's decided she doesn't want to invite you to the wedding. Which is why I called you here.'

His suspicions had been right. He was in trouble. He sat in silence, feeling his heart beat faster.

'You know Solomon, when you first told me that you were going to be a pastor for this church, I wasn't very happy because it was one of these new age churches and not a proper Anglican church. But then I thought, you know, maybe it would be good for you to teach people about God's word and to live a proper life in accordance with it.' Her eyes flashed with anger. 'But now, I'm hearing all sorts of things about what you're doing there. I'm seeing on TV, on TV, that you're telling people not to take their medicine? You're telling people to give you money to cure them, and I don't know what you're doing with all this money because you have not even given us a cent here when you know we need it.'

'Now, Mama—'

'No!' She snapped. 'Don't interrupt me while I'm talking to you. You... you are even calling yourself a prophet! A prophet Solomon? When the Bible warns against false prophets and here... my own son!' She was shaking. 'I know people here who have gone to your church and you are telling people lies!'

'I'm not telling them lies, Mama,' he was getting flustered.

'Don't lie to me Solomon. I've heard of some of your sermons. I know how you're twisting the word of God to suit yourself.

'And as for telling people you're healing them, well, I know you. You have never had a gift, not once, and now suddenly when it's time to get people's money, you have such a gift for healing? I know all about pastors who pretend to raise people up from the dead and say all sorts of nonsense to trick hardworking people out of their money. I just never imagined I could raise one, when I never raised you to love money.'

'But Mama, the healings are real,' Solomon insisted. 'I'm not tricking people!'

'Oh really? If you have a gift for healing then why don't you walk into the bedroom right now and heal your father? Go on and do it! I want to watch you.'

He paused. Every word from her was a stab in his chest. His skin had turned hot. He didn't know what to do. He was tempted to call that woman and tell her to bring her child immediately.

'Mama, I can't just do that. There's a process—'

'Oh, what rubbish!' She yelled. 'You are talking rubbish! There's no such thing! Did Jesus have some big ceremony when he raised Lazarus? When he healed the blind man and the lepers? Did he demand money from them or did he just put his hand on them and do it?'

'Mama... I... I.'

'I so disappointed in you Solomon. You are a scam artist! You are a false prophet and what does the Bible say about false prophets? Come now, you're a big pastor now so you must know. Doesn't the Bible say to beware of false prophets who come to you in sheep's clothing but inside are hungry wolves? Doesn't it say you will recognise them by the fruits they bear? What fruits have you borne Solomon? People have bankrupted themselves and are killing themselves because of you! Doesn't that sound like the work of a false prophet?'

Solomon said nothing. He felt himself grow smaller under her gaze.

She continued, 'I didn't raise you to be this way. This needs to end today. You can sit here and tell me you'll quit this church and find a proper, honest job. Or you can walk into that bedroom right now, heal your father, and I'll never doubt you again. Or you can walk out that door, go back to your church and never come back here.

'But know that I'm not going to tolerate criminals, or false prophets or anything of the sort in my house. If you leave you can never come back. I mean it, Solomon. So what will it be?'

After two hours of begging and pleading with his mother, he left her house. He had walked in with his head bowed and emerged as a pillar of salt.

TWENTY-SIX

Thato felt cold all the time. It wasn't just because winter was there, drying up all the leaves and bringing frosty grass that the other kids raced to slide on. Even when she wore a vest and a sweater or her school tracksuit she still shivered. She shivered even when she sat next to the heater. She had more bad days than good days. The strings she saw attached to people shone so brightly they were like rays of sunlight burning her eyes. She saw the white dog with gray spots sitting in the corner of her room with its ribs sticking through its skin, walking next to her at school. She saw the woman in the yellow dress standing in corners watching at her. She saw the woman in her dreams. What scared her most about the woman was the long string that came out of her and tied itself around Thato. It was thicker than any rope Thato had seen and flickered like a lightbulb. The string scared her. I don't know her, Thato thought. How can I be the thing she's missing?

One day Thato was walking through the school corridor but when she got to the end she wasn't near the hall like she should have been. She was in a field with a lake on one side and a big rocky hill on the other. In front of her was the woman in the yellow dress. Thato blinked. The lake was covered in small green, roundish leaves and a thick, swampy, muddy smell came from the water. On the other side of the lake there were big, pretty houses. She saw some small boats wading through the leaves on the water.

'Where am I?' She asked the woman in the yellow dress. But the woman just looked at her. And then she was being dragged back, watching the woman and the lake get smaller and smaller, until she landed with a thud on her back. She opened her eyes and saw eyes huddled around in a circle staring at her.

'Alright everybody, move,' she heard her teacher's voice yell. 'Give her some space!'

She was being lifted up onto her feet and taken to the school nurse. The teacher and the nurse were saying things to her but she couldn't hear them. The woman in the yellow dress was looking at her through the window.

'Thato?' Her teacher said to her. 'Thato? We've called your Mom and she didn't answer. So we called your granny and she's coming to pick you up, okay?'

Thato didn't say anything.

'Why don't you lie down and have a little rest?' The nurse said. 'We'll call you when your Granny gets here? Okay?'

She nodded and lay down but couldn't sleep. The woman in the yellow dress was staring at her through the window. She heard a familiar voice outside the door that made her sit up. She cried out when she saw Koko walk through the door.

'Koko,' she said leaping off the bed.

'Hey sweetie,' Koko said, picking her up and holding her. Thato felt Koko's heartbeat, breathed in the scent of her perfume, and started to cry. She hadn't realised how much she had missed her until she felt herself melting into Koko's hug.

'It's okay sweetie,' she said, stroking Thato's hair. 'I'm here now.'

Inside the car, Koko kept trying to ask her questions about the church. But Thato's head was too foggy from the yellow dress lady's face, and the swampy lake smell to answer. When they got to Koko's home, Thato went straight to her old bedroom and fell asleep. She woke up with a start when someone shook her shoulders, pulling her out of her dreams and back into Koko's house. She turned and saw Mommy's face.

'Come on Thato, it's time to go,' she said, pulling on to Thato's arm.

'Kgethi, you can't take her,' Koko said. 'Where do you think you're going?'

Thato had fallen asleep and woken up in World War Three. Her mother, grandmother, and some strange man she'd never seen before were all arguing. Mummy was pulling her by the hand out of the house while the other two were telling her to stay. Telling her not to take Thato back to the church. She felt scared and confused. The emotions piled up making her head feel as though it was about to explode. She couldn't understand what was going on or why Koko looked so upset or why her mother was throwing her into the car before she had a chance to even say goodbye to Koko. She looked out the car window at Koko's face and felt herself shaking. Mummy was dead silent in the front.

'Mummy, what just—'

'I don't want to talk about it, Thato,' she snapped back.

The car was silent. Thato wanted to say something but the words were stuck in her throat.

She almost jumped up in surprise when Mummy asked her, 'What's been going on with you? They said you were sick at school.'

'I felt funny,' Thato said. Her heart was still pounding against her chest. She breathed in and out to try calm herself down.

'What kind of funny? Are you feeling sick?'

'No. Just funny.' Thato didn't know how to explain it. She didn't feel vomity funny. She felt run away and hide funny. Her heart was beating hard enough to jump out of her chest. She was cold but her hands were clammed up with sweat.

'Do you feel okay to go to church today?'

She nodded her head. She didn't know how to tell Mummy, but she didn't want to go to the church anymore. She was fed up of feeling tired all the time. She was fed up of seeing all the dead people there who looked at her like she did something wrong. Because she was doing something wrong.

I hate the Pastor.

She felt bad as soon as she heard the thought echoing in her head. She remembered Koko telling her she should never say she hates anybody. 'Hate is a horrible feeling that hurts you more than it hurts the other person,' Koko once told her when they still lived together. 'You're too young for that, baby girl.' But she did. She didn't like the way the Pastor took all that money from people. The way he made people feel like it was their fault when Thato's powers didn't work. She thought back to the boy with epilepsy. She felt awful when she couldn't cure him. She wanted to tell his Mom, 'I'm sorry. I don't know what that is. I can't help him.' But the Pastor told his mother it was her fault when Thato knew that wasn't true. When she saw the mom cry afterwards she wanted to cry with her. By keeping quiet, she felt like she was lying too. She couldn't fix every problem. She couldn't give people jobs, or give them money to pay all their bills. But the Pastor told people he could if they came to his church, prayed the way he told them to, and gave him money. She even remembered the Pastor saying he could give some woman a husband. How was Thato supposed to give anyone a husband?

Every time she went to church she felt like crying because she knew they were all lying. She didn't care what the Pastor said. It was a lie, and she kept hearing Koko's voice saying, 'You should never, ever tell a lie. Because one day the truth will come out and then it will be much, much worse than if you had been honest the whole time.' She missed Koko. She missed her smile, her warm hugs, the sound of her voice, and the smell of her cooking. Mummy bought her sweets more often as a reward for helping people at church. Now Thato hated the taste of sweets. She didn't want them anymore. She wanted to go home.

She walked into the prayer session with Mummy but this time something felt off. There weren't any men around. A lot of the women there looked young. Even younger than Mummy. They looked around the same age as the big kids at school. Mummy stopped in her tracks and looked around the room squinting. 'What the?' She asked.

When they found the Pastor she asked him what was going on. 'Things today are going to be a little different,' he said.

'Different how?'

'Well,' he said, 'we're starting with our youth sessions. These are the kids who are going to be confirmed.'

Mummy looked around. 'And where exactly are the boys?'

'We've decided to do gender segregated sessions,' he said. 'You know how they are at this age with all those hormones. We thought it was better this way. Fewer distractions.'

Thato felt nervousness swirling around her tummy. Something was wrong. She looked up at the squint on Mummy's face and knew she felt it too.

'If this is just for confirmation then why does Thato need to be here?'

The Pastor looked around him to check if any of the girls were listening and then leaned closer. 'It's extremely important for her to be here. These girls are about to commit themselves to the church. We must encourage them to do that by showing them what God can do. You know what teenagers are like—'

'Actually, I don't.'

Her waved her off. 'These days they have social media and Netflix and all these other things telling them God doesn't exist. That being a Christian isn't cool. They need to see Thato's powers in action so they can see for themselves that God does exist.'

Mummy looked at him for a long time. She didn't seem sure. 'You know, we still need to talk about our call earlier.'

'I know,' he said in a lower voice. 'But not now. We'll set up a time to talk about the details properly. In the meantime, how about we get through tonight and I'll even give you a portion of her fees in cash?'

She looked from him to Thato and sighed. 'Okay, fine.'

'Good,' he said, straightening up. 'And the young ones have said they'd prefer it if there aren't any grown-ups in the room.'

'I'm literally in my twenties,' Mummy protested.

He shrugged, 'Twenties is still grown. Especially to a fifteen-year-old. You understand?'

She glanced at Thato. 'And what happens to her?'

'Don't worry, she's done this a million times before,' he said. 'It'll be the same thing she always does.'

Thato didn't want to stay. Not without Mummy. And when she looked at Mummy's face she could see she didn't really want her to stay either. Thato wanted to throw up. Something was wrong. She looked at Mummy and hoped she felt it too. Instead, Mummy looked at her and said, 'Fine. I'll wait in the car.' She turned around and left. Just as Thato watched the door slam she felt the Pastor's hand on her on shoulder. 'Come on,' he said. They walked a few steps before he turned and looked at her. He kneeled until his eyes were straight in front of hers and dropped his voice.

'This person we're going to heal,' he said slowly. 'This is a very private thing. You know what private means, right?'

She nodded.

'Tell me what does it mean?'

Her throat turned dry. She had to force the words out. 'It means no one else can know. Like a secret.'

The Pastor smiled. 'Yes. Exactly. It's exactly like a secret. And you know how to keep a secret right?'

She nodded again.

'That means no telling Mummy. Or Koko. Or teacher. Okay?'

He stood up, held onto her arm, and pulled her forward. She felt like she was going to be sick. She wanted to run out the door. But she kept walking next to him towards the group of girls.

'Sanibonani mantombazane,' the Pastor said to the girls with a smile on his face.

They turned to him and greeted him back.

He forced Thato to sit at his feet while he took them through the history of the Old Testament. She wasn't listening. She looked at the faces of the girls around her who also stared at her. They weren't like the other people, who looked at the Pastor like he was Jesus himself. They looked bored, as if they were being forced to be there like Thato was. After what felt like forever he told them he would start with a special healing session. 'Now, which one of you is coming first?' A shy girl stepped forward. Thato saw it was the thin, light skinned girl who always led the prayer session. What was her name again?

'Lucille,' the Pastor said with a smile. 'Please come with me.'

The three of them walked down the hall in silence. Thato looked at the girl next to her. She was looking at the floor, like she wished she wasn't there. Thato felt like she and the girl were connected, sharing a string tied to the both of them that the Pastor couldn't see. He took them into his office. The room didn't look anything like the place where she had healed the sick boy. He'd swapped out all the furniture for big oak pieces and plush leather sets that were too big for the room. Framed paintings hung on the wall in elaborate golden frames. There was a massive dark wood bookcase stretching from the floor to the roof with rows of dark red books on it but Thato had never seen the Pastor read any of them. She'd never seen him read anything except the Bible. Every time she walked into the room she felt like the furniture was slowly getting bigger, suffocating her, until one day it would swallow her whole.

This felt wrong. The healing sessions were never in his office. They were usually in one big room filled with people. Thato didn't like it.

'Lucille, lie flat on the floor,' he said. She looked confused. 'Why is she here?' She asked pointing at Thato.

'Because I always bring children to my healing sessions, and she's the only one who could make it today,' he said. 'Now lie down.' His voice was much sterner.

She looked from him to Thato and then lay on the floor. Slowly. Like she was a mouse who was afraid of being pounced on.

'Now,' the Pastor started, 'your mother tells me that you're dealing with a very special kind of sickness. She says that when you're menstruating you get very sore?'

'Yes,' she said. She didn't look at Thato or the Pastor. 'The lower part of my back and my stomach gets so sore. I can't really sit or stand.'

'And you know,' the Pastor continued, now kneeling down next to her, 'that these pains are not caused by medical reasons but rather spiritual ones?'

She kept quiet.

'Did you know that when Adam and Eve ate the forbidden fruit, God punished Eve by deciding that she and all other women would have extreme pain during childbirth?'

She nodded. Her face paled.

'And the Bible also tells us that when a woman experiences her menstrual blood, for that period she's unclean. Impure. And so your pains give us no other choice but to believe God must be using your time of uncleanliness to punish you for whatever sins you have committed. Just like he punished Eve. So what we will do tonight is to purge you of your uncleanliness. To do that, I will need you to remove your underwear.'

Lucille looked at him in shock. Thato felt her heart sink to her stomach. She remembered her teacher telling the class about good touches and bad touches. She could hear teacher's voice in her ears saying, 'If a man who isn't your doctor wants you to take off your clothes for him, you must tell a grownup you trust, like Mommy or Daddy, or a teacher or even the pastor at your church.'

Who should she tell now? He was the Pastor. She felt a shiver go up her spine when she saw the girl take off her panties. She looked away. She wanted to run away but her legs were glued to the floor.

'Now, come closer Thato,' the Pastor said. 'Help me pray for this girl.'

She didn't want to be near him. She looked at the girl and thought of how much pain she was in. She didn't know what menstruating meant but with the blood and pain it sounded really bad. Maybe she could cure the girl so she wouldn't have to menstruate again. Maybe she could do that. She kneeled next to the Pastor and put one shaky hand on the girl's shoulder. The Pastor told her to bow her head. Just before she did she could see his hands go between the girl's thighs and up her skirt. She felt the girl become very still. Like she was frozen. She heard her gasp loudly for air. Thato's whole body turned cold. She was frozen. The twisting in her tummy spread through her, turning her arms and legs numb. She wanted to stop. She wanted to run away. But she couldn't. She realised the whole room was silent and opened her eyes. The girl's cheeks were wet with tears. Thato wanted to crawl into a hole and hide away. She looked at the Pastor and her skin burned. She hated him. She hated him. She didn't want to help him anymore. She wanted to leave the church and never come back. When he was done the Pastor turned to her one last time. 'Remember,' he said to her. 'This is our secret.' She didn't say anything to him.

When they walked out of his office she saw see-through people standing in the hall. She looked from side to side and saw old faces, young faces, angry faces, sad faces, faces that were half covered by hands clasped over mouths. Every one of them belonged to a woman. Some were bright coloured with strings that had only just wilted like the leaves of plants in need of water. Others were dull with faded colours and withered, dried strings. Some wore pretty dresses with hats while others wore jeans and t-shirts. Thato walked down the hall with the Pastor on one side and Lucille on the other and looked only at the changing expressions on the women's faces. One of them spat at the Pastor but it flew straight through him, disappearing into the floor. Another reached out as if to grab Lucille's hand but Lucille walked through her arm without notice. She saw the straw-hat lady standing ahead of her, staring at her with an unreadable expression. The moment Thato saw her face the words My dear sweet child!

You're helping the pastor more than anyone else, my darling! echoed in her ears. Thato looked into her face, into every face and knew the secret wasn't hers alone but was spread out all around her in a hall of invisible women who in that moment were all as powerless as she was.

She felt numb inside. She wanted to escape her numbness, away from the church forever. She left through its doors and walked to Mummy's car.

'Took you long enough,' Mummy said when she got in. 'How was it?'

She didn't say anything at first. But later that night she burst into tears, crushed under the weight of the secret.

That night she dreamt about the yellow dress lady again. The pungent smell of the swampy water enveloped her in sleep. The lady looked at her, reached out her arm, and said, 'Thato.' When she woke up her nostrils were still filled with the lake's scent. She felt like she was being pulled away from the house, far, far away to the lake itself. To the lady. Then she realised what was happening. The lady in the yellow dress wanted Thato to find her.

TWENTY-SEVEN

Kgethi saw Thato's face as she climbed in the car. She didn't look tired. Instead, she had turned into stone. Her face was bloodless. Her expression unreadable. She looked battle scarred, like the Sierra Leonian child soldiers Kgethi had seen pictures of during her History lectures. 'How was it?' She'd asked. She was met with silence. Thato had always been a shy child but this wasn't shyness. This was something else. And whatever it was sent shivers up Kgethi's spine. It didn't help that Kgethi was already on edge. She was still reeling from the ambush, no, the blatant attack she had endured from both sides of the fence.

The first had been from the Pastor. It has been yet another slow, boring day at work when she heard her phone vibrating against the desk, picked it up, and saw his name on the screen. She looked around to make sure no one was watching before stepping outside. 'What do you want,' she said in place of a greeting.

'Is that how you greet me?'

She rolled her eyes. 'When you call me at work then yes, it is.'

'Listen, I have a proposal for you.'

The red flag went up and everything went downhill from there. He told her that his YouTube channel was doing much better than expected. In the few short weeks the channel had been up he had already amassed hundreds of thousands of subscribers and millions of views, mostly in Africa. As a result, the church committee had decided it would be a good idea to begin organising a tour of sorts. The first leg would be a national tour to all nine provinces. Then, if that went well enough, they would expand into the continent, starting in Botswana and stretching upwards towards the grand finale in Nigeria.

She paused, taking his words in. She was confused. 'Um...' she started.

'Yes? That won't be a problem, will it?'

'What exactly is supposed to happen to Thato? She's at school now and her holidays won't be for another couple weeks.'

'Well then, you'll just have to let her have an extended holiday.'

She was taken aback. She heard the little voice that lived inside her head firmly, decisively, saying, 'No.'

'That's... that's not what we agreed,' she started. 'This arrangement isn't supposed to mess up school.'

He laughed. 'Trust me, Mamokgethi, by the time we're done here we'll be making so much money she won't need to go to school. How about we talk about it more the next time we see each other, hmmm?'

It was out of the question for her and she said as much. But he had already dropped the phone on her. Her confusion turned to anger. How dare he even ask that of her? She'd made it clear that their arrangement could under no circumstances mess with Thato's education!' She started thinking about all the nights she had done Thato's homework for her. All the times Thato had woken up still exhausted from healing people the day before. Even with Kgethi's efforts, it was taking a toll on her schoolwork. Her last report showed that her marks had dropped.

'Is Thato getting enough sleep at home?' Her teacher had asked Kgethi at the last parent teacher conference she had attended. 'She seems depleted when she comes into class lately. Perhaps an earlier bedtime might help?'

She had fooled herself into thinking the arrangement

wouldn't affect Thato. What was she doing? Her uncertainty about all of this grew daily. Every time the Pastor handed her money, every time she did Thato's homework, every time she looked into the empty eyes of someone who had paid everything they had to be healed, she felt a deep sense of shame permeating her body. She felt dirty. She scrubbed her skin raw in the shower but that did nothing to make her feel clean. She wanted to shout, to break down, to say something, but she had to be brave for Thato. And she couldn't tell her mother.

Then, the second attack happened. She looked at her phone and saw that she had a message from her mother. 'Thato fainted at school and the teachers couldn't get hold of you so they phoned me. I took her home. When you come fetch her, we need to talk.' She went stiff. Fuuuuck she thought. She checked her phone but didn't see any missed calls. They must have phoned while the Pastor was calling her.

Since when did Thato faint in school, she thought. She didn't know how much her mother already knew. She thought of Thato and began to wonder if she had told Mom anything, what she had said, and how much detail she'd going into. She felt a cold sweat icy on her skin.

She got into her car and drove to her mother's house. Stay calm, stay calm, stay calm, she told herself as she drove. When she arrived she saw an unfamiliar black BMW parked in the front. When she walked into the house she saw a familiar face that made her freeze in her tracks. A man was sitting at the kitchen island drinking tea with her mother. His hair was turning grey and his skin was beginning to sag but his face was still unmistakable. It was the first time she had seen her father in years.

'What is this?' She asked them.

'Is this how you greet us now?' Her father responded. Even his voice had changed. It had become hoarser, as if his years of smoking had finally caught up with him.

'I'm sorry, who are you?' She said squinting. 'I don't think I recognise you. Have we met before?'

'Don't be like that Kgethi,' her mother said, turning to face her. 'He's here because we're both very worried about you and Thato.'

Kgethi glared at her father before settling on her mother. 'Where's Thato? What happened to her?

'She fainted outside the school hall,' Mom replied. 'It was nothing serious thank God, but they still wanted someone to pick her up. And your phone was busy when they tried to call you so they called me instead. Now can we talk?'

Being in that house and seeing her father and mother in the same room again triggered unpleasant memories. She saw herself walking inside, school bag in hand, to enter a room pregnant with tension. The sound of her parent's voice in the corridors, the smell of her father's cologne as he walked past her, and the sound of him slamming the door came back to her and suddenly, she felt weak. As though she were a 15-year-old schoolgirl again.

She pulled up a chair at the island. 'Fine, but as long as it's quick,' Kgethi said. 'Seeing you both here together is starting to get weird.'

Her father turned to face her. 'Trust me, young lady, I'd rather not be here either. But your mother has told me that you've gone and gotten yourself into serious trouble. And you've involved that poor little girl in it.'

'That poor little girl is your granddaughter. You'd know that if you ever bothered to meet her.'

'Kgethi, that's enough now,' her mother snapped. 'Can you cool it with the attitude and take this seriously for once? We are seriously worried about you. What were you thinking getting Thato involved in a cult?' Their words cut into her. She resolved to remain firm but her parents chipped away at her, exposing the Pastor for who he was.

'Do you know how many people I've had to help who got into debt because of men like him?' Her father thundered at her. 'He is exploiting vulnerable people, poor people, and you're sitting there helping him do it!'

'Jesus Christ Dad,' Kgethi said exasperated, 'It's not a cult! It's a church! People give money to churches all the time and anyway, Thato likes helping sick people!'

'Kgethi,' Mom said, crossing her arms. 'I spoke with Thato's teacher when we picked her up. She told me Thato's been coming to school exhausted. Falling asleep in class. Struggling to concentrate. And apparently, the homework she's submitting looks like someone else's handwriting. As if someone has been doing it for her. And now she's busy fainting in school.

'You can't seriously think this is fair on her, can you? She is nine years old, Kgethi. Nine. She should be playing outside with kids her age, not stuck in some 'church' helping a horrible man take advantage of desperate people. That you even brought her into this is unforgivable. How could you do this to her?

How could you do this to her? The question echoed in Kgethi's mind. For the first time she had nothing to say. No rude or sarcastic quips. And no real justifications.

'You know what, I don't need this from you two,' she said. 'You kicked me out,' she pointed at her mother. 'And you abandoned me years ago,' she pointed at her father. She stood up, picking up her handbag and keys. 'So you guys don't get to act like you care now or like you're some kind of team when you can't even fucking stand stand each other.'

'Kgethi,' her mother said getting up. 'We're worried about you!'

But she wasn't listening. She went upstairs to shake Thato awake. Her parents walked in after her, telling her to stop and trying to convince her to stay. But she had switched off from them. She was stubborn until the end. Despite her parents protests, and the mounting tide of guilt eating her from the inside out, she walked past them, frog marched Thato to the car, and left.

While Thato had been inside healing, she had been sitting in the car replaying the argument in her head. How could you do this to her? She saw her mother's face warped in anger hurling accusations. You can't think this is fair. She saw Thato's face at breakfast being propped up by her arm, drooping into sleep while her cereal milk turned cold. He is exploiting vulnerable people, poor people, and you're just sitting there letting him do it! She saw a sea of hungry faces, emptying out their pockets and looking up at the Pastor as though he were God himself.

She heard someone tap on her window. She looked up and saw Bongani waving at her. The sight of his face annoyed her instantly. She so did not want to speak to him right now. She rolled down the window, trying to figure out the best, most polite way of telling him to fuck off.

'Kgethi,' he said. 'How are you, sisi?'

'I'm fine thanks and you?' She said through gritted teeth.

'I'm doing fine myself thanks. Lalela sisi, I think we must talk.'

Her suspicion grew. What was he up to? 'About what?'

He looked around to check if anyone was in earshot. Then he leaned in closer to her, resting his arm against the window. 'Sisi, are you still sure about this healing thing with Solomon and your daughter?'

She was taken aback. 'What do you mean?'

He opened and closed his mouth a few times trying to find the words. He shook his head. 'I mean… I don't wanna lie to you, I'm worried. You know, there's people who aren't taking their medicine anymore. I mean old people with diabetes and stuff because they think Solomon is gonna cure them and look, I don't know how Thato's powers work. Maybe she can cure diabetes, I don't know. But I'm uncomfortable with this, yaz'. I think maybe we're playing with fire here. And the money people are taking out to get cured! I've been speaking to some of the people at the church and there's people here going to amashonisa just to be able to pay to get cured and I don't like it. I really don't like it.'

She looked into his eyes and for the first time saw that they shared something. That someone was feeling the way she had been. Maybe this man wasn't as far up the Pastor's asshole as everyone else was.

'Should… shouldn't you be talking to him about this? The Pastor – I mean the Prophet?'

He flinched. 'Eish that's another thing. I don't know how I feel about this prophet business. Here's the boy I grew up with eKasi busy calling himself a prophet. You know, I tried to talk to him about it but he got so defensive. So I thought maybe I must talk to you. Thato is your child and I've been watching her. She doesn't look so good. I was looking at her face earlier and I could see, this one? Uyagula.' He looked straight at Kgethi with eyes filled with worry. 'Are you sure this whole thing is okay for her? I don't want to tell you what to do because this is your child. But are you really sure about all of this?'

She sat back in stunned silence. Bongani of all people was questioning her? She couldn't believe this. 'Bongani I know what I'm doing,' she said, a little more harshly than she intended it.

He gave her another look before saying, 'Okay. If you're sure. I'm just saying I don't think she looks okay. Maybe you must think of taking her to see a doctor?'

Her defenses went up. She had just spent the day having her parenting skills questioned by her parents. She wasn't going to have them questioned by Bongani too. 'Yeah, okay Bongani. Next time I need parenting advice I'll be sure to ask you.'

He looked wounded by her words but he left her alone after that. A few minutes after he left Thato returned to the car. As they drove away from the church she kept glancing in the rearview mirror at her daughter. 'Thato,' she said.

'Yes, Mummy?'

'You would tell me if you didn't want to do this anymore right? With the Pastor?'

Thato went quiet. The longer the silence dragged on, the tighter and tighter Kgethi's chest felt.

'Thato? Don't you want to do this anymore?'

She glanced at the rearview mirror and saw the tears forming. Her face scrunched up, she opened her mouth, and the tears were matched with large, loud sobs.

'Thato! What's wrong?'

But her daughter was inconsolable. She could not be reassured in the car, or back in their home. No matter how many times Kgethi asked her what was wrong, or how many hugs she gave until her shirt was wet with tears, Thato wouldn't tell her what happened. Eventually, when Thato's voice became too hoarse to sustain her sobbing she quietened down into a whimper.

'Thato,' Kgethi pleaded. 'Talk to me. Tell me what's wrong. Did something happen?'

Her daughter's tear-stained face looked up at her and nodded.

She felt her heart sink to the floor. She suspected she knew the answer but she was too scared to hear it. She had to force the question out her throat. 'What happened? Did the Pastor do something bad during a healing session?'

Thato nodded. After Kgethi coaxed her and guaranteed she wouldn't get into trouble, Thato told her everything. Kgethi forced herself not to scream.

TWENTY-EIGHT

Kgethi admittedly didn't remember much from her six short months at Wits University. Half the time she had been too drunk to remember anything. Another quarter had been spent chilling with her friends on the Library Lawns or at the food court known as The Matrix, meeting new people, making weekend plans, and relaying the funniest stories from the last party. Of the things she did remember, she thought that maybe less than ten per cent consisted of anything she actually learned in her lectures. She couldn't even remember whether she had taken Sociology or Anthropology, or what the difference was between the two (mostly because she'd never attended a lecture).

But one of the things she remembered clearly was a Psychology lecture on ethics in psychological experiments. She still remembered the day clearly. It was second term, first semester. The stark grey concrete walls had trapped in the chilly autumn air, turning the entire campus into a freezer. The only reason she'd bothered to turn up to this lecture was in the hope of seeing Psych Hottie, AKA Luvuyo, AKA Future Deadbeat Baby Daddy. Once she'd turned up on campus, frozen her ass off, and realised he wasn't even there, it was too late to turn around and go back to bed. The lecture topic sounded like it was supposed to be unbearably boring. Supposed to be. Until their lecturer, a petite Coloured woman with a high-pitched voice, began explaining the experiments in horrific detail. The Stanford Prison Experiment. The Harlow Monkey Studies. And finally, the Milgram Experiment. The final one was the one that hooked into her. It went something like this:

In the mid-twentieth century, a Yale University psychologist named Stanley Milgram was, like the rest of the world, watching the Nuremberg Trials. Former Nazis stood before a military tribunal to be held accountable for the atrocities they had committed during the Holocaust. Many of them had the same excuse. The same justification. 'I was just following orders.' The tribunal didn't buy the excuse. Neither did Stanley Milgram. Milgram asked himself, can obedience really go so far that it pushed people to do what they know to be evil? Where does the line between obeying authority and obeying one's conscience get drawn?

So in 1963 he conducted an experiment. Three rooms were set up: one where the participant would sit with a 'scientist', a switchboard, and an intercom attached to the wall; one with a 'test subject'; and one where Milgram sat and observed. The scientist and the test subject were paid actors. The forty-odd participants were volunteers who were told they were helping test a new teaching technique. They were told that in the other room was a test subject who was connected to the switchboard that sat in front of them. The switchboard was capable of delivering electric shocks ranging from a slight shock to 450 volts, enough to kill a healthy adult. The more the switch was flipped, the higher the volts would go.

The test subject would read out answers over the intercom. Every time he read out an incorrect one, the participant was ordered by the scientist to flip the switch. When they did, the subject's scream could be heard coming through the intercom. The more wrong answers were read, the more the switch was flipped, and the more intense the bloodcurdling screams would be. Each time a participant looked at the scientist with uncertainty he would say, 'Please continue.'

Another scream.

'The experiment requires you to continue.'

Another scream.

'It is absolutely essential that you continue.'

And another.

'You have no other choice but to continue.'

Until the intercom went silent. At least two thirds of the participants continued up to 450 volts, well after the screams had stopped. Allegedly, there was one participant who stopped well before that point. Who looked at the scientist and said, 'I have already gone too far, and I am afraid I can no longer continue.'

After the lecture, Kgethi had wondered who she would have been in that experiment. Would she have been among the 65 per cent who chose to continue delivering shocks even after the subject was passed out, or worse, dead? Or would she have been in the 35 per cent who stood up and said, 'I have already gone too far, and I am afraid I can no longer continue.'

Ten years later, Kgethi felt like she was one of the volunteers sitting in that room. In the scientist's chair she saw the Pastor. When she flipped the switch she heard Thato's voice screaming through the intercom. And for the first time in years, Kgethi burst into tears. Her whole body shook under the weight of her grief. She had already gone too far. And she could no longer continue.

PART FOUR

REVELATIONS

TWENTY-NINE

October, 1986
Soweto

Mahlatse couldn't sleep. She kept tossing and turning until she felt a pillow hit the back of her head. 'Stop that,' Dineo mumbled in an irritated voice. 'You're annoying me and I can't sleep!' Their narrow single beds were in such close proximity that they could hear every movement, every sound every breath the other took right on the backs of their necks. It couldn't be helped. The bedroom was too narrow. At least we have a bedroom, Mahlatse often thought. Unlike Molefi who'd been relegated to sleeping in the living room before he'd left them for his new, exciting life in Braamfontein.

Resigned to sleeplessness, Mahlatse lay on her back and listened to the sounds around her. The neighbourhood had gotten much quieter at night ever since the state-imposed curfew started. She used to hear the sounds of drunk people having loud conversations on their way home from the tavern. The odd car driving through the streets. Loud music playing from a neighbour's house. Now all she heard were crickets. The dull whining of a distant dog. And occasionally the heavy sound of a casspir rolling past. She watched the fluorescence of the tall streetlights illuminate her curtain. It was ironic. They hadn't had electricity for three weeks straight, so while all the houses were dark, lit only by dim yellow candlelight, the tall lights guarding the street shone brightly.

'It's so they can see everything we're doing,' Dineo had

explained. 'They're watching us all the time, you know.' Dineo knew the answers to all the questions Mahlatse and Molefi were too scared to ask Mama. While Mama had explained the rudimentary aspects of the birds and the bees, it was Dineo who told Mahlatse what an orgasm felt like. What cigarettes tasted like. How being drunk felt. Dineo flouted every one of their mother's rules for being a good Christian woman. She drank alcohol. She smoked away from the prying eyes of parents and neighbours. She refused to go to the hair salon with Mama to have her hair chemically straightened into submission.

'You can relax it or you can cut it off,' Mama told her plainly. So Dineo went to the hair salon that weekend and cut it all off, cutting it periodically every few months until she left school and dyed it peroxide blonde. Mahlatse turned to look at the back of her sister's head. She could just about make out her silhouette in the dim lighting. She didn't know why but looking at Dineo made her feel uneasy. She felt restless. Unsettled. As though she should have been standing up and pacing the room. Her chest tightened more and more. Something was wrong. She didn't know what but she felt it in her veins. Something was wrong. She lay in bed until she saw the pale blue-grey light seep through the curtains, becoming brighter and brighter. She knew it was morning when she heard Mama clattering in the kitchen.

It was Saturday. Saturdays meant helping Mama do the washing and laundry in the mornings or taking over completely on the weekends she was working at the clinic. They meant attempting to catch up with the schoolwork she had fallen behind in during the week. They meant watering the vegetable garden outside, which in the October heat had started to ripen. They used to mean going out with friends or begging Dineo to let her hang out with hers, but she didn't do much of that anymore. When she stepped into the kitchen she saw Mama in her navy blue nurses uniform. Odd. She wasn't supposed to be on duty that weekend.

'I've been called in,' Mama explained. 'There have been

more clashes with men from the hostels. It sounds like it was bad.'

'Oh,' Mahlatse said. Violence had erupted in the hostels, spilling into the streets and houses of nearby residents. The hostels across from Dube train station were an IFP stronghold. Every so often they would clash with UDM men, shedding blood of both their opponents and of bystanders. Mahlatse knew of some families close to the hostels that had abandoned their homes to escape it.

Mama walked up to her. 'I need you and your sister to be responsible today. Papa is going to a boxing match with his friends, so make him some breakfast. And wake up your sister so she can help around the house. I don't know when I'll be back but it should be before the curfew. Okay?' She was annoyed at having to make Papa breakfast but she didn't complain. She couldn't exactly argue with her own mother. 'Yes, Mama,' she replied. She hated being the responsible one. That was meant for Dineo, who threw pillows at her when she tried to nudge her awake. She was halfway through making Papa's breakfast when Dineo sauntered into the kitchen.

'Mama gone?' She asked in a lazy voice.

'Yes. She left a couple minutes ago.' She didn't want to ask why Dineo wasn't at work. She had gotten a job as a hairdresser shortly after completing matric and Saturdays were supposed to be a hairdresser's busiest day. Yet here she was standing in the kitchen in her pyjamas. Mahlatse was becoming suspicious.

'And Papa?' Dineo asked.

'He's still here. But he's going to watch boxing soon,' Mahlatse responded. They both knew their father would rather cut his arm off with a blunt knife than miss a boxing match.

Dineo looked at her and nodded. 'Okay,' she said before walking off. There was a shiftiness to her demeanor. Dineo usually walked around with long, languid movements but that morning her movements were smaller, quicker, with her head kept down as though she were hiding something.

Mahlatse prepared breakfast and delivered it to her parents' bedroom on a tray. Her father hardly looked at her, instead speaking loudly on the telephone positioned on the bedside table.

'I'm telling you, Milton will take it! Tau won't make it past the third round, I can feel it!'

Very few things excited Papa in life, and one of them was boxing. He lived for boxing, speaking about men like Baby Jake and even Muhammad Ali all the way in America with so much detail and passion one would have thought they were best friends. Years ago he coached young boxers, including Molefi, while Dineo went across the road for dance classes at the YWCA. Until June 16 1976, when thousands of high school students took to the streets in protest of the Afrikaans language policy. So many of the young boys Papa coached died, went missing, or were thrown in jail that he gave it up. On that day Mahlatse knew he would be unable to think of anything else but boxing. She left his room quietly. She went and opened her bedroom door.

'Neo,' she said. 'We have to do the laundry!'

Dineo was reading a letter, her face creased in concentration. 'Go away, Hlatse,' she said without looking up.

'But Neo—'

Dineo looked up at her. Her eyes had turned dark. 'Jesus Christ Hlatse, can you just hold on? I'm busy now!'

Mahlatse was stunned by the sharpness of her voice. Dineo could be temperamental, especially during her teen years, but there was something weird about her. She had been off ever since some man named Ernest Magubane had been executed for murder a few weeks prior. Mahlatse had watched Dineo sit in the living room reading the story in the newspaper with her finger touching Magubane's face and a hollow look in her eyes. After that the light in Dineo's eyes dimmed.

Ask her what's going on, a voice inside her said. Instead, she closed the door. She wiped the countertops with Handy Andy, dusted the shelves, and started mopping the floor. At some point

Papa entered the living room, took his hat and jacket, and left after a hurried goodbye. Where was Dineo? She felt tempted to go barging into their room again but after the look she'd seen on Dineo's face, she thought better of it. She walked into the front yard. She could smell the tomatoes ripening in the sun. She preferred being outside. Caring for the family's vegetable patch was no small business. They all depended on its produce come mealtime and whatever they didn't use could be given to the neighbours or traded for something else.

There was a complex bartering system in place. Borrow an egg from one neighbour and they'd lend you carrots next week or some maize meal. Ownership over food wasn't rigidly defined but shared in a neighbourhood stokvel. She picked up a plastic watering can and filled it. She started with the tomatoes, which were slowly turning from green to orangey red. The winds at least weren't too bad so not too much dust from the mine dumps was blown into her face. After Mahlatse had been watering the vegetables for a few minutes, Dineo walked into the garden wearing a mustard yellow dress and holding a cigarette in her hand. Mahlatse turned and looked at her for a moment. Dineo had a crease in her forehead, as though something were troubling her. She never usually smoked in the garden. She would walk far away towards one of the open fields out of fear that if her parents didn't catch her a neighbour certainly would. There were few things worse in people's eyes than a young woman who smoked.

'Papa will kill you if he sees you smoking,' Mahlatse said.

Dineo shrugged. 'There are worse things,' she replied.

Mahlatse finished watering the tomatoes and moved to the spinach. 'Worse than death?'

'Worse than Papa.' She finished her cigarette before moving to Mahlatse.

'Listen Hlatse,' she said. 'I need to leave for a couple of hours. If Mama asks where I am can you tell her I went to the bioscope with Mbali? Tell her I went to watch that new Sylvester Stallone movie if she asks.'

Mahlatse froze. Something felt off. 'Can I come with?'

'No,' she replied firmly. 'I'll see you later, okay?'

She watched Dineo leave. She walked down the street, her yellow dress becoming a smaller and fainter blur on the horizon, eventually turning a corner. The whole time she wanted to call out to Dineo. There was a hollow feeling of impending doom growing inside her. Ordinarily, Mahlatse would have been frustrated at having been dumped with all the housework. A part of her was. But she couldn't ignore the twisting feeling in her stomach. The subtle red flags. She finished watering the garden. After carefully weighing up her unwillingness to do the laundry with her unwillingness to face Mama's wrath if she came home and found the laundry not done, she decided to do the laundry. Doing the laundry by hand over a basin was no easy task. Every time she picked up an item of clothing she recognised as her sister's she thought next week, I'm letting Dineo do all this by herself!

Of course Dineo had skipped out on laundry to go out with her friends! The two sisters were day and night. Mahlatse was a home body, bound to their bedroom knitting, trying to do homework, and listening to radio dramas until Papa came home and told her to switch that thing off.

Dineo, however, was a social butterfly in full flight. She always had friends either knocking at the door or calling the landline to ask for her. Before the curfews, she'd go out with her friends and walk home late at night. The neighbours would always ask after her. There was a line of boys stretching from Dube train station to their home in Orlando West waiting for a chance to take her out.

Mahlatse passed the time by picturing herself lounging on her bed, knitting or listening to the radio dramas broadcast on Radio Bantu, a cup of rooibos at her side while Dineo was outside doing the washing and scrubbing. She felt herself melting into daydreams the way she did whenever she did something repetitive, until she looked down and saw there were no more clothes to wash. By the time she hung them on the line and it sagged a little with their weight, it was late afternoon. Papa was the first to come home. He had a spring in his step that immediately told Mahlatse the person he bet on won the match.

'Dumela, Papa,' she said when she saw him.

'Dumela, Hlatse.' He peered over her. 'Is Dineo inside?'

She shook her head. 'No. She went to the bioscope with Mbali to watch that new Sylvester Stallone movie. I think it's called...' she wracked her brain. She knew she had heard the boys at school talk about it but what was it called? 'I think she said it's called Cobra?'

Papa paused. 'As long as she's back before nine.' He walked into the house.

Mahlatse was starting to get a little concerned. She didn't know what movie Dineo had gone to watch or even what time she'd gone. She tried to suppress the nerves in her belly. She'd probably gone to see one of those boring long movies and would come back soon, she thought. The afternoon light turned from orange to blueish grey. Dineo was still not back. Mahlatse's worry started to deepen when she looked down the street to see if Dineo was coming. But there was no yellow blob on the horizon. A boy on a bicycle came cycling towards her. She recognised him as Vincent, one of the boys from her class, and waved her hand. He came to a stop in front of her gate.

'Heita, Hlatse,' he said. 'U-right, sisi?'

'I'm okay, thanks. Vince,' she said, leaning closer to him over the gate. 'Have you seen my sister?'

'Seen her where? You mean now?'

'Yes, now,' she said, slightly annoyed. Vincent could be slow at times. She knew he lived in Molofo, not too far from Eyethu Cinema. If he had been cycling in this direction maybe he'd seen Dineo on the way. 'She went to watch a movie with friends. Maybe you saw her?'

'Uh,' he said, scratching his head. 'I don't think so. But I haven't been looking for her.'

'Are you sure? Maybe you saw a woman in a yellow dress?'

He looked at her for a moment. 'I have to be honest, I haven't seen her and I came straight from Eyethu. I wouldn't worry if I were you though. She'll probably come back soon.'

She paused. 'You know what, you're right. Thanks anyway, Vince.'

'Sho-sho Hlatse. See you Monday,' he got back on his bike and left.

She waved goodbye to him and looked again at the sky. It was starting to get late. She looked down the street again and saw a dog walking towards her. It was thin and white with grey spots and the outline of its ribs visible through its skin. She'd seen the dog hanging around her sister numerous times. It was an unclaimed neighbourhood stray that birthed a litter every so often. It seemed to really like Dineo, who fed it scraps of food. Mahlatse had always been too scared of ticks, rabies, and God knows what else to go near it. The dog stopped in front of her and whined. Odd. It had never done that before. It started circling before standing up on its hind legs, leaning against the fence and whining again.

'Hhayi, voetsek!' A voice shouted. She turned and saw Mama aggressively waving her arm at the dog, yelling 'Voetsek! Voetsek! Nxa!' at it. The dog whined and ran away.

She opened the gate. 'I hate these stupid dogs!' She looked up at Mahlatse. 'Hlatse, what are you still doing out here? Let's get in before it gets dark. Is your sister inside?'

Her throat turned dry. She swallowed and said, 'No, Mama. Dineo isn't back yet.'

Mama looked at her with a confused expression. 'What do you mean she isn't back yet? Where did she go?'

'To Eyethu.'

'With who?'

'Mbali.'

They walked into the house. It was starting to get dark and the tall Apollo lights were turning on. Mama looked at the wall clock in the living room. 'She must come back soon.' An hour later Dineo was still not home. Unless she magically appeared in front of the gate right that moment, she was going to break the curfew. Mahlatse knew her sister was smart enough to come home undetected. So many people took the chance and made it. But if she was caught, the consequences could be severe. She had a million things running through her mind. She was sitting on edge. She kept glancing at the door hoping Dineo would walk through. But she didn't. Mahlatse heard Mama on the kitchen phone. 'Dineo isn't there?' Mama said in a strained voice. 'She said she was with Mbali! Didn't they go to the bioscope together?' Mahlatse stood in the doorway and watched her mother. Even Papa turned down the radio from his seat in the living room. The only noise they could hear were crickets.

'Mbali is there? She's with you now? And Dineo isn't?' Mahlatse's heart sank to her stomach. She numbed over. If Dineo wasn't with Mbali then where was she?

'Okay, okay. Ke a leboga, Mme,' Mama put the phone down. Her face had taken on a grayish tone.

'Where did she say Dineo was?' Papa had appeared behind Mahlatse, nudging her into the kitchen.

'She doesn't know,' Mama started. 'She says she hasn't seen Dineo at all since yesterday and that Mbali has been home the whole day. Mbali was there with her and said she never saw Dineo today.'

'Bathong,' Papa exclaimed. 'Then where is she?'

The room went silent. Both of them turned to Mahlatse who was leaning against the counter, arms wrapped tightly around her torso.

'Mahlatse,' Mama started. 'I want you to tell me exactly what Dineo said to you.'

Their expectation weighed against her skin. Her throat had turned to sand. 'I... she... she told me she was going to the bioscope with Mbali,' she half mumbled.

'Is that it?' Papa said. 'What else did she say?'

Mahlatse shook her head. 'Nothing, Papa. That's it. That's all she said.'

'But this doesn't make sense!' Mama said. She was beginning to work herself into a state. 'She obviously didn't go there so where did she go?'

'Look Sylvia,' Papa started. 'I think we must try to calm down. Dineo is a smart girl. Maybe she went to watch a movie with some other friend and now that it's past nine she's staying at the friend's house until morning.'

'But why would she tell Mahlatse she was going with Mbali if she wasn't?' Mama protested. 'That's what I don't understand.'

'I don't know. Maybe let's wait until morning and then if she hasn't come back we can go to the police.'

It wasn't a comforting idea. The police didn't care about missing black people. Black people had gone missing all the time since the student protests and the police either didn't care at all or were covering up that the missing person had gone missing because of them. No police officer was going to help them. As far as they were concerned, the more blacks that turned up missing or dead, the better. But they still held onto hope. It was all they could do.

Mahlatse didn't sleep at all that night. A million scenarios played out in her mind. What if Dineo had been caught by a group of boys and gang raped? What if she had been caught in the hostel men's crossfire? What if she had been on her way home after nine and was caught by the military? She tossed and turned, replaying the earlier scenes with Dineo. The troubled look on her sister's face. How adamant she was that Mahlatse could not come with her. Even the stray dog unnerved her. Something about the way it whined and leaned against the fence bothered her. Had it been trying to tell her something? Mahlatse got up, lit the paraffin light next to her bed, and went searching for the letter Dineo had been reading. She found nothing. She looked in the small corner dustbin and saw ashes and a torn piece of paper that had clearly been burned. Whatever Dineo read in that letter was something she wanted no one else to find. That was when she knew for certain Dineo was not at a family's house. Wherever she was, she was likely in danger.

Dineo never turned up the next morning. It was the first Sunday in years that no one in the household had gone to church. Instead they waited with baited breath, jumping every time they heard what sounded like a noise at their gate. Mahlatse lost track of the number of times she had run to open the door, hoping to find her sister, and instead finding no one. The next morning, Papa announced that he would go past the police station on his way back from work.

'They won't bother looking for her. You know that,' Mama said in an empty voice.

'Yes, but maybe they've found a body,' he said before closing the door behind him.

The idea of Dineo being dead was too much for Mahlatse. Instead of walking to school, she ran down the street, turned the corner, and kept running until she reached TK's usual spot. TK was one of those boys. The ones their mother was always warning them against. The ones who dressed in smart clothing, gold chains, and drove around in their cars neither going to work or school. The jack rollers. Mahlatse knew TK was a criminal. Everyone did. But for some reason, that didn't stop Dineo from climbing into the passenger seat of his blue Colt. He had taken a liking to her and, by extension, Mahlatse. 'Don't worry,' Dineo had told her. 'He'll protect you. Make sure no one else bothers you.' And he had. He called Mahlatse his little sister. He sometimes walked her to and from school with Dineo at his side. Since he came into their eyes, the boy who used to wait at the street corner for Mahlatse and twist her arm until she agreed to be his girlfriend had left her alone. Mahlatse had admittedly enjoyed the relative peace he brought into her life, but still looked at him with sideways glances. But she supposed, if Dineo thought he was safe then perhaps he was. He was standing with his friends, listening to one of them tell a story. Usually they scared her, but she wasn't scared this time. Now, she was angry.

'TK!' She shouted. They all looked up at her.

'Look who it is,' TK said with a smile. 'How are you doing sis' wam? Shouldn't you be going to school?'

She walked towards them with a defiant stare. 'TK, where is Dineo?'

He looked taken aback. 'I should be asking you that. I haven't seen her since Friday. We were supposed to meet up yesterday but she never showed up.'

'Well, she never came home on Saturday,' Mahlatse said. She was on the verge of tears but was determined to fight them back. 'Last time I saw her she said she was going to Eyethu. She didn't go with you?'

He shook his head. 'No, she didn't go with me. Like I said, I haven't seen her since Friday. She'll probably show up soon, though. I wouldn't stress if I was you.'

The nonchalant way he said it, the complete lack of concern or care in his face just made Mahlatse angrier.

'Well, if you see her please tell her we're looking for her,' she said before turning away. She walked away from him, ignoring him as he called after her.

She didn't know where to go. She couldn't go to school. She would get lashings for being late and besides, she would never be able to concentrate in class. Not with this happening. Going home wasn't an option as she was supposed to be at school. She walked the streets, asking a few more people if they had seen Dineo and ignoring their questions about why she was bunking school. She felt as though she was going mad. As she walked past Dube station she saw some soldiers milling about carrying guns. Two pimple-faced blonde boys were speaking to each other. The one looked up at her and then nudged the other. They both turned and stared at her, speaking to one another. She was too far away to hear but she felt she understood. An electric current of shock coursed through her body. The burnt letter. The lies. Mahlatse had heard whispers of her sister being involved in the ANC, but dismissed them out of hand. Now, it all came together. They had taken Dineo. She didn't know how she knew, but she knew. Dineo hadn't disappeared. She had deliberately been taken.

Over the course of the next few weeks her family rang up everyone they knew asking about Dineo. Papa went to the mortuary every time they heard of another black female body that needed to be identified, but none of them were Dineo. Every time she saw the soldiers, every time she smelled tear gas or heard a heavy casspir rolling past her window, she thought of Dineo. She pictured her sister being thrown in the backs of those cars, hands behind her back, to be carted off to John Vorster Square. She felt the anger grow inside her, forming a solid base, and igniting the day of her sister's memorial service held 18 months after she went missing.

* * *

Three years after Dineo disappeared, Mama passed away. Despite what everyone expected, Papa didn't remarry. Years later when Mahlatse tried to convince Papa to leave Soweto and move somewhere safer and closer to her, he shook his head.

'If I leave then how will Dineo know where to find me?' He would always ask. 'I'm staying right here until the day she comes back.'

THIRTY

Kgethi was in a hell of her own making. The walls were closing in with no place for her to turn. For months she had told herself that she was in control but that lie was unravelling around her. She had ignored the red flags. She saw the Pastor was screwing people over but figured damn it, that's how this whole capitalism thing works. Who hadn't screwed over someone less rich, less educated, lacking in common sense or whatever to make a bit of money? She almost had a grudging respect for it. She finally had to admit that the 'harmless' pastor wasn't as harmless as she thought. Under that meek exterior was a cold, calculating monster. She had spent too long ignoring how he controlled people. How he had gone from helping people to seemingly only helping himself, while gaslighting everyone around him to convince them he hadn't turned rogue. The way he upgraded himself from Pastor to Prophet. She'd seen it all happen.

The red flags had turned into sirens. Kgethi felt as though she had been sleepwalking. Now that she was awake there was nothing else for her to do except pick Thato up and run. The night Thato told her the Pastor had been sexually abusing his congregants, Kgethi threw up. She could count the number of times she had thrown up in her life on one hand, and most of them had been in the first trimester of her pregnancy. She remembered leaning against the toilet bowl, silently cursing her body for betraying her. She hated her pregnancy more and more with each retch. Each wave of nausea reminded her that her body was no longer hers alone. Every breath she took was no longer for her lungs alone, nor was every mouthful of food for only her stomach, but was being shared with a clump of cells growing larger and more complex by the second.

It was strange. Not once throughout her pregnancy, nor the first few months of Thato's life, had Kgethi felt the primal protective urge that was said to be instinctual with motherhood. She would look at her stomach growing larger, pressing against her clothes, and be aware of all the people who stared through her and at her stomach instead. The amount of people who would simply walk up to her and rub her stomach until she fought back the urge to shout, 'Hello, I'm here! I'm a person! This is my body!' She wanted to run. But how can you outrun something growing inside you? When the baby was born she felt as though every moment she spent looking at Thato's face was sucking away precious time she would never get back.

She would go on Facebook or Instagram and watch as her friends and former classmates graduated, travelled, and moved abroad to teach English in Asia or complete Master's degrees at prestigious institutions. They went to Rocking the Daisies and Oppikoppi. They watched her favorite artists perform live. They became social media influencers, artists, lawyers, and doctors. They posted pictures of themselves laughing with their friends, holding glasses of champagne, and showing off their perfectly flat, stretchmark free stomachs and perky breasts in gorgeous bikinis. They got married to partners they met in university, showing off stunning diamond engagement rings in closeup photos.

All the while Kgethi felt stuck. Her life was stuck in first gear on an unrelenting work baby work baby 24/7 routine. She never travelled nor went to music festivals. How could she when every spare cent went to Thato and besides, who would watch her? She never posed with friends by the pool. She lost most of her friends when Thato's birth brought a new language her friends couldn't understand. She no longer felt comfortable in bikinis anyway with her sagging breasts and stomach marred by stretch marks. She had been walking through the past nine years of her life with her eyes half open. Just enough to do the bare minimum expected of her and even that left her drained. She had sleepwalked through motherhood and her dead end job. Through her nonexistent dating life consisting of temporary men who bolted when they found out Thato existed.

Now she was awake.

She saw the Pastor for what he really was. He was a monster, sucking the life out of Thato to feed his own appetite and he would never be full. She decided she would let Thato sleep. In the morning, she would sit her down and tell her they were never going back to the Pastor again. This had gone too far and they were done. Kgethi was done. When she walked into Thato's room the next morning she immediately saw that something was wrong. Thato's face was grey. She was shivering under her blankets. Her skin was hot and sweaty under Kgethi's touch.

'Thato!' She yelled. No response. She started shaking her. Thato's eyelids opened and dropped shut again. She mumbled something inaudible.

Kgethi stared at her in shock. 'Thato? Thato!' She yelled again. Thato slumped over in her arms like a doll. Kgethi laid her flat and listened to her chest. Her eyes filled with tears as she listened to the steady but faint heartbeat. She sat up and did the only thing she could think to do. She pulled out her phone.

'Mom!' She burst as soon as her mother answered. 'Something's wrong! Thato won't wake up!'

'What do you mean she won't wake up?'

'She won't wake up!' Kgethi said through tears. 'She has a temperature and she's shaking and she won't wake up! I don't know what to do Mom!'

'Kgethi, you need to take her to hospital. Right. Now,'

Mom said sternly. 'Call your boss and explain what's happened. I'll come meet you at the hospital.'

Kgethi lost track of time. Picking Thato up, driving to the hospital, sitting in the ER all blended together into a nightmare sequence. She felt like she was floating above watching her body below signing papers, watching her motionless daughter lie in a narrow, white hospital bed, and listening to the doctor's words without taking any of it in. Even her mother looked lifeless as they sat together listening to the doctor and watching over Thato.

'This can't go on Kgethi,' she said without looking at her.

'I know Mom, I know,' she said.

'So then why don't you go to the police? You must get a protection order! I'm sure Molefi will be able to help you.'

'Don't worry Mom, I'll sort it out on my own.'

'And just how are you going to do that?' She asked in a sharp, raised voice.

'Mama,' said a nurse who'd poked her head around the corner. 'Please keep it down. We can hear you down the hall!'

She leaned forward, covering her face with her hands. She heard her mom mumble an apology to the nurse. She didn't want to have to deal with her mother. Her head was still swimming. She was still piecing together the past few days. How did it all go so far south so quickly? They had met the pastor in February and it was only October. Had it really only been nine months? It felt like decades had passed.

'Kgethi? Are you listening to me?'

'Mom, please' she said, sitting back up. She didn't want to talk about this. She couldn't talk about this. Not now when shame burned so hot in her throat she wanted to scream. 'I haven't slept and this is really overwhelming for me! Can we please not talk about it right now?'

Mom opened her mouth to speak and closed it before she said anything. 'Okay,' she finally said. 'But we must speak about this soon.'

They sat in silence side by side until the nurse came back.

She gave a sympathetic smile to Mom. 'Ng'yaxolisa mama, only parents can stay after visiting hours,' the nurse told her.

Kgethi breathed a sigh of relief when she left. The child down the hall had finally stopped screaming leaving the hospital ward eerily quiet. She looked at Thato's face. She was lying perfectly still. Her skin had a grayish pallor and she had dark circles around her eyes. She had always been small but she looked shrunken in the bed. The hospital gown they had put on her drowned her. The machine she was connected to recorded her steady heartbeat, but Kgethi felt the urge to reach over and feel for herself if it really was there. When did she lose so much weight and how had Kgethi not noticed before? What had she done? Her whole world was crumbling around her. She hadn't always made the best choices but she'd always made it out okay. Thato was in this hospital because of her. Because she had failed to protect her. She had driven a car off a cliff and now the most innocent person she knew was bearing the consequences. She held Thato's hand. It felt cold and clammy. She could feel Thato's whole body vibrating against her palm. Kgethi's vision turned blurry from tears which formed warm streaks down her face.

'Thato,' she said in a soft, broken voice. The child didn't move. 'I don't know if you can hear me but I'm so sorry. I'm so sorry I did this to you. I didn't mean for this to happen. I...' She choked back a sob. And then another. And another. The floodgates had opened sending rivulets of tears pouring down her face. She cried over Thato, over the church, over her own complicity, her own stupidity, over everything. There was only one thing left for her to do. She looked at Thato again. 'Don't worry, I'm going to fix this,' she said. 'I'm going to make sure that man never comes near you again.'

THIRTY-ONE

Thato saw blurry colours. She saw a person-shaped blob of brown, black, and blue that had Mom's voice. A blob of purple that was small, soft, and squishy like her favourite teddy bear. Blobs of green outside the window where the trees should be. She was so tired. She felt both hot and cold. Her face was hot and sweaty. Her body shivered under the sheets. All she wanted to do was sleep. Sleep and shiver. Shiver and sleep. She was between this world and somewhere else. In the other world she saw herself walking with the Pastor on one side and her mother on the other. 'See, look at those arches,' he said gesturing upwards. 'I always liked the buildings in Sandton and wanted to take that modern look. To show that this is us, taking God away from all those old churches with their pagan rituals and into the modern age.' Everything was covered in a film of grey and white dust but through it Thato could see a white marble floor. She could see the smooth cream walls with sharp-edged rectangle arches jutting out. She could see five rows of light wooden benches wrapping around the room facing towards a raised platform. Behind the platform was a wall made out of bright differently coloured shards of glass all arranged into a pattern. The glass wall was throwing coloured light that sparkled all over the room. She looked up and saw a ceiling that stretched into the sky. A giant chandelier had been fixed in the centre with delicate gold tendrils that dripped down like rain.

‘I’m thinking of hanging up a few portraits on some of the walls,’ the Pastor said. ‘Religious portraits but by local artists so we get that African feel. There’s a whole centre for youth, ages 4 to 17, with Bible study rooms. Offices for the staff. We’re building a smaller chapel where we’ll have the christenings and weddings for people too cheap to pay for this room.

‘We’re also building a food court and allowing some of the entrepreneurs in the congregation to open up small food stalls and pay rent. We’re even thinking of having a monthly market, you know like Neighbourgoods or Fourways Farmer’s Market, to raise a little more money for the church. And we’ve built a library and a bookstore so everyone who does Bible studies can get their books there.’

He led them out of the room into the marbled foyer and pressed a button on the glass elevator. ‘There are six floors,’ he said excitedly, swiping a card on the keypad. The button for the fifth floor lit up in a red circle. Thato clutched on to Mummy tightly. She didn’t know where they were going and the was scared. They shot up to the fifth floor. When the doors opened Mummy gasped. They stepped out into an apartment. It was spacious with slick lines, large windows and a big modern kitchen to one side.

‘It’s got two bedrooms and two bathrooms,’ the Pastor said. ‘And I know you’ll like the walk-in closet in the master bedroom.’

Thato stepped slowly into the living room. The soft carpet felt like a cloud under her feet.

‘Solomon, what is this?’ Mummy asked.

He turned to them with a strange look on his face. ‘Isn’t it obvious? This is your new apartment.’

Everything became fuzzy. She felt herself slipping, becoming weak until she collapsed on the ground. When she came to she looked up and saw the lady with the yellow dress. The lady reached towards her and pulled her up by the hand. She stood on a road she’d never seen before. The yellow dress lady was standing in front of her. The thin white dog with grey spots was panting at her side with its tongue lolling out of its mouth. In front of them was something that looked almost like a big field covered in little green plants. On top of the plants she saw bottles and plastic bags. When she looked closer they almost looked like they were gently floating in the breeze. The air smelled swampy. She realised it wasn't a field at all. It was a dam. There were big houses on the one side of the dam with red roofs, some of them as big as the houses with high walls that she passed on her way to school. She could see small boats floating, battling through the green plants.

The lady in yellow was stroking the dog. 'Good girl, Spotty-spotty,' she kept saying. 'You've been trying for a long time haven't you?'

'Where are we?' She asked the lady.

The lady looked up shrugged her shoulders. 'This is the place they brought me to.'

'Who?'

'I'm not sure. I don't remember exactly how I died. The last thing I remember was being at a farm. Then I woke up here.'

She started walking and Thato noticed she walked with a limp. The dog walked next to her, wagging its tail. They walked next to the road until Thato saw a big sign which said 'Welcome to Harties!' In big, joined lettering.

'Harties?' Thato asked.

'Yes, dear. Hartbeespoort Dam,' the lady said in a flat voice. 'My Papa's family village isn't too far from here. I used to hate coming past here. But now that I'm stuck here, I think it's quite pretty. Don't you?'

Thato didn't say anything. There was something about the woman's face. Thato had seen her before. The lady had always been familiar looking to her but now Thato was sure.

The lady turned to her and kneeled until they were looking each other in the eye. 'Thato,' she said. 'I'm sorry if I ever scared you. I've been trying to figure out how to ask you this.

You're so small and I know all of this, everything, has been scary and unfair. But I need something from you. You do one thing and all of this can be over. I need you to get your Koko and your uncle and bring them here to come find me.'

Her eyes widened in surprise. 'You know my Koko and Uncle?'

'Yes, sweetie,' she said with a smile. 'You still don't know who I am?'

Thato shook her head.

The lady put her hand on her shoulder 'I'm your auntie. Your Auntie Dineo.'

Thato knew that name. It was the name Koko couldn't say without her eyes clouding over. Someone said Dineo and the room would go quieter. The light from the sunshine would turn grey. She woke up. Her tummy felt hollow and sore. She was in a hard, white bed. There were clouds, birds, and trees with pink flowers painted on the wall in front of her. The sides of the beds had a hard, metal frame made out of white poles. She heard Mommy and Koko's voices nearby talking to each other.

'This can't go on, Kgethi,' she heard Koko say.

'I know, Mom, I know,' Mommy replied. 'I'm going to get rid of him.'

'So then why don't you go to the police? You must get a protection order!'

The two voices mixed together, echoing like they had been thrown down a concrete hall. The voices were moving further away. The lights were getting brighter, spreading across the ceiling like exploding stars until everything turned white. She was walking in the whiteness. Was she dead? She felt like she was floating. Maybe this was where all the see-through people went when they finally disappeared. She kept walking and as she walked, the room started changing. She could see shadows that grew bigger, forming into lines, curves, and corners until they were house-shaped. The white underneath her felt solid like a floor and turned into a grey, gravelly strip. The leftover parts between the grey strip and the house-shaped shadows turned brown and dusty. The white above her turned blue bathed in orange.

She kept walking. She put up her hand for cover from the wind blowing dust into her face. The house-shaped shadows became solid brick houses that squat against the dusty pavement. Some had little grey wire fences while others had proper walls with metal gates. There were people walking past. This looks like Ntatemogolo's street, she thought. She looked up and gasped when saw his house. The lady in the yellow dress walked out through the gate and closed it behind her. She walked with her shoulders up and her head bowed down. The white dog with gray spots and sticking-out ribcage walked across the road to meet her and started walking next to her.

They kept walking. 'Heita, Neo,' someone said to her with a wave as they walked past. She greeted them back and kept walking. They turned around a corner and walked into an empty street. The empty street petered into dust and then a big open field. As they walked Thato realised the distance between them was growing. She tried to run but the distance grew, turning the lady into a doll-sized figure on the horizon. Thato kept running. She saw a car slowing down and stopping in front of the lady. Two men with dark hair and red faces got out. Before the lady could react they grabbed her and forced her into the car. The dog sprinted ahead, barking at the men but it was too late to save her. She was gone.

Thato watched the boxy, black car drive off in shock. Everything around her started to change, changing shapes and colours and sizes until she blinked and saw she was back at the lake. It was nighttime now. The lake looked creepy covered in darkness and was quiet except for the sound of dirt being shoveled. There were two figures standing in the clearing. One was digging into the ground with a shovel while the other one watched. The man held his hand near his mouth and moved it to blow tobacco smoke into the air. They were talking but she couldn't hear what they were saying. The man put down his shovel. The two of them walked off and returned holding something too big and too long to be just a bag. It looked person-shaped. Lady in yellow-shaped. They threw her into the pit and shoveled dirt over her.

Thato blinked. The world started changing again as though someone had taken a remote and hit fast-forward. The men shoveled dirt at super speed and then left. The night sky became lighter while a round sun rose into the sky, sinking again moments later and leaving the sky dark with only a slice of moon and a few twinkling stars to light it. She watched the sun go up, down, up, down. She watched as cars and people whizzed by, as boats sped about the lake, as new houses went up in seconds. Then everything slowed down, looking exactly the way she had always seen it. The lady in the yellow dress, her Aunt Dineo, was standing by the lake staring at her.

'Thato,' she said. 'You need to come find me. Tell your Koko and Uncle Molefi to come find me.'

She blinked one last time and was back in the hospital room. She heard the beep-beep-beep of the machine next to her. She felt the needle from the drip digging under her skin. She turned and saw her Mom, her Uncle Molefi, and her Koko sitting and standing around her.

THIRTY-TWO

Kgethi stared down the ugly, brown building for what she knew would be the last time. Its ugliness looked more hostile in the sharp spring light. Rage welled up inside her. She wanted to grab stones and throw them through the church windows. Reach into her handbag for her lighter, douse the building in petrol and burn the whole thing down. She wanted to hear the Pastor's screams inside the burning building washing her regret away. She looked at it, took a deep breath, and walked forward. She rehearsed the script in her head. Just keep cool Kgethi, she told herself. Remember why you're here. Don't take no for an answer. Don't listen to his bullshit. She walked into his office and found him bent over a thick wad of papers. He looked up at her as she closed the door.

'Kgethi,' he said with a smile. 'Good, you're here. How are you doing?'

She had never been more disgusted at the sight of a smile. His shamelessness offended her. His ability to sit at his desk and smile, as though he had done nothing wrong, as though he were no different from anyone else, sent shivers down her spine.

'I wanted to show you something,' he said holding up the pile of papers. 'Do you want to come see?'

'What is it?'

'These are the plans for the new church. The architect sent them this week for approval,' he started looking through them, excited as a little boy on Christmas morning.

'You must come and see the plans for the auditorium! We're going to import marble for the floors from Italy. There's going to be a whole wall made out of stained glass right behind the altar—'

'Solomon,' she interrupted. 'I really don't care about this.'

He looked up at her. 'That's because you haven't seen your apartment yet.'

Did she mishear? 'What do you mean 'my apartment'?'

'I mean I was thinking it might be easier to have the two of you living in the new church. That way you won't have to rush to take Thato home, so time won't be such an issue. And if we have any emergencies we can just call for you and you'll bring her down.'

For once, she had nothing to say. The script in her head was replaced by radio silence. She felt… violated. The room was claustrophobic. The air stale and tainted by him. Her next words pushed their way through like vomit. 'Are you fucking crazy?'

His smile disappeared. 'Excuse me?'

'You're insane if you think I'm moving into a church with my daughter. Insane. You think I'll just agree to give you 24-hour access to my daughter? You? A fucking child molester?'

He stood up. 'What did you just call me?'

'I know, Solomon,' she stared him square in the eye. Her face turned hot. Her heart drummed against her chest. 'I know what you did. Thato told me. You're a sick fucking bastard and I don't want you near my child. So I came here to tell you that we're not doing this anymore. Me and Thato are done. And if you contact me again, I'm calling the police.'

He stared at her in silence. Was she imagining guilt on his face? If he had an ounce of shame left he would have been constructing a heartfelt apology which Kgethi was preparing to reject. Instead he laughed in her face. 'The police?' He said between laughter. 'What are they going to do? They're the same ones who lose dockets if R5,000 makes its way into their pockets! You wouldn't do that. If you did then I'll tell them how you sold your own daughter. How I was just trying to save the poor girl from you. Who do you think they'll listen to? The whore who sells her daughter to any grown man who asks or the Prophet who has healed hundreds of people with his bare hands?'

'You're so full of shit, Solomon,' she snapped back. 'You know that? You didn't heal anyone. You've been using Thato this whole time and when people find out the truth it's over for you.'

'And how are they going to find out? Are you going to tell them? You?' He laughed again. 'You tell anyone and they'll take her away from you. I'll make sure everyone knows what a bad mother you are. How you knew and agreed the whole time because you wanted money. You didn't give a damn about Thato because this was convenient for you.'

'That's not true. Stop lying!'

'Where is the lie Mamokgethi? Isn't it true you came to me to make the deal? Isn't it true you came every week to get your money from me? How many clothes have you bought with that money? How much makeup? How many wigs? How much of that money have you spent to make yourself look like a whore? How much of it actually went to Thato and not you? Now you want to act all innocent? Don't make me laugh, please! There's a verse in Proverbs that describes people like you. It goes, 'the greedy bring ruin to their households, but the one who hates bribes will live'. And here you are after your greed has brought ruin to your household trying to blame me when the only person you have to blame is yourself!'

A surge of guilt stupefied her. She was breathing too hard to think. She pictured Thato collapsing in the church and realised that on one level, the Pastor was right. She had gleefully traded Thato for everything he promised her.

'Fuck you, Solomon,' she said. 'Fuck you. I should never have agreed to any of this. You can manipulate your little sheep all you want but I'm not going to sit here and use my child to help you do it anymore! So you can threaten me all you want but I'm done. And I'm never letting you come near my daughter again.'

He started to say something but she was beyond caring. She started walking towards the door. He grabbed her arm to try pull her back. She turned around and punched him so hard he fell backwards, knocking his head hard into the desk. He looked forward with a dazed expression and blood trickling down his nose. Before he could say anything she left. The ground shook under her feet as she walked but she kept going, down the hall, out the entrance, and out the church doors.

'Kgethi!' She heard a voice call out. She turned around and saw Bongani walking towards her.

'Leave me alone, Bongani,' she said. 'If he sent you here I don't want to hear it.'

'Just wait!' He half-walked, half ran towards her. 'I heard you two fighting. What's going on? Is everything with Thato okay? Did you manage to take her to a doctor?'

She sighed. 'No. Me and Thato aren't doing this anymore.'

He paused before nodding. 'Good. I think you're doing the right thing. I'm surprised he's letting you leave when the tour is starting in a few weeks.'

She'd almost forgotten about that stupid tour. It would begin in Soweto, move south to Durban, continue west through to Port Elizabeth and Cape Town, rounding back through Upington, Bloemfontein and Rustenburg. Once they arrived back in Johannesburg they would prepare for the international tour starting a few weeks later. She had never had any real intention of getting on that bus. Now she was finally killing the dream. 'I made it clear to him that I don't care, Bongani. We're not going anymore. He's going to have to find someone else.'

'God willing he won't be able to find anyone else,' he said. She stared at him. She noted the resigned tone of his voice. The defeated downward tilt of his head and slump of shoulders.

'The Solomon in there isn't the person I grew up with. He's changed so much and I...I'm glad you're leaving. I actually think he needs to get out of this thing. I've been thinking for a while that Solomon has lost his way. When he started this he was so excited about helping people live in accordance with the Word. But now, hhayi I don't know,' he shook his head. 'And the sad thing is people are now starting to get hurt. It's like he cares more about having power than God. I think he must end this thing with Thato and just go back to the basics and preach the Word. I've actually been thinking maybe we must even tell people the truth—'

'No!' Kgethi shouted. He looked at her in shock. She calmed herself down and started again. 'I mean, Thato is a child! The whole reason we agreed to this was because we thought, I thought that if Solomon pretended the powers were his it would keep her safe. There are crazy people out there. We don't need them to know that Thato has powers.'

'Okay,' he said nodding. 'I see what you mean. But I do want to help you.'

'I'm sorry Bongani but I don't know if I can trust you. You're his friend.'

'No, I understand. But if maybe you decide you need my help, just know I'm here. I'm actually thinking of leaving now. There's something very dark about this place. I don't want to be here anymore.'

She looked at him. Bongani was a lot of things but an actor was not one of them. There was a sincere sadness in his eyes. She wasn't sure she could trust him with details but maybe, if she needed a favor, she could consider him.

'You have my number,' he said as if reading her thoughts. 'If you need anything, anything at all, please give me a call.'

She nodded. 'I should go now. Take care Bongani.' She turned and walked towards her car. As she drove away from the church she saw him standing in the same spot, staring at the entrance with an unreadable expression on his face.

THIRTY-THREE

Mahlatse was at the end of her rope. She was mad as hell at her irresponsible daughter. At that awful predator she'd attached herself to. She knew without being told that he would try squeeze his grip even tighter around Thato. He was not going to let her go without a fight. Thato was his cash cow. His Hail Mary. The lifeboat that had both saved and birthed his career. Anyone with two brain cells to rub together could have predicted this would happen. And Mahlatse had the misfortune of birthing a daughter who did not even have one. How could she be so stupid? Mahlatse could barely look at Kgethi. Her blood had turned to ice when she heard Kgethi's panicked, tear-filled voice on the phone. She had fought to keep a veneer of calm in her voice while inside she panicked. When she arrived at the hospital and saw Thato lying motionless in bed, she wanted to slap Kgethi in the face. At least Kgethi had the decency to look guilty with eyes swollen from the tears that spilled down her cheeks as she admitted she was wrong. That the Pastor was a dangerous man who should never have been allowed near Thato in the first place. 'This can't go on, Kgethi,' she said. Kgethi told her she was going to get rid of the Pastor on her own but Mahlatse couldn't see how. Didn't she realise it was her foolishness that got Thato into this situation in the first place? And if she was serious, why hadn't she gotten a protection order? Mahlatse was seething.

The three of them were squished into a sterile hospital room with three other sickly children and their stressed out, drained families. A baby had been screaming on and off for the past hour somewhere down the hall. Mahlatse identified parents by the large bags under their eyes they wore with their stricken expressions. When the baby's mother walked down the hall Mahlatse saw her own past reflected in the mother's face. She had brought Kgethi to a different hospital in a different time, when the sounds of her daughter's constant screams rang in her ears and convinced her something was irreparably wrong. Why else would the baby not stop crying? She had sat there mostly alone. Itumeleng had come and gone two hours later. Something about work. Mahlatse had sat next to the hospital bed too exhausted to move and watched her pink faced child screaming with little hands balled into fists. Now over 20 years later she was watching her granddaughter. And once again she was exhausted. She hoped that Kgethi had medical insurance. Otherwise the hospital visit would cost an arm and a leg. 'And I'm not in a position to pay for it,' she told her daughter.

'Kgethi, you need to press charges,' she insisted. Kgethi kept telling her she would fix it. But Mahlatse wasn't convinced. She stared at Thato who had been trapped somewhere between consciousness and sleep. The thought that she might not wake up seeded itself in her mind. As the hours dragged on it began to sprout. Mahlatse had been the mother for so long that handing over the parenting reigns to Kgethi still felt strange to her. Especially now. Kgethi was knocking on 30's door but she was still so childlike. So unthinking. So selfish. If Mahlatse had it her way she wouldn't trust her with a pot plant let alone a child. When she saw Thato lying in the hospital bed, a living monument to her daughter's irresponsibility, she wanted to scream out, 'Fuck it! I'm the only adult here!' She spoke briefly to Molefi who had just returned from a business trip to the Cape Town office and promised to visit Thato in hospital the next day. He was cancelling a dinner date with someone named Emile. Mahlatse knew that name sounded familiar, but she was too tired to dig deeper.

She looked at her phone and considered phoning Itumeleng. She still hadn't told him what happened. She had involved him in this. She couldn't very well not involve him now. She looked at his number but something held her back. Perhaps it was preemptive disappointment. Perhaps it was the memory of being in hospital alone. Whatever it was, it prompted her to push the responsibility of informing him onto Kgethi. She messaged Kgethi to tell her if she wanted her father to be there, she needed to phone him herself.

She didn't sleep at all. She couldn't. Her head had filled up again with visions of the worst possible scenarios. She imagined strangling the Pastor. How good it would feel to wrap her hands around his neck and squeeze until there was not a single breath left in his body. She could, if she wanted to, go to Hillbrow right that moment and find some boys who would kill the Pastor for as little as R5,000. The economy was bad, people were desperate, someone was sure to do it. Considering how useless the police were, who would catch her out? Though knowing her daughter, she would probably have to save that R5000 for Thato's medical bills.

On the second day, she walked into the room to find Thato still sleeping. Kgethi wasn't there. Mahlatse scowled. Surely she could have taken off work to be at her sick daughter's side? The nurse walked in a few moments later and greeted her warmly.

'Is Mom here?' The nurse asked. It took Mahlatse a few seconds to realise she was referring to Kgethi. 'Uh… no, I don't think so. I just came and I haven't seen her.'

The nurse walked to the IV drip and machines Thato was attached to. 'She was awake earlier,' she said. 'You missed her.'

Mahlatse's disappointment displayed itself openly on her face. 'Oh. How was she? Did she speak? Has she eaten?'

'She didn't say much. She ate a little but we've mostly been feeding her through the drip.'

She sat down in the tired armchair next to Thato's bed. 'Sisi, do you know if the doctors have figured out what's wrong?'

The nurse gave her a sympathetic smile and shook her head. 'Her tests so far have come back fine. I think the doctor wants to run some more but she'll speak to your daughter about that. Honestly, mama, she seems to be very tired.'

Mahlatse sighed. 'She spends a lot of time at church,' she said in a voice tinged with bitterness.

The nurse looked confused. She opened her mouth to say something but the sound of Kgethi's footsteps as they walked through the door interrupted her.

Mahlatse turned to her. 'Where have you been?'

'Hi to you too Mum,' Kgethi said, setting her bag down.

'I'm serious, Kgethi.'

Kgethi glared at her. 'I was sorting out our issues with the Pastor. I told him me and Thato were done.'

'And he just said, 'Okay'?' Mahlatse asked incredulously. 'Have you applied for a protection order like I told you to?'

'No, Mom,' Kgethi said through gritted teeth. 'I figured if he keeps harassing me I'll be able to use those phone logs and messages to build a proper case. If he leaves me alone then we don't have to waste the time and the money.'

Her frustration flared up again. 'If? If? Kgethi, you can't seriously think—'

'Can you two please tone it down!' Said Molefi's voice, stopping both of them in their tracks. They turned to see him by the door carrying a Woolies plastic bag and a teddy bear.

'I could hear you two down the corridor! Thato is lying in a hospital bed and you're still going at each other like this? Still?'

'Molefi, please talk some sense into her!'

'I want to see my niece first.' He walked into the room and looked over Thato. 'I brought her those disgusting sour sweets she likes. Has she still not woken up yet?'

'She was awake when I saw her this morning,' Kgethi said. 'And when I spoke to the doctor she said all her tests came back fine. They're just keeping her for observation.'

'Poor thing,' he said looking at Thato. He placed the teddy bear next to her and the packet on her bedside table. 'She looks so tiny.'

Thato started to stir. They all focused on her. Mahlatse forgot all thoughts of a protection order and held Thato's hand. When her granddaughter came to she started babbling about, strangely enough, Hartbeespoort Dam. Mahlatse had no idea where she had even heard of Hartbeespoort Dam. She couldn't recall anyone ever expressing any interest in it.

'Can we go?' Thato asked, her voice still heavy with sleep. 'Can we go see the dam?'

'When you're better, baby girl,' Mahlatse cooed. 'And then we'll all go together.'

Her eyelids started drooping again. 'Okay,' she said. 'But can we go soon? Auntie Dineo wants to see us.'

They all stood in shocked silence. Molefi looked wide-eyed from Mahlatse to Thato. 'What did she just say?' He asked. But they didn't get an answer. Thato had fallen asleep again.

They looked at each other. So they had all heard. For once even Kgethi had been rendered speechless. Mahlatse felt a shiver run up her spine and spread outwards, tingling under her skin. She searched through her memory but couldn't recall ever mentioning Dineo to Thato. So how could she? What did she mean?

'Do you think—' Molefi started.

'I don't know. I actually don't know,' Mahlatse said slowly. 'Kgethi did you ever tell her about your aunt?'

'Who? Aunt Dineo?'

'Yes, Dineo,' Molefi said, switching to full interrogation mode. 'Did you ever speak to Thato about her? And what did you say?'

'Um…' Kgethi paused. Her eyebrows furrowed in concentration. 'I don't think so? I don't really know much about her, so.'

'I don't think I've mentioned her either to Thato.' He turned back to Mahlatse. 'What do you think?'

'I don't know,' Mahlatse said. 'And why Hartbeespoort of all places? We've never taken her there. And why would she place Dineo...'

She felt a jolt so powerful she almost jumped. An electric current coursed through her veins, firing the synapses throughout her nervous system. At that moment memories flashed in front of her. Two-year-old Thato toddling into a room dangling a set of missing keys. Four-year-old Thato warning her of a minor car crash that later happened exactly as described. Six-year-old Thato telling her she sees ghosts. Molefi pulling her aside to tell her of eight-year-old Thato healing a bird. All these events stitched themselves together like a quilt, taking form behind Thato's curious eyes that were identical to the ones her sister once had. She excused herself, ran to the bathroom, and threw up.

THIRTY-THREE

Kgethi looked at her phone and saw she had ten missed calls from the Pastor. She needed to buy time. She suspected he already had people looking for them. She half expected to look up and see him walking down the hall towards them. She went outside and smoked. She'd been slowly weaning herself off cigarettes but Thato's hospitalisation had meant a pack of ten had turned into a pack of twenty. One pack turned into two. She stood far enough from the hospital entrance to avoid the security guard's scowl and considered her options.

She could call her father. Her mother had left the responsibility of informing him of Thato's hospitalisation to her. She took out her phone and looked at his number. Realistically speaking, when was the last time she could depend on him to do anything? How many times had he dropped the ball on her throughout school? Her whole life he had been there in name only. She was even convinced the intervention in her mother's kitchen had less to do with his concern and more to do with him having missed a chance to scold her.

She thought about her mother. Ever since Thato had mentioned Aunt Dineo, Mom had been in a kind of trance. She was determined to go to Hartbeespoort. Kgethi had dismissed it as craziness before. But now… She looked at her phone and found Bongani's number. She hesitated. He was the Pastor's friend. He had been by his side through all of this. Then again, he was the only one at the church who had shown concern for

Thato's wellbeing. The only other person who knew. And he had told her to get out. She thought again of their conversation outside the church the night of the assault. She could hear his voice saying 'This one? Uyagula.' And he was right. Thato was so sick that she was lying in a hospital bed clinging onto the last shred of life. 'Are you sure this whole thing is okay for her? Are you really sure about all of this?' He had tried to warn her right before shit hit the fan. She remembered the look in his face. The sincerity of his concern. While he was the Pastor's friend and she couldn't trust him with everything maybe she could trust him a little. At this point she had no real choice.

She took a deep breath and phoned Bongani. 'Listen, were you serious about helping me?' She said.

'Yes I was. Where are you? Solomon has told people that you're missing. Church members are looking for you. They know where you live,' he responded.

She took a deep breath. 'I need you to stall them. Make up places you've seen me. Rosebank, the South, I don't care. Tell them you saw me in Krugersdorp if you have to.'

'But where are you?'

'You know I can't tell you that,' she said. She still wasn't one hundred per cent sure she could trust him. And even if she could, she wasn't sure he wouldn't let her true location slip. 'I just need you to help me buy some time.'

He hesitated before saying, 'Okay. I'll stall him. But in the meantime you must stay safe. Don't go home, Kgethi. You must stay in a place he doesn't know. Call me if you need anything else.'

She dropped the phone, finished her cigarette, and went back to the hospital room. 'And you're sure she'll be fine?' She heard her mother's voice ask. She walked in and saw her mother standing with the doctor. Thato was out of the white hospital robes and in her regular clothes again, sitting on the bed with her bag at her side. All of her tests had come back normal, leaving the hospital little choice but to discharge her with advice that she rest.

'I don't see what the problem could be,' her doctor said. The doctor was a young, pretty dark-skinned woman with close cropped hair. 'A visit to Harties might help her relax. I've heard the dam can be quite nice. Very quiet. It might be just what she needs.'

With a single look her mother told her that the matter was settled. They were going to Hartbeespoort. Kgethi couldn't remember the last time she had been. Back when her parents were still married and the three of them were still playing happy family they used to pass the dam on their way to Sun City. But she couldn't remember ever staying there, and she had usually been too excited at the thought of going to the Valley of the Waves to even look.

'Go back to your house and you can pack some things for you and Thato and drop off your car,' Mom told her. 'We'll take mine. I'll fetch some things quickly and come meet you.'

'Bongani told me they know where we live.'

'Who is Bongani now?'

She paused before saying, 'Someone at the church. A friend.'

Her mother raised an eyebrow at her. 'I don't think you should give this Bongani character more information. I still have some of your and Thato's things at the house. Let's leave from there together.'

And once again, Mom was in charge. Kgethi had to admit she felt a bit relieved. Things had been a shit show since she'd left home. She could finally admit to herself (but never out loud, obviously) that maybe she didn't have things as figured out as she thought she did. Here she was in her late twenties with a child and she still didn't know how to adult. Go figure.

Kgethi heard her phone ringing incessantly as she drove and ignored it. She glanced in her rearview mirror and saw a car tailing close behind them. Her skin turned cold. She turned into a street and the car followed. She made another turn and seconds later saw the car turn behind her. She clutched her steering wheel hard, trying to keep her gaze on the road in front of her and returning it every so often to the rearview mirror. She made a final turn and waited to see if the car would follow. When it didn't she almost gasped from relief. We need to get out of this city, she thought.

She looked back at Thato who was gazing outside the window. 'You excited to go to Harties?'

'No,' Thato said.

'Why not? You're the one that wanted to go.'

'Ja, to find Auntie Dineo,' she said. 'I don't want to find anything anymore.'

Kgethi didn't know what to say. She imagined the Pastor waiting for them at the apartment and felt a chill run down her spine. Her heart skipped when she pulled up to her mother's house and saw a short man walking past until she realised it was a neighbour. She was starting to lose it. They needed to leave now. They didn't have much time. Kgethi found a spare bag in the downstairs cupboard and threw Thato's things and hers into it. She didn't know how long they would be gone for, but that wasn't her biggest concern.

Should she be more afraid of what she would find when they got there or what would face them when they got back? The question remained at the forefront of her mind. She knew from her mother's and daughter's faces that this wouldn't be a fun, relaxing family holiday. But whatever they were doing needed to be done. She was decidedly not in control. There was something else at play. Perhaps whatever had given Thato her powers was pulling them there. Thato's powers needed to be paid for and Kgethi wasn't entirely sure it was a price they could afford. In other words, she was scared shitless.

She sat on the bed in what used to be her bedroom and turned warm from shame. In the corner was the drawer she had searched through when she looked for her bracelet. The door creaked from her repeated slamming. She looked out her window and remembered the white butterflies that had flown through the garden and how Thato had tried to capture them. On her bed lay the pillow she had used to help her sleep more comfortably when her belly was uncomfortably big and round in the final stages of her pregnancy. She looked up and saw the three dark brown patches on her ceiling she used to stare at when her parents' arguing kept her up late at night. Her old life was imprinted in every corner of the room. She wished she could fall back into it, throw the covers over her head, and wake up to find her current life had been a bad dream.

She looked at her phone. There were a dozen messages waiting for her, each more aggressive and threatening than the last. She read through them all. She would have to go to the police. She didn't have a choice anymore. She didn't answer any of them.

She walked into the kitchen. Her mother was sitting at the counter with her head bent over her phone. She looked up when Kgethi entered.

'I managed to find a guesthouse that will put the three of us up,' she said. 'We're all sharing one bedroom but it has a cot for Thato so we should be fine.'

'What about Uncle Molefi?' Kgethi asked.

She shook her head. 'He's not coming. He has some business he has to attend to. It doesn't matter anyway. It's probably better that it's just the three of us. Anyway, let's get going,' she said, straightening up. 'We should try to get there before dark.'

There was an uneasy silence between the two of them. Kgethi could see from the look in her mother's eyes that they were both thinking the same thing, but neither could vocalise it. 'Mom,' she eventually said. 'What do you—'

'I don't know Kgethi,' she said quickly. 'I don't know. But we need to go. I have a feeling about this.'

The three of them climbed into the car and set off for Hartbeespoort. A cold tension hung in the air. Kgethi's breath caught in her lungs every time she thought she saw a car following them. When the car turned a corner she exhaled. It had been months since the three of them had been in the same car together. Now they weren't sure what to do. Talk about the past? Talk about the unknown they were heading towards? Mom put on Brenda Fassie. After three songs she changed her mind and played Mariah Carey instead. Kgethi couldn't stand Mariah Carey. She screamed too much and the whistle notes she was famous for sounded torturous. Kgethi half expected all the glass windows to shatter when her mom started playing Emotions.

She would rather have listened to someone like Beyonce or Travis Scott but she knew how Mom felt about her music. 'What is this noise?', Mom used to say with her nose wrinkled like the music smelled as bad as it sounded. 'Back in my day musicians used to actually sing! Now they record any nonsense and call it music!' The memory took her by surprise. Snippets of their pre-war pre-Pastor life came back to her. She hadn't always been happy. There were times when she wanted to kill her mother. But they were undeniably better off. The three of them had a life that while not perfect was at least stable.

She glanced at her mother and saw her hard, locked jaw. For the first time she noticed the fine lines around her eyes and the dark circles underneath them. She noticed how her mother's hair which was usually neatly pulled back was tied up in a messy, discoloured doek. Mom had never been overly concerned about her appearance, but she had always made sure she was presentable when she left the house. For the first time Kgethi became aware of the toll these past few days, weeks, months had taken on her. The guilt she had felt for Thato now extended itself and shrouded the recent memories she had with her mother. Thato fell asleep in the back sleep leaving Kgethi and her mom with a pregnant silence interrupted only by the vocals of Mariah Carey.

'I sold the blanket, you know,' Mom said.

She was confused. 'The blanket? What blanket?'

'You don't remember? That one I knitted. The one you said was too expensive.'

Now she remembered it. The image of the soft, cream, wool blanket came to mind. She cringed at the memory of their argument. 'Come on, Mom. It was expensive.'

'Well, I sold it. To some housewife whose daughter was going to Rhodes.'

'Oh.'

'At full price.'

'Well good for you, Mom.'

Mom smirked. 'Good for you? That's all you're going to say, Miss no-one-would-pay-that-much?'

Kgethi resisted the urge to roll her eyes. 'Okay Mom, I was wrong. I shouldn't have said that.'

'Thank you,' there was a pause. 'And I shouldn't have kicked you out the house. I've kept thinking that maybe if I didn't you never would have met that man in the first place. But you have to understand Kgethi, you haven't always been an easy person to deal with. I don't know why you do it. There's being honest and there's being cruel. And for years you've been very difficult. You cross the line. It's felt like you save up all your cruelty just for me. And it's frustrating for me because I've always tried my best with you.

'And I excused it when you were younger. I thought you'd grow out of the tantrums. And then you became a teenager and I thought it's just the hormones. You'll grow out of those too. And then you had Thato, and you just didn't stop. I felt so overwhelmed by you sometimes. I just wished...'

Kgethi leaned forward waiting for the end of the sentence. When it didn't come she slowly realised the implications of it. She filled in the missing words herself. 'Did you wish you hadn't had me?'

'Kgethi, I never said that.'

'But you're not denying it. You did, didn't you? You wished you hadn't had me?'

'Of course I wanted to have you!'

'Oh my God!' Kgethi said. She became angry. 'You're such a hypocrite!'

'Excuse me?'

'This whole time you made me feel like there was something wrong with me because I didn't want to be a mother—'

'Kgethi!' Mom interrupted in a horrified tone. 'Your daughter is in the backseat right now!'

'She's sleeping, Mom! It's all she ever does these days. She'll be fine. This whole time you've made me feel like I'm some kind of monster for not thinking motherhood is rainbows and sunshine and unicorn farts—'

'No one expected you to think that, Kgethi. At least I didn't. I told you for years and years to wait until you were stable to have kids for exactly this reason! But you didn't want to listen to me. You instead decided to do your own thing, like you always do, and come home from your first year of varsity pregnant by God knows who!

'And fine, I'll admit I didn't want to have more kids. I had my hands filled with you and I didn't want to start all over again with another child. I just couldn't do it again. So I got an IUD. And I never told your father because he wanted another one and I didn't.

'I took precautions to make sure I didn't have another child. And you couldn't even bother to use a condom. But it was fine, right? Because I was there! You lived in my house. I helped you raise your child and a lot of the time I was raising Thato for you. But you never appreciated any of it. Instead you consistently disrespected me in my own house! So yes, I snapped! And I'm sorry that all of this has happened to Thato. I should have seen that you would do this. But I'm not sorry for just wanting a fucking break!'

For once Kgethi didn't have a sharp retort. She wasn't mounting a defense. She thought about all the times she had spat venom and how often it had been targeted at her mother. 'I... I don't know what to say,' she finally said. 'I don't know why I say the things I do. I guess I've just been upset that nothing's worked out the way I wanted. First you and Dad broke up and then I had Thato and I just... I feel like nothing's ever gone the way I thought it would.'

She looked at her mother. 'But Mom, I'm really sorry for making you feel like I didn't appreciate you. For being such a bitch. I don't know how I could have done any of this without you. I mean look at how much I've messed everything up!' Fresh hot tears stung her eyes.

'I've been on my own for a few months and I've fucked up so bad! And I just wish,' the tears were flowing now, 'I wish we never left. I'm sorry for fighting over that blanket with you. I'm sorry for everything, Mom. Please can we come home?'

Mom blinked rapidly in the way she often did when she was holding back tears. 'Of course you can come home, Kgethi. You can always come home.'

They started speaking again of all the things that had happened since Thato and Kgethi left home. They spoke as the cityscape of Johannesburg petered out into rolling plains and hills with sparse shrubbery. There were few other cars on the road. It took them under two hours until she saw the red roofs typical of homes by Hartbeespoort Dam. When was the last time Kgethi had been here? She couldn't remember. The town was quiet with money tucked in corners. Old money. The money in the town didn't scream the way Sandton money did. Instead it gave itself a veneer of quaintness, mock humility, which shone through the size of the immaculately maintained homes nestled on hills between green shrubs, trees and private boats that floating lazily on the green algae scented dam. The town looked Afrikaans. There was no other way to explain it. It gave itself away by the prevalence of Afrikaans and English language signs and suspicious lack of black people. Whenever Kgethi left Johannesburg and stepped into a small town further north she could feel the Afrikaans bristling against her skin. She could see it in the faces that walked past. She anticipated it before anyone opened their mouths to confirm her suspicions.

'Koko,' said a little voice in the back. They both jumped when they heard it. Neither of them knew when Thato had woken up but there she was, wide-eyed and energetic. Kgethi couldn't remember the last time she had seen Thato look this alert.

'You have to turn here, Koko,' she said.

'But baby girl, the guest house we're going to isn't down this road,' Mom replied.

'You have to turn here,' she insisted with a determined point.

Mom made the turn. They had fully handed over control to the youngest person in the car.

'Should we be doing this?' Kgethi asked.

'We're already here,' Mom responded. 'And I've put the guesthouse address in the GPS. We can always turn back if we need to.'

Kgethi had entered the twilight zone. Her mother, who rarely listened to her, was now taking directions from a small person. It would be annoying if it wasn't so odd. Thato took over alert and authoritative, saying in her small voice, 'Turn this way here Koko,' gesturing with her left hand, 'and then go straight for a while.' The longer they drove, the more Thato's energy seemed to pick up until she was practically bouncing in her seat. Kgethi couldn't remember the last time she had seen her daughter look so excited. So alive. They were driving closer, circling around the edge of the lake but further from the town. Kgethi was starting to get concerned. The road became dustier and more pothole ridden until the tar disappeared and they were driving on a dirt track. What if the car broke down and they needed help? What if there were dangerous men waiting to jump them?I sound like my mother, she thought. How ironic that she had turned into her mother while the usual worry her mother wore was gone. Whatever Thato was leading them to, Mom was determined to find it. Kgethi just hoped they would make it out okay.

They stopped at a clearing. They were surrounded by more nature than houses. In front of them was the dam water, sparkling in the sun. In the distance they saw the boxy, Roman-esque brown and grey arch of the dam. If anything happened to them, no one would know. No one would be able to get to them in time. Kgethi pushed down the thought. Thato unbuckled her seat belt and pushed out the car before

Kgethi could stop her. She ran towards the dam. Mom also unbuckled and left the car.

'God damn it,' she thought. So they were really doing this. She took a deep breath and got out the car.

'Don't you think this is a little dangerous?' She yelled after them. She was walking towards them, but slowly. She still wanted to be close enough to the car to reach it in case… something happened. Neither of them responded to her.

'Come on you guys, I'm not playing,' she said again, inching closer. 'Shouldn't we at least call the guesthouse? Tell them where we are?'

Thato stopped. She turned around and pointed at the ground. 'Here,' she said.

'Here what, Thato?' Mom asked her.

'Auntie Dineo. She's here.'

There was silence. Kgethi was creeped out. No, she wasn't creeped out. She could feel herself shivering. She had just walked into a horror movie with her eyes open and wanted out. She wanted to turn around and run without stopping until she reached Johannesburg.

'Mom, what's going on?' Kgethi said. 'This is creepy!'

But Mom wasn't listening. 'She's here?' She asked in a breathless voice. 'Are you sure?'

Thato nodded.

'Can you speak to her? What is she saying?'

'Mom, this is insane! Can we please go?'

'Not now Kgethi,' she snapped. 'I want you to tell me if she's saying anything? What does she look like? Where is she?'

Thato pointed down again. She fixated on the spot Thato was standing at. Suddenly they all understood.

Mom reached into her pocket and pulled out her phone. She punched in a number and waited. 'Molefi,' she said. 'You need to come right now. As in right now. It's an emergency.'

She glanced back at the spot Thato was pointing to. 'And we need you to bring a shovel.'

THIRTY-FOUR

They waited for Molefi to arrive. Kgethi stayed in the car, chain-smoking with the window open. No way, no fucking way, she kept thinking to herself. She didn't want any part of this. She wanted to slide herself behind the steering wheel, start the car, and go home. She wasn't a superstitious person. Before Thato she never even believed ghosts existed. Never believed in anything that went bump in the night other than the stuff that fell off her bedside table. But this was too much even for her. This was some white people shit. And she wanted to leave.

Mahlatse walked to and fro. Anxious. A hollow feeling gripped her stomach. She wanted to throw up. But more than that, she wanted to dig with her bare hands.

Thato stood and watched her Koko. She had never seen her like this before. Koko reminded her of the insects that the boys at school would catch. How much they fought to escape before the boys crushed them in their hands. Koko looked like she wanted to flee something. Thato stared at the long thread that left Koko and planted itself in the spot where she'd pointed. The thread was thick and strong, shining brightly in the sunlight.

Molefi came against his own better judgement. The shovel from his garden shed was sitting in the boot of his car. This is the most insane thing I've ever done, he thought. He had resolved to save his sister from herself. His only living sister who was in the middle of nowhere with one small child and one dumb one as though they weren't three black women in this dangerous country. He would let Mahlatse do a little digging so this madness would be laid to rest once she found nothing there. They would get out before sunset. He was not willing to entertain the thought that Dineo was there. His chest felt hollow. He saw Dineo's face in his mind and felt the gentle pressure of her pressing against his skin. The last time he saw her she had hugged him tight at Dube station. 'Don't worry, papa will come around,' she had assured him. 'Just give him time.' He shook the memory away. Dineo was gone. And Mahlatse needed to see that.

Mahlatse watched her brother's silver Mercedes park next to her car. He got out and strode towards her. She saw Kgethi climb out of her car as well. The four of them stood in the clearing. Mahlatse practically wrenched the shovel out of Molefi's hands, ignoring as he protested, 'Mahlatse, what are you doing? This is insane!'

She walked towards the patch of earth and pointed, looking at Thato. 'This is it? This is the spot, right?'

When Thato nodded, Mahlatse sank the shovel into the dirt with so much force it sent ripples through her whole body. Instead of wiping her out, the ripples re-energised her, giving her the strength to continue. She dug wildly, flinging the dirt to the side in blind determination. The other three watched her. Three silent witnesses. The only audible sounds were the birds chirping in the background, Mahlatse's heaving, and the sound of loose dirt hitting the ground.

Molefi gave in first. 'Here, let me help you,' he said. He could see she was becoming tired and he wanted this over with. The best way to deal with disappointment was as quickly as possible. He took the shovel and began digging into the hole she had made. She stood hunched over, hands on knees and breathless from exhaustion. She watched him shoveling bigger mounds of dirt than she could manage and disposing of them tidily on the side. When he became tired she took over. They swapped in and out until suddenly Mahlatse spotted something. It was hard and off white. It looked suspiciously like…

Like…

Like…

'Molefi!' She yelled. 'Molefi look!'

He looked. Kgethi stepped forward. When Thato tried to do the same, Kgethi held out a protective arm to push her back. Molefi and Mahlatse paused and looked at each other in shock. A jolt of electricity passed through them both, connecting them together like one of Thato's threads. In unison they dropped to their knees and began pushing away the dirt revealing a femur. A tibia. A humerus. A clavicle. Ribs. And finally a skull, partially worn away, with two gaping holes staring at them that had once housed eyes.

Mahlatse looked and saw a torn piece of mustard yellow fabric. She picked it up and held it. At that moment time stood still. There was no other sound, no other sensation, than the weight of the fabric in her hand. She sucked all the air in the clearing into her diaphragm and spat it out in a loud, drawn cry. The sound ricocheted off the water, the ground, the trees, and the three people who stood there stunned. Tears formed and spilled down her face. She leaned down until her forehead touched the ground and cried into the earth. The three stood and watched her. Molefi through stunned tears. Thato through round, curious eyes. And Kgethi through grave silence. She moved forward, put her arms around her shaking mother, and held her while she cried out Dineo's name.

THIRTY-FIVE

They buried Dineo a week later in a small, private funeral with just the four of them, Ntatemogolo, and Dineo's childhood friend Mbali who had never left Soweto. Although Molefi and Mahlatse had insisted on paying for the arrangements together, it was Ntatemogolo who insisted on having the final say on everything. He had the final say on the coffin. The venue was his home. Dineo's home. Molefi had wanted to bury her at a costly cemetery just outside of Soweto. But it was Ntatemogolo who insisted she be buried next to her mother. 'This is where she belongs,' he said.

Mahlatse felt light. So much lighter that she often lost her balance more than she had before. The heavy stone she carried in the lining of her stomach was gone. She stopped snapping as often as she had. The lashes whipping against her insides ceased. Her annoyance at life's every day inconveniences felt less intense. She felt quiet. There was an emptiness inside her that made room for peace. She saw a change come over her father. He looked… younger. The creases on his face cast less severe shadows. He walked with a lightness in his step she hadn't seen in years.

'Are you okay, Papa?' She asked him.

'Now, I'm at peace. I can rest now,' he said. 'Dineo has come home. She has come home.'

He died in his sleep two weeks later. Molefi discovered him. He had walked into the Soweto home to retrieve his serving platters he had brought over for the funeral. He hadn't wanted to be the one to do it but with Mahlatse's hands tied up in helping Kgethi stay away from the Pastor he had no other choice. He had planned to exit as quickly as he entered while saying as few words as possible. But seeing his father laying in his chair had rendered him motionless.

'Papa?' He said. After he received no response he moved closer and shook his shoulder. He lay his hand against his father's neck and felt no pulse. He pulled away and stared at his father's body, allowing his death to sink in. In that moment he saw his father standing in front of him 30 years prior with a face twisted in rage screaming, 'Get out of my house! Leave and don't come back!'

He saw his graduation from Wits, LLB in hand, his mother and his sister clapping for him and taking pictures with him outside the Great Hall while his father was nowhere in sight. He saw 30 years of Christmases spent with friends. Of being asked by colleagues if he was going home for the festive season while knowing he had no home to return to. He saw his father arguing with him right until the end, dismissing his opinions on Dineo's funeral arrangements.

'He'll come around, you know,' Dineo had reassured him just three months before her death. But he never had. And now he never would. Molefi felt rage and pain building up inside of him, entwining with one another in an unholy marriage. His childhood home had been stolen from him, and now the thief lay dead.

He felt hot tears spilling down his cheeks. He buried his face in his hands and started to sob, shaking at the loss of all the memories that had been stolen from him. Molefi had always told himself that he could never reconcile with his father, but in that moment he truly felt it. He composed himself and looked once more at his father's face for a long time. When he felt ready, he walked into the kitchen, picked up his serving platters, and called his sister.

They buried him near his wife and daughter. Father,

mother, and child lay together in a row at last. While the priest was droning on during the burial, Thato's mind was focused elsewhere. She was looking past the rows of guests seated around the grave to a patch a little further away. She was looking at Ntatemogolo. He stood without a cane wearing loose cotton clothes. He was now see-through. He wasn't alone. He was holding Aunt Dineo in his arms and the two were laughing together. His hands were wrapped around her face. The two of them hugged for a long time. Then they turned to look at Thato. Aunt Dineo waved at her and Thato waved back. The two of them turned around arm in arm and walked away. Thato watched as they walked into the distance, disappearing into the white light of the other side.

The next day Thato walked out into the garden. She was at Koko's house. They were moving back in and Thato was already starting to sleep peacefully in her old bedroom again. She was up before anyone else and stepped outside to see the world still tinged in blue-grey light. The grass was still wet from the morning dew. She took a few steps forward and collapsed.

When Kgethi looked out the window she screamed. She ran outside and saw Thato lying on the ground. A perfect circle of white dandelions had formed around her. The white seeds of the dandelions were floating in the air, settling on Thato's hair, clothes, and skin. Kgethi ran to her side and shook her awake. She woke up, looked at Kgethi, and said in a soft voice, 'It's finished now, Mummy.'

EPILOGUE

5 January 2029

Dear Aunt Dineo,

I have to admit, I don't really know how to do this. I've never written a letter before, and I don't think the ones I wrote in my university application forms really count. Koko told me that you used to write letters to each other all the time and wait a week or more for a response to be sent through the post office. I can't imagine what that must have been like. I get impatient when someone takes a few hours to respond to a message; I can't imagine how I'd feel desperately waiting that long for an answer.

Still, I am writing a letter. I know I won't get a response to it even if I wait a week, or a month, or a year. But I'm writing it because it's been a long time, about ten years now, since I last spoke to you and I think I need to speak to you now.

I've been having dreams about you. In them you're wearing your yellow dress, standing next to the dam, telling me to come find you. At first I thought it was a sign that maybe my powers were back. I lost them just after we buried you. I still remember it. I woke up in Mom's arms with white dandelions in my hair, on my face, and on my clothes. I said to her, 'It's finished now' because that's what you and Ntatemogolo said to me. I still remember hearing your voices say that to me before I woke up. The funny thing is, I still don't remember how I got to the garden. I woke up surrounded by dandelions and I felt like something was missing. I felt lighter. Like I'd cut off all my hair and was only just starting to realise how heavy it had weighed on my neck. I tried, you know. I couldn't see the threads anymore. I couldn't see ghosts anymore. I've never had a vision since. Worst of all, I've never healed anything again. I felt useless afterwards. Like I had lost my purpose.

That's basically what the Pastor said. He tried to fight to get me back. I didn't know it at the time but when I was older Mom told me that just before your funeral she had to get a protection order. He sent people from the church to look for me. Our neighbours said he came to our apartment building demanding to be let in until security chased him away. He threatened to report her to the police if she didn't bring me to him. Everything changed when Uncle Bongani came. I still remember seeing his face marked with concern and his massive, imposing figure stuffed into a chair in Koko's kitchen. He came to our house to tell us that the Pastor wasn't prepared to stop. He said maybe we'd be better off moving until everything died down. He used to gesture with his hands when he spoke and in his urgency he accidentally knocked over a hot cup of tea and burned himself. So, me being me, I tried to heal him. And it didn't work. I didn't feel the power flowing out of me like it was supposed to. I didn't feel anything. I took my hand off of his and the burn was still there. I remember Uncle Bongani saying, 'What happened? What's wrong with her?' And that's when I knew I had lost them.

The good thing is when I lost my powers so did The Pastor. When he couldn't cure anything anymore people realised that the Pastor wasn't a prophet. He was just a man. Just like them. He was a greedy, predatory, awful, awful man. His church lost many of his followers, while others stayed on in hopes he would gain his powers back and they would be rewarded for their loyalty. Months later people started laying charges against him for all kinds of things. Fraud, sexual assault, even culpable homicide. Some of the people who stopped taking their medicine because of him died, and their families held him accountable.

Mom didn't let me at the time but I've gone back now and watched some of the old news clips. Would you believe he had loyal supporters until the end? They would stand outside court, singing hymns and holding up placards saying he was innocent. A couple of them were even interviewed on TV saying they believed the charges were a plot from Satan and this was a test of faith. They truly believed it. They could not understand why the state was punishing a black man for the crime of being blessed by the hand of God while so many evil white men went free. I wouldn't be surprised if they still send him letters in prison to this day. He'll be there for a long time. Fifteen more years to go until he's eligible for parole.

As for us, we've mostly been okay. Koko lost her job after the pandemic but she's started her own boutique store of bespoke knitwear. You won't believe how much she charges for a scarf, and people pay! She has clients from West Africa and even Europe because she found an interesting way of incorporating African patterns into her knitwear. It's very pretty. She promised she would give me a blanket to keep me warm when I go to UCT, where I'm starting in a few weeks' time. Also, she's gotten herself an admirer. There's a very handsome customer who keeps coming back. She says he's just a customer but you should see the way her face lights up when he walks in. Mom and I think Koko's dating him but you know Koko. She'll never say.

Mom's been fine too. I won't say things have become perfect but she's become more present. She's been annoyed with me less. She listens to me and has been there for me more. She keeps saying that now that I'm grown and leaving the nest she'll finally get to do whatever she wants, but I think she'll still miss me. She's already started planning a solo holiday to Spain. She finally got her degree from UNISA and now she helps Koko run the business. You should see them together. They get along much better now than they did when I was little.

Uncle Molefi is Uncle Molefi. He doesn't even live here anymore. He did one of those conversion exams and now he's in London working as a lawyer there and living with his partner Uncle Emile. He still won't get married. And he says I'm the closest thing to his own child he'll ever have. They send me presents for Christmas and birthdays. They invited me to visit them two years ago but it rained from the moment I left Heathrow to the moment I was dropped back off to catch the flight home. Still, his apartment is warm and beautiful and he still has all his bits and pieces cluttering the shelves.

As for me, I won't lie, it was difficult losing my powers. I lost a part of myself. As messed up as the Pastor's church was, I felt like I was contributing to people's lives when I was there. I loved healing people, but more than that I loved giving people hope. That was the draw of the church. It kept hope alive at a time when hope was a rapidly fading light. It gave people answers to complicated questions. The Pastor wasn't just a man. He became in their eyes a saviour, sent from God to deliver a third testament. A new testament that uncomplicated the complicated, that took difficult concepts and heavy symbolism and translated them into easy, comfortable answers. Answers they could wrap around themselves to insulate against the bitter cold of reality. But in life there are no easy answers. Sometimes there are no answers at all.

I still have so many unanswered questions about my former powers. Why they led me to you but never showed me what happened to you. If I could really see the dead or if they purposefully chose to present themselves to me. I used to think that the people all around me were the puppets and their past was the master. They couldn't move forward with the strings of their losses pulling them back. But now I've started to wonder if I was the puppet all along and my powers were the strings pulling me back towards you. And maybe they weren't a burden but a harness, holding me between two worlds and making sure I never lost my grip and fell into one of them. By severing the strings you trapped me in this one.

Most of all, I wonder why you chose me.

I'll probably never know the answer. I used to think it was my responsibility to heal the world but now I don't think I was ever meant to. I think I was just supposed to bring peace to my family, and in doing so bring a little more light onto this Earth. I do miss healing people, though. Which is why I'm going to UCT. I want to be a doctor. I worked really hard and got into medicine there. It's going to be a long seven years but I'm ready for it. I got my acceptance letter a few days ago. Since then I've been dreaming about you every night. And I've been trying to figure out what it all means. Koko says it means maybe you're coming to fetch me for another mission. Maybe it actually means you want me to be a sangoma now or something. I wouldn't know.

But what I do know is this. I miss you, Aunt Dineo. You were a big part of my life. You gave me the courage to go to Cape Town. You showed me that no matter what happens I will always find my way home. Because there will always be someone who loves me waiting here for me, just like we were waiting for you.

Give a big hug to Ntatemogolo for me.

Love,
Thato

ACKNOWLEDGEMENTS

Writing a book has been a lifelong dream of mine. Achieving this is the greatest honour of my life and it is not something that I could have done on my own.

I have received the most incredible support from all four of my parents who have encouraged me to push myself further since I wrote my first manuscript at 17. Thank you to Mom for teaching me about life in Soweto under Apartheid, to Dad for helping me translate phrases into isiZulu, to Daddy for providing historical and legal feedback and context and to Aunt Tsholo for your warmth, energy and for accompanying me to my residency.

I could not have written this without the support I received from Blackbird Books, starting with the Casa Lorde writer's residency and ending with a book deal. Thank you to Natalia and Andres for opening your home to me to allow me the space and time to write. Thank you to my publisher Thabiso Mahlape and the team at Blackbird for investing me through your skill and expertise. You have believed in my writing from day one and I could not have asked for a better publisher.

To my editor Efemia Chela for offering your invaluable insight throughout the editing process. Your thoughtful input helped me flesh this story out into one I am incredibly proud of and for that I will forever be grateful.

To Remy Ngamije for reading the unreadable first chapters.

Thank you for providing your kind words and pieces of advice while I was still finding my voice.

To my sister Kopano for being my number one cheerleader, my beta reader and my confidante throughout this process. Thank you for supporting me, for reading my manuscript when it was a mess of a first draft and for telling absolutely everyone you meet that I'm a writer.

A special shoutout to all ten million of my siblings: Siphelele, Oratile, Tshiamo, Sihle, Lungi, Mbali, Lwazi and Mandisa.

Thank you to my grandmothers for your warm hugs, prayers and love. Thank you to Mawe for always taking pride in my achievements. Thank you to Koko for always believing that I would achieve my dreams. I wish you were still here to see that I've finally done it.

Thank you to Hussein for reading my manuscript, providing me with feedback and encouraging my writing since we met at Rhodes.

A special thank you to my cat Luna for keeping me company during the evenings and on my toes during the day.

And finally, thank you to my offline and online community for cheering on my writing journey. Knowing that there were people out there eager to support my work was one of the major motivations that kept me going and allowed me to finish this book.

I hope you all find joy and pieces of yourselves while reading this book.